KNOTTED

Also by Louette Harding

Two Into One
Women Like Us

KNOTTED

Louette Harding

Hodder & Stoughton

Copyright © 2000 by Louette Harding

First published in 2000
by Hodder and Stoughton
A division of Hodder Headline

The right of Louette Harding to be identified as the Author of
the Work has been asserted by her in accordance with the
Copyright, Designs and Patents Act 1988.

10 9 8 7 6 5 4 3 2 1

A CIP catalogue record for this title
is available from the British Library.

ISBN 0 340 70842 5

Typeset by Hewer Text Ltd, Edinburgh
Printed and bound in Great Britain by
Mackays of Chatham PLC

Hodder and Stoughton
A division of Hodder Headline
338 Euston Road
London NW1 3BH

For the girl on the grey pony

Chapter One

At first, Suzy was happy waiting. It had been an age since she'd been invited to a wedding, so there was a certain novelty about the proceedings. She'd decided against a hat, but as she watched the procession of pastel women filing up the aisle in their wide straw brims and froths of net, she felt naked. A hat would have been elegant and grand. She shouldn't have listened to Luke and Daisy; they were at an age when they considered it amusing to undermine their mother at every turn. A hat would have made her feel like someone different. She would have walked taller in a hat.

She glanced over at Paul. He looked younger, scrubbed like a young boy and unnaturally close shaven. His hair was newly cut, too, the tips of his ears flushing in the shaft of sun that fell through the stained-glass window: the Holy Family on their flight into Egypt. Joseph was leading the donkey on which Mary was perched decoratively, her head gracefully bent above the babe in her arms. The artist had gone to a great deal of trouble to paint Joseph's beard in different shades of grey, and he was stooping, Suzy noticed, as if, with his new wife and his new baby, the cares of the world were lying on his shoulders. His eyes were fixed on the road ahead; the only way he would manage the journey was in small stages.

It was a pretty church: Anglican, of course, with its plain white-washed walls, its Gothic arched window above the altar, its brooding dark oak pulpit, the ramshackle, wheezing organ on the other side on which a bald-headed man was pressing out churchy music, little loops of notes that rounded on themselves and went out.

One of the ushers, the one with the heavy tortoiseshell glasses who had been glancing over in their direction, appeared at the end of their pew.

'It's Paul, isn't it?' he said.

Paul looked up. Suzy noticed a tiny pimple on the back of his neck.

'Nigel,' said the usher. 'Nigel Browning. Garth's friend from way back when?'

'Nigel!' Paul exclaimed. 'Well, good to see you.'

Suzy turned away. A woman in a baby-blue suit was edging past the occupants of the pew in front. 'Thank you, thank you,' she said, as they bobbed to their feet to let her pass. When they sat down, Garth became visible in profile, some distance in front of them, leaning to catch something his best man was saying, something light-hearted because Garth smiled. There was the faintest family resemblance, the same aquiline nose, the same blond hair and grey eyes, but you'd be hard pressed to guess that Paul and Garth were cousins. It had been quite a surprise when Suzy had opened the envelope addressed to Mr and Mrs Paul Winslow and found Garth's wedding invitation inside. He was only a few years younger than Paul, and they had both thought of him as a confirmed bachelor, a pottery, apologetic man with hunched shoulders whom girls tended to reject. But now, it seemed, his luck had changed. Suzy glanced round at the main door behind them. The tall, spare vicar was waiting there, silhouetted against the light, his splash of red hair incongruous against his sober robes. Suzy was nosy to see the bride, who was called Tania, or possibly Sonya. The script on the invitation had

curled and spiralled so determinedly, it was impossible to be
sure.

She checked her watch. Tania was twelve minutes late, the
bride's prerogative. Suzy had been ten minutes late for their
wedding; Paul had told her afterwards that each of them had
been a torment for him. 'Nincompoop,' she'd said. And here they
were, sixteen years on, a happily married couple ready to be
reminded of the day they took their vows.

The flowers were simple and fresh: freesias and tulips in
mixed posies hanging by an ivory ribbon at the end of every other
pew. By the pulpit, tulips drooped gracefully from a glass vase on
a wrought-iron stand. She noticed Garth push back his white
cuff, unobtrusively checking the time. He seemed unperturbed;
he turned and winked at his family in the pew behind.

The music changed. 'Jesu, Joy of Man's Desiring.' Now, a
plump woman in a navy polka dot dress was sailing up the aisle.
Tania's mother? No. No mother of the bride would make such a
rushed and ungainly entrance. She cannoned into Nigel's
shoulder as she hurried on – for a second they stared at each
other, round-eyed with surprise – and then the woman pushed
past without so much as a sorry.

Little ripples flowed through the congregation.

'That's Tania's mother,' said the woman in blue.

'Why, whatever is she—'

And now Suzy saw that the vicar was hustling after her, his
cassock swinging around his squeaky black shoes. He knocked a
tulip head from its place; it fell on to the encaustic tiles, a sad
little pod.

Suzy gripped Paul's sleeve.

'It's probably just a problem with the transport or something,' he said.

Gosh, she hoped he was right. She hardly knew Garth but she
had no wish to see anyone so humiliated.

Garth was standing up. So were his parents. Suzy couldn't see

Garth's face but his ear had turned ashen, a ghastly fungus sprouting on the side of his face. The group around him appeared to steer him through a side door towards the vestry and after a moment's hesitation, Tania's mother followed. It wasn't looking good.

The vicar pulled at his nose. He stepped to the front of the aisle, staring intently at the floor. Someone had a word with the organist and the music faltered in the middle of a phrase and went out.

'Ladies and gentleman,' said the vicar. 'I expect you've gathered that there has been a hitch.'

Well, that didn't sound so bad.

'In fact the wedding will not now take place.' He paused here, frowning, and murmurs passed through the congregation. 'I would ask you all to say a prayer for Garth – and for Tania – before you leave,' the vicar finished.

'Good God!' Paul said in a low voice.

'Jilted!' said the woman in blue.

There was an instant of complete silence and then someone else said, 'I wonder if they'll be returning the presents.' Everyone began to shuffle and talk. A man in an ivory silk suit sprang to his feet. Only Suzy bent her forehead to her hand and did as the vicar had asked. She didn't believe in God but it seemed the least she could do.

Their alarm was set for 6.40. Sometimes, when the world burst into activity, the local radio hammering news bulletins into her semi-comatose head, she lay flattened by the eternal weight of gravity to her mattress.

Could I be sick today? an inner voice asked.

Almost immediately the vision this conjured – of reading in bed, of rising in the afternoon – exploded and dispersed, particles in the cruel shafts of light striking the pillow. The

universe was so arranged that it did not function properly
without her.

Each morning she took her shower, every other morning
washing her hair under the spluttering stream. Wrapped in her
bathrobe, she towelled springy hanks of hair dry and folded them
into a precarious towel turban. She always used the downstairs
shower room, tracing her way past the closed bedroom doors,
trying not to wake the family. Also, she relished this quiet,
undemanding prelude to the day.

She barely registered the faint, hollow grumble of his platform bed as Luke turned over, or the seething hiss of the shower.
Afterwards, though, she noticed a bird in the garden, its raucous,
insistent peep of hunger, and the wind, which had strengthened
overnight and was circling the trees, preparing for a tussle. Now
a car, a heavy car, pulled past. Through the small, square hall
window the brake lights of the newsagent's van halted further up
the close. The world was waking. She was no longer alone. Soon
she must break the sleep silence of her lips and surface from her
trance.

In the kitchen, she filled the kettle. The dog rose and
stretched, his tail beating air. She slapped his bowl of kibble
by the back door. Daisy appeared speechlessly behind her,
stretching in the doorway so that her commodious T-shirt rode
up to display further inches of tawny, sturdy thigh, marked a few
inches below the hip with a peachy bruise. She raised her
eyebrows in two startled circumflexes, blinking five times in
succession.

She caught Suzy watching her. 'Facial exercises,' she said.

Suzy went to kiss her, receiving a hint of floral shampoo
underlain by the spices from last night's chicken Kiev.

As she stirred instant coffee, a ceiling-quake informed Suzy
that either Paul or Luke had got up.

Last night's dream returned to her with a spasm of embarrassment. Robin Cook had been screwing her in her bed upstairs,

his beard prickling her cheek. *Really!* Suzy scolded her subconscious. *What did that mean?* Why was it that her occasional, night-time seducers were never anyone she truly found desirable? Were invariably men she thought repulsive? (Although it was shameful how aroused she'd become in her sleep.) It didn't seem fair, somehow. Whereas bedding Colin Firth in your dreams would seem an acceptable trade-off for sixteen years of blameless marital fidelity.

Paul appeared in the kitchen in his grey suit. He took a few quick swigs of his coffee, bent to peck Suzy on the cheek. A tide of soap had dried where left cheek met ear.

'Have a good day,' she called as he retreated.

'Hmph.'

'Drive carefully.'

The front door slammed. By the sink, Daisy was dreamily eating an apple pie, its foil tray cupped in one hand beneath her chin. As Suzy watched, a dollop of effulgent filling, poised at the brink of the pastry crust, fell in slow motion, missing the container, landing on the green linoleum tiles where it lay, a phosphorescent slug.

The Winslows lived in a box, a pink brick and white clapboard box, one of six in a cul-de-sac that had been bulldozed through a water meadow in the centre of their straggling village in the sixties. Over the years the inhabitants had made little attempts at individuality — a panelled hardwood front door, an extension, a new porch — brave make-up on a plain façade. Suzy and Paul hadn't done much to their house, it was true, but in this they might be fulfilling their neighbours' expectations. The general habits and characteristics of each family were well known to their fellow dwellers in Sylvan Close. They knew so much about each other, and so little.

Each family came with a set of unspoken adjectives. The

Mundays were the fusspots; Will was forever mowing his lawn or pruning his roses. The Mortlocks were the organisers, could be relied upon to take charge of the harvest festival supper or the jumble sale collection. The Winslows, Suzy suspected, were the busy, slapdash ones. People were fond of them in the way you might be fond of a clumsy, dilatory younger brother; they gave everyone else an effortless sense of their own superiority.

The Winslows' paint blistered, then peeled away from their window frames like dry skin. Their grass grew lush and tall before Paul cut it. Their lettuces bolted. Even their apples were ruined by worms and wasps, which gnawed furtive holes or hollowed pale craters in the thick red skins. Will's apples wore nylon stockings to protect them, like bank robbers.

The postman appeared. The letterbox squeaked. The mail completed its Fosbury flop on to the mat. There was a hand-written note for Paul, which aroused Suzy's curiosity, but it was only a subscription reminder from the golf club. She wondered whether she should reseal the envelope.

After the postman came the dustcart, with its heavy clanging and grinding. The dustmen, fluorescent jackets above their overalls, swung the bin bags into the lorry's screaming metal mouth. Will Munday placed his black bags outside at eight in the morning precisely, before climbing into his Daewoo Espero and driving to work. The new couple who had moved in a year before – young, unmarried, not as much a part of the close as the marrieds – put theirs outside the night before. (Will grumbled that this attracted vermin.)

Suzy compiled a To Do list. Her lists were something of a family joke, especially at Christmas or holiday time when there were master lists and sub-lists, dynasties of lists pinned to the cork board behind her glass desk in the conservatory.

The telephone rang.

'Suzy,' said a woman, her voice melodious and very deep, almost masculine.

'Mother!'

'Thank the Lord I caught you. I've got to get away. Will you get my room ready for me?'

The spare room, she meant.

'I can't stand life with your father a moment longer,' her mother's voice continued.

'What's he done now?'

'Ah, don't you put it like that. You're a one for always taking his part,' said her mother.

'No, I don't. Tell me what he's done.'

'Oh, you know what he's like . . .'

'Well,' hedged Suzy.

'Ah! He's back!' Her mother dropped her voice. 'I'll be seeing you tomorrow then.' Suzy replaced the receiver, a smile pulling at the corners of her mouth. Only a few years ago such a conversation — for they were not unusual — would have thrown her into a distressed flurry of preparations. Now, she knew better. She would receive another call, perhaps tonight or tomorrow morning. 'Suzy?' her mother would say. 'How are you? . . . Us? Oh, we're grand. Your father and I, we were just talking about you . . .'

It was Suzy's day off: she ironed, vacuumed, shopped, found a garden centre to service the lawn mower and helped out for an hour at Riding for the Disabled. At four, she picked up the children from the nearest station. The afternoon degenerated into an attempt to signal to Luke to stop mumbling to Baz on the telephone and devote his attention to the French Revolution. To discuss the horribleness of her peers with Daisy, who today had been called 'sad'. To prepare a meal that would meet with the approval of a boy who hadn't eaten tomatoes and mush-rooms since babyhood, a girl whose class had recently watched a video on factory farming methods, and a man with an atavistic urge to face red meat on his plate each evening.

The hunter-gatherer returned.

'Did you get my dry cleaning?' he said.

At nine, Suzy loaded the dishwasher. At ten, she went to bed with a magazine. The evening was chilly. Their bedroom was perpetually too hot or too cold and tonight its air held an antiseptic, early summer fragility. The skin of her bare toes looked puckered. She undressed hurriedly, pausing only to examine the red, embossed mark around her middle where her jeans did not appear to fit her any more. She pulled the duvet in its baggy yellow cover right up around her shoulders. Downstairs sounds infiltrated the bedroom: television dialogue punctuated by eruptions of music, the rolling of a kitchen drawer.

The magazine was an American publication, which she had brought back after the family holiday in Florida, and the women featured within its pages had a peculiarly glossy quality. Their hair was lustrous, their teeth and eyes would glow in the dark. She was entranced by a set of photographs of a minimalist interior. It was the bathroom that particularly attracted her. The sink was made of glass and posed next to it, in a steel vessel, like a pair of exotic orchids, were two stainless steel toothbrushes. That was all. The other rooms were similarly bare. The owners, an architect and his musician wife, had two young children. Suzy wondered how much the stylist had carted away before they took the pictures: boxes and boxes of bits and accumulations, she would guess. Despite telling herself this, she embarked on a fantasy in which she redesigned their house in a minimalist style. She brushed her teeth with a stainless steel toothbrush.

'Rescue Cure for a Tired Marriage' declared the headline on the next page to which she flicked. Oh, Suzy loved features like this. They carried the pleasures of gossip without the aftertaste of guilt. This one resembled an elongated problem page: you got her side, his side and a counsellor's overview. In this issue, Marcie was feeling under-valued. She had too much to handle. Doug was miffed, nursing a sense of rejection because Marcie never seemed to want to make love nowadays. Several sessions with the counsellor were detailed.

'If I had my time again, I wouldn't marry Doug,' Marcie declared dramatically in the first.

Woo! Talk about honesty! Talk about candour!

Impossible not to feel a squeeze of empathy for Marcie when she began to explain how perfunctory Doug was. 'He comes in and it's "I did this" and "I did that". He never asks me how my day went.'

'Now, Marcie, that is simply not true,' Doug interjected.

'It is so. Since I first noticed, I've been counting. It has been one hundred and forty-three days and you haven't once asked how my day went.'

'Well, that doesn't mean I'm not interested, honey.'

Marcie ignored him.

'Then there's his assumption that I'm responsible for running the house.'

'Hey, hang on a minute here. Who is it that mows the lawns? Who is it that takes the trash out?'

'Could you iron me a fresh shirt for tomorrow morning? Could you pick me up some new socks while you're in town, hon? It won't take a minute. Could you choose my mother's birthday present?'

'I didn't think you minded running a few errands for me. I happen to work pretty hard,' Doug said tightly.

'I happen to work too,' Marcie said.

Naturally, Doug retreated into a sulk. How very male, Suzy thought. She was beginning to dislike Doug and to hope that Marcie might leave him. But it appeared that the counsellor was highly skilled. At the end of the sixth appointment, Marcie and Doug tentatively suggested that they were ready to discontinue the sessions. The counsellor noted they made eye contact as they left her room.

Suzy let the magazine slip to the floor. She found the happy ending a touch contrived, even though she wanted Marcie to be happy. Anyway. She was drowsy. She was shattered . . . She was asleep.

The sag of the bedsprings awakened her. In the darkness, Paul's arm dropped across her ribs, heavy and restricting. He burrowed against her. A furtive life form, fluttery, swelling, rubbed against her bottom. Rigid now, it insinuated itself between her legs, rasping against her pubic hairs. Paul's hand was kneading her right breast.

'Suzy?' he whispered. 'Sooze?'

She exhaled in what she hoped was a dormant manner.

'I know you're not asleep . . .'

She lay still.

'Hey, Sooze,' continued the whisper. 'My little strumpet. How do you fancy a bit of rumpy-pumpy?'

A kaleidoscope of images wheeled before Suzy's sleep-sozzled mind: a couple in a consulting room; the luminous green numbers of the alarm clock, its central colon blinking out the seconds; tomorrow's To Do list.

She was a happily married woman.

She decided to ignore him.

Chapter Two

The bell shrilled.

Suzy, who was editing transparencies on her light box, uttered a silent swear word in her head. Working from home translated into continual intrusions. Her neighbours announced complacently, 'I'm not interrupting you, am I,' as they strolled in to discuss the latest campaign against the traffic on the bypass, or to borrow something trifling. They knew about her job, of course, but they didn't quite grasp that when she wasn't on an assignment, photographing someone's house or, occasionally, someone's garden, there was administration to catch up on: invoicing the magazine, editing, telephoning. It was her own fault. She wasn't very good at rebuffing them. She had never learned the art of gently closing a door in someone's face. She always worried about their feelings.

She put down the eye glass and straightened her track-suit bottoms, tucking in her white T-shirt. She ran her fingers through her hair, which was more than usually static.

The wavy glass panel in the centre of the front door allowed her a fugitive inspection of her caller. She made out a woman of medium build, stooping to set down a navy case. Robust, springy, vixen hair. A Mrs Punch nose in profile. An olive-green raincoat, new probably, for it stood out like a tent.

She knew that figure. That figure caused a violent fluctuation of emotions to slop around inside. It was as if some agent of the mischievous fairy folk had pitched up on her doorstep and there was nothing for it but to welcome her in.

'Sweet Mary above!' exclaimed her visitor. 'What a journey!'

An ivory saloon with a taxi sign on the roof, like an illuminated lozenge, was completing a neat three-point turn in the hammerhead of the cul-de-sac.

'Mum!' Suzy said. But her astonishment might sound ungracious. She hugged her mother quickly, the coat giving a waterproofed scrunch. The faint odour of rubber was reminiscent of new wellington boots, or Durex.

'I wasn't . . .' Tact stopped her revealing that she hadn't taken her mother's telephone call seriously.

She glanced round the empty close as she pulled the door to, checking whether there were any witnesses to her mother's arrival. An illogical anxiety, something to do with maintaining her father's dignity, even among those who had never met him, fluttered within. The pink boxes were silent and deserted, their blank windows reflecting clouds to infinity. She closed the door. Poor Dad. What had he done? Her mother couldn't be serious about this.

Paddy had already ripped apart her heavy poppers to a jolly, syncopated tempo and was folding her intransigent coat as best she could, leaving it jack-knifed over the bottom of the banisters.

'Do you like my new mac?' she said. 'I bought it for country walks.'

'You don't go on country walks,' Suzy said.

Paddy glanced at her, turned her attention to the hall. All of a sudden, it seemed poky and Suzy noticed the ruck in the runner, which the unwary might trip upon, and the overflow of greying knickers and limp socks drying on the radiator. Chester was sniffing Paddy's bum.

'It was a living nightmare,' Paddy was saying as she batted the dog's nose away. 'There was a delay. They said one of the units had a fault.' (She extended the syllables in a parody of an official accent – 'yoo-nits'.) 'This absolute brat kept bouncing up and down on the seat next to me while its mother did nothing, and this man spilt his coffee all over my newspaper so I couldn't read. Will you put the kettle on and ply me with biscuits? I need the lavvy.'

Suzy went to do as she was told. She had the sensation she had been outflanked in some way.

'That's better.'

Paddy wore a washed and brushed composure and a fresh coat of toffee-coloured lipstick, a shade chosen to complement her brown skirt and buttoned beige blouse. She drew out one of the beech-ply chairs and sat herself down at the kitchen table among the breakfast things. Two black lines outlined her lashes. She looked grand and newly theatrical. She glanced up, aware of Suzy's inspection.

'So do you like my hair?' she asked. 'I was bored after I had it cut the last time, so I walloped that henna stuff all over it. It made a right filthy mess.'

'Henna?'

'I thought it looked more natural.' She rotated her chin, fanning her layers through her fingers, trying to examine her own handiwork.

'Oh.'

'Do you remember that time you and Gerard hennaed a smiley face on your father's bald spot after he nodded off?' Paddy was continuing. Sadness settled on Suzy, a brief shadow.

'That was Gerard's idea,' she murmured. She turned her attention to the kettle, its water churning, the steam stinging her face. No point dwelling on that. Besides, Paddy was diverting her from the matter of the moment. Suzy began:

'Mother . . .'

'You didn't find that cleaning woman then,' Paddy replied. She was stabbing at stray bread crumbs with her forefinger, rubbing them off above a plate. 'Not to worry. I can make myself useful while I'm here.'

Paddy looked up at Suzy and smiled, the delta of lines under her rouge deepening. On closer scrutiny, the make-up could not disguise how drawn she looked, or that her pale eyes were tinged with yellow. Did this indicate some serious strain? Long, slow months reaching unhappy conclusions?

But the notion of her parents splitting up – at their ages, after forty-odd years of marriage – was risible, surely? And *while I'm here* didn't sound very permanent.

Behind various packet soups and the tins of low fat rice pudding, Suzy located a pack of Rich Tea biscuits. A chink of pottery suggested that Paddy was scraping and stacking the breakfast plates. Suzy started again:

'Do you think you'll be? . . . Mother, what exactly has happened between you two?'

Paddy was lining up cutlery very precisely in a row.

'Oh, Suzanne,' she said. 'Oh, Suzy.' She stared very hard at the plate. 'I know you're not going to understand.'

A wobble in her voice, a nakedness of emotion, elicited a flash of panic in Suzy. There was a long silence that she was at a loss to break. She spent some moments gazing at two globes of the dog's kibble, which were collecting fluff by the skirting board.

'Do you remember Judith?' Paddy eventually asked.

'Who?'

'My friend. Surely you can't have . . .'

'Yes, yes, of course I remember her.'

Judith was Paddy's oldest friend, a tall, thin blonde who had lived two streets away during Suzy's estate childhood, who had been a nearly permanent presence over cups of coffee in the kitchen when Gerard, Suzy and Clare arrived home from school. She had featured on the guest list for every family celebration in her capacity as an honorific aunt.

'She's got breast cancer,' Paddy announced. 'She found out last January.'

'Oh . . . well, will she be all right?'

Paddy gave an anxious grimace. 'So they say.' She made a tiny sign of the cross in the air above her bosom; it wasn't a serious gesture, she hadn't been to Mass in a decade.

'Um, well, she had trouble before, didn't she? I seem to remember. Lumps which turned out to be benign.' Suzy set to clearing the table of the plates and bowls, scraping crusts into the pedal bin. Her face was reflected darkly in its chrome lid – her round, grey eyes, her fringe hanging heavily – before the lid swung upwards and she was replaced by crumpled cartons and a banana skin.

'I'd say she was expecting the same diagnosis, this time,' Paddy continued. 'She was very shocked when they told her it was cancer. It made her think. You know she doesn't love Michael, not for these long years she hasn't. Ever since that affair when she came entirely too close to a nervous breakdown, in my opinion.'

'Michael was unfaithful?'

Paddy shot her a look.

'An awful business, it was. Didn't you know? I thought I told you. But perhaps she asked me to keep it quiet? Anyway, she's kicked him out and she's starting anew.'

'Ah.'

Judith was frozen in Suzy's mind at some point in her fifties, when she and her husband had sold up and moved to a detached, non-estate location on the other side of Stevenage. This must have been after the tumultuous breakdown. She tried to imagine her at sixty-something, starting over as a single woman. What was happening to people?

'Michael's living in their caravan in a caravan park outside Bristol.'

'A caravan park?' Suzy thought she could see where the conversation was leading, an idea that produced a defensive palpitation.

'But Daddy hasn't had an affair!'

Paddy sniffed, an exhalation of muted scorn that implied he didn't have it in him, but in a placatory tone she added only, 'Ah, Suzy, you know how he is.' There was another pause. 'It's the same old cycle,' she continued slowly. 'We rub along quite peacefully, a week, a fortnight goes by. Then a row breaks out over nothing. He says to me, "Are you booking the car in for its service, or am I?" Well, he knows full well I am, I'd said I would. It's his way of nagging. He tells me I nag, but he's like an old woman himself. "Are you doing this? Have you done that?" It drives me to distraction. He says, "I'm only ask-ing." ' She drew out the syllables in a way Suzy had heard her father do a hundred times. She had to suppress a little grin at the accuracy of the impersonation.

'Then, of course, he starts to sulk . . .' Paddy tailed off. She cupped her fingers around her mouth. 'It's wrong of me to say so.'

'No, it's not.'

'Wicked, even. Anyway,' Paddy said. 'Anyway . . .'

'Perhaps you should go for counselling—'

'He's gone down to the cottage for a fortnight to see about painting the exterior, which, I may tell you, he only painted last summer. I said to him, I told him: "I've had enough. Do not expect me to be here when you get back." '

Suzy felt a rush of relief. 'He's gone to Cornwall? When?'

'What? Oh, yesterday . . . yesterday evening it was . . .

'Compromises,' Paddy added slowly. 'I am fed up to the back teeth with making compromises.'

Everything had become clear to Suzy. A fortnight, she

repeated to herself. Paddy would return home in a fortnight's time; of course she would. Her father would be banking on that, too. She imagined him pottering around the narrow, terraced cottage with his paint pots and his brushes, serenely daubing colour on bowed walls, content in the knowledge that his wife was with their daughter. Paddy wouldn't have wanted to accompany him. She was a possessive person, resenting him giving his attention to any object other than herself; nor would she want to be left alone. That was her predicament. She hated being without attentive company, always had done; the Irish half of her was as gregarious as it was boisterous.

Suzy admonished herself for being so foolish. Why did she always take these ruptures of theirs so seriously? She'd been observing them for thirty-eight years; she should have learned their pattern by now.

Paddy required tending, somehow. She needed to be hosted. She wanted a different sort of lunch, not a sandwich, but something more substantial on a plate. ('I'm not fussy, just a little green salad with a slice of quiche, say, or a bowl of soup and a roll,' was how she put it.) Also, she expected Suzy to break from her desk to come and eat with her. She said she would make up her own bed, but five minutes later, just as Suzy had resumed editing her last shoot, she reappeared in the doorway, expectantly. Suzy was trying to decide between two images of a white porcelain bowl, switching the magnifying glass from one to the other, her Chinograph hovering over the left-hand shot . . .

'Suzy? Are you busy? I don't know my way around. You'll have to come and show me which sheets I can use.'

Oh yes, for the next twenty-four hours, Suzy was aware that Paddy's arrival had altered something within their pink-brick walls, as the molecules of air rearranged themselves to accommodate the bulk of a fifth body.

The children were pleased to see her, of course. They seemed to take her sudden appearance in their stride, unsurprised by the turbulent track of adult relations.

'Gran! How's you?' Daisy cried, hurling her bag into the back seat of the car. Her fine, fair hair was dishevelled after the day at school, a central section of her fringe standing up as if statically charged. She inserted her navy shoulders into the gap between the Golf's front seats and stretched a kiss on Paddy's cheek. 'I didn't know you were coming. How long are you staying?'

'Well, I'm not sure. You're not trying to get rid of me, are you? I've only been here five minutes,' Paddy teased. But Daisy took her literally:

'Of course not, Granny,' she said earnestly. 'You know I'd never do that.'

'Lo, Gran,' said Luke. A grease mark had appeared in the exact centre of his grey-and-green, diagonally-striped tie.

Paul, on the other hand, spat out, 'Christ! I hope she's not going to be emotional,' and slammed his car door so hard that the light cast from the street lamp appeared to wobble.

'I hope she doesn't think she's staying,' he hissed.

'Well, of course she's staying.'

'For long, I meant. For good.'

'Of course she's not staying for good.'

'Why doesn't she just grow up?' he asked, before stumping indoors and up the stairs. He was never normally so vehement. Only her mother seemed to rouse him to such passion.

It's not as simple as that, Suzy answered his question silently. She was shivering. It was a clear night and the stars had emerged, pale spangles in the deepening dome of the sky; looking at stars always made Suzy sad and wistful. She followed Paul across the window shape of warm light stencilled on the porch tiles, clicked the door quietly to. In the kitchen, steam had condensed on the windows; the washing machine chugged comfortably in its corner. She had ignored Paul's overtures last night, she remembered, that was the root cause of his bad mood.

A preposterous ebullience bubbled up in Suzy that evening. It was as if she hoped to carry the others along with her energy. She went to more trouble than usual, laying the dining table, with glasses on coasters and the beans and potatoes piled into the heavy, blue serving dishes. Melting knobs of butter formed oily rivers, which flowed over the green logs and floury slopes. She set the ivory pepper mill and the silver salt cellar in the centre of the table. Candles might be a notch too far.

A tune she liked was playing on the kitchen radio. She began to sing along. '*Ooh! Think twice! Just an-other da-ay in par-a-dise!*' Beads of blood formed on the grain of the steaks in their pan. She danced backwards through to the dining room, partnering a stack of plates.

'This is nice.' Daisy had pushed her way through the stiff double doors from the sitting room.

Suzy smiled at her. 'Well, thank you!' she said, dealing green rimmed plates onto each woven place mat.

Luke barged in behind his sister. He was still in his uniform, the white shirt ferociously crumpled, the grey trousers fanned with creases at hip and knee.

'Why are we eating in here?' he cried. 'I want mine on a tray.'

Suzy's spirits stuttered. 'Not tonight, Luke.'

'But there's something really good on the box!'

'Just this once we're going to eat as a family.'

'Oh, bollocks!' He made a viperish, stabbing motion with his chin. 'I don't suppose we've got such a thing as a blank video tape in this household,' he demanded of no one in particular as he barged his way out.

Paddy's voice, raised above the newscaster on the television, asked, 'What is it that you're looking for, Luke? You're blocking my screen . . . Sorry?' There was a rumble from Luke. 'Ah, well, eating in front of the television is a slovenly way of living, I always think.'

Paddy and Daisy appeared within moments of Suzy calling out that supper was ready.

'Hungry?' Paddy asked.

'Starving.'

But they hovered with their hands on the backs of the chairs until Suzy told them to sit where they wanted. Luke, when she summoned him again, hollered back, 'I'm tuning the video.' '*Special, digitally re-mastered version,*' said the television set and loud theme music played.

'Turn it down, Luke.'

'I only want the tichiest steak,' Daisy was saying, as she mounded vegetables on her plate. 'Oh, Gran, sorry! Do you want vegetables?'

'I'll wait my turn,' Paddy said.

Daisy finished with the serving dish and passed it carefully to Paddy. Then she picked up her knife and fork to slice into a potato. There was a clatter as she dropped both on her plate, remembering her manners. She cast an enquiring gaze at her mother.

'Start, both of you,' Suzy ordered.

Paddy asked for a napkin.

'Luke!' Suzy yelled, as she rose to her feet.

This time he appeared, edging into the room backwards, straining his neck for one last tantalising glimpse of the TV set before taking his place.

'I've got a bottle of good red somewhere. Would you like a glass, Mum?' Suzy recalled, as she handed Paddy a somewhat linty paper serviette excavated from the bottom of a drawer.

'That would be lovely.'

Suzy retraced her path to the kitchen.

At last, Paul had put in an appearance. He was wearing his

faded cotton trousers and an old, soft shirt, with splurges of the apricot emulsion from Daisy's bedroom on the sleeves. He was attempting to press a wedge of polystyrene packaging into the overflowing bin. The lid wouldn't shut flush.

'What are you doing?' Suzy hissed. 'Don't do that now.' In the background, she was aware of Paddy quizzing the children about school and only Daisy answering.

The Châteauneuf-du-Pape was tucked behind the carousel in the corner cupboard.

'I was saving that bottle for our anniversary,' Paul told her as she pulled the cork.

'Will you go through?' She hoped he wasn't going to be curmudgeonly.

'Paddy,' he declared in a controlled way, stooping by her chair.

'Paul!' she said, a little warmer. They touched cheeks, Paddy pursing her lips to the air a few centimetres from his skin. Suzy relaxed a degree.

She had selected the largest steak for Paul from long habit: largest for Paul, second largest for Luke. She passed it across to him. A juice, buttery and brown, streaked with blood, had collected in the dish.

'I saved you a nice half-pounder,' she told him. 'Do eat up. Before it gets cold.'

Paul prodded at the meat with his knife.

'This is much too big for me,' he said. 'I'll never get through this.'

'Just try.'

'So,' Daisy told Paddy, 'they showed us this video and all the girls were going, "Leo! Leo!" and it was just, like, totally obvious that no one was taking any notice of the actual play . . .'

Paddy was wearing a bemused smile, studying Daisy carefully as she spoke, as if she were deaf and having to lip read.

'Well,' said Suzy brightly, as she sawed into her steak. 'It's been a long time since we had a proper family supper.' She glanced at the familiar faces spaced around her table. 'Isn't this nice?' she prompted.

There was no response except from Daisy, who offered her a nervy smile, a kink at the corner of her mouth, which might have been of agreement, or which might have been of sympathy.

For a while there was no sound but the chink and scratch of cutlery on china and a slow mastication. A yell came from the television. Suzy found she couldn't think of a thing to say.

Chapter Three

Paul contemplated moving to the sofa that night but was visited
by an intuition that Paddy would discover him – if he overslept,
for example, or if she came down to fetch a glass of water. This
moored him to his own mattress. Oh, yes, Paddy'd sniff him out
all right. He could sense her moving in for the kill.

Christ! He was fed up. He had worked up an angry, bilious
churning in his gut. If not, it was that ruddy great slab of a steak.
What a lousy cook Suzy was! You'd have thought her skills
would have improved over the years. Other women seemed to
enjoy cooking, were forever watching television programmes and
throwing together Tuscan feasts. But not Suzy . . . He tossed
and turned. He scratched a random itch on his backside. He
pounded the pillows a couple of times. But Suzy exhaled
peacefully, serene on her side of the bed further from the door.

He was being a prick, he knew, which made him all the
angrier with Suzy somehow. He couldn't blame her for having a
mother, of course, but Christ! This was his own home! He was
acutely aware of Paddy's presence just metres from where he lay,
a respiring entity behind the thin plaster walls. He thought he
could detect her snoring, a chesty, rhythmic rumbling right at the
edge of hearing. No wonder he couldn't sleep. And he was facing
a heavy day tomorrow.

It was at times like this he examined his wife for early symptoms of maternal metamorphosis. Recent signs suggested that she was not the sunny, energetic, complaisant girl he had married, who had seemed so different to either of her parents. Now he saw that she was an amalgamation of them both. Sometimes, he thought she incorporated their better points, missing out on the bad, but increasingly, he had his suspicions.

He'd been twenty-four when they'd married, a mere stripling. Back in the early eighties, that was what people did. There had been a sense of relief in having settled the matter. Phewph! No more dating. No more uncertainties. No more disappointments. Time to get on with adult life. So he had plunged into marriage impatiently.

He'd been paddling frantically beneath the surface ever since. That was how it felt. (He was visited by a sudden flash of his long white legs with their bony knees and ankles, treading water.) He was one of the rear guard, the last of the last generation to act in such a spontaneous, daring fashion. These days, people dithered at the edge, dipped a toe in and as often as not retreated. Or they seemed to be proceeding according to a scheme, something that was considered, sage and sensible, so much more so than his way of doing things. But it was odd: on the one hand, he was proud of his decisiveness; on the other, small regrets stung him. And he didn't want his children to rush into marriage as he had done. Twenty-seven was the ideal age, he thought. Maybe twenty-eight. What about thirty?

They had met at her parents' house. Gerard had effected a listless, garbled introduction. Suzy said, 'Hi,' in a friendly enough fashion, but almost immediately slipped out of the kitchen. He was left with an impression of red gold hair, of large grey eyes and wide cheek bones and of a figure that caused him a summary satisfaction. There was something resilient about her that Paul grew to like: the spring of her wiry hair, the set of her shoulders, the way she wrinkled her nose right up when he said something she disagreed with.

She was fervent about matters that were never discussed in his household: the environment, the shape of a tree. 'Don't you love the shades in that bark?' she said to him once, gazing out of Gerard's bedroom window at her parents' commonplace back garden. And yes, she was right; it wasn't brown, it was chestnut, rich and polished. How come he had never noticed it before? He remembered her perched on the back of the kitchen chair telling him that Anne Boleyn was the first feminist, and Gerard saying, 'Oh, shut up, Suzy.' But Paul was attracted by the elliptical shape of her thoughts, that she produced so many odd, quirky abstractions that she could scatter them on everyday landscapes or on Tudor queens. It had been in the back of his mind to ask her out one day, if Gerard didn't object.

After Gerard's death, they'd been thrown together a lot. Naturally, he had wanted to support the family in whatever way he could. He had sat in the passenger seat while Suzy learned to drive. Her mother had given up driving, so Suzy practised with her father at weekends, or with Paul in his beaten-up Beetle on weekday evenings. Once they drove to Thetford forest and she had parked in a rutted lay-by beneath the still shade of a conifer forest. When she cut the engine it was absolutely quiet, all noise absorbed by the thick, spiny carpet of needles on the forest floor. On impulse, he stooped and kissed her, a chaste brush of her lips. She tasted of lipstick, that sweet, waxy smell. The make-up around her eyes was clumsily applied, which made her look younger and more vulnerable than ever. It seemed to him that that was the moment he had fallen in love with her, though it was years before he kissed her again. He'd progressed to Sheena, who had cheated on him, and Charlotte, who began to find fault with him, and Jan, who had clung to him. Then, when Suzy was older and they were both free, he had asked her out. It was a relief to be with Suzy, who seemed familiar as an old friend.

'We have to go,' she'd said, after he'd kissed her in Thetford forest.

'Already?'

'My parents might be worried,' she said. 'We've been an hour driving up here.'

'Of course.'

Back then, her consideration for their feelings had impressed him. He hadn't foreseen that she might regard this pair of wounded people as her responsibility for ever after. To be honest, back then, in the aftermath of the accident, he had regarded them as his responsibility, too.

Rationally, he knew he was the only member of the party who was not to blame for what had happened. His had been the one small voice of moderation. He had driven the following car. And he had been sober. He reproached himself nevertheless. Over the intervening years, Paddy seemed to have divined this feeling of his. She had come to regard him with suspicion, as if there must be some basis for his guilt. As if he was keeping a murky secret.

Oh, he admitted it: the years had made him more reserved. He had grown to doubt people. He was wary of spending his affection on them. Frankly, it didn't seem to be worth getting to know them. His and Gerard's contemporaries from university had scattered to the far reaches of the country and had gradually slipped off Suzy's Christmas-card list. A settled friendship with a colleague became obsolete the moment he left the company. The man never telephoned. He never replied to invitations.

Those foreign students Suzy had met at church in Cambridge, keeping what amounted to open house and open larder for them – they had all vanished to their respective countries when their courses finished. These were people who had invited themselves to Daisy's birthday party. One of them, the girl called Rosa, had said, rolling her r's so fiercely that Paul's throat stung in sympathy, 'I am wanting to see a traditional English celebration.' It had made him feel like part of a freak show. And then: not so much as a postcard from any of them. It was as if these people had never existed.

It was Suzy's brother who had died, but it was Paul who had grasped how tenuous people were, how temporary.

She had been hurt by those foreign students, he knew. One day, examining the post, she'd said sadly, 'You would have thought Rosa at least would have dropped me a line.' And part of Paul had welled with sympathy for her, and most of him had itched with irritation.

The trouble was, Suzy's wide, open face was naturally friendly; she looked attentive without even trying, so that strangers gravitated towards her.

'I knew,' the Spanish woman had confided, scoffing cake at his table, 'the first time I saw your wife, I said, "That is a good woman." '

'Yes,' Paul had replied, flatly.

He usually wore a closed expression, he realised, and other people, even those who knew him fairly well – some of the neighbours, for example – found him forbidding. But if he nodded or grinned when people addressed him, he felt false and . . . gushing, that was the word. Often, he was simply wondering how to reply. He liked to weigh his words before letting them loose. It was better than prattling, wasn't it?

And on many occasions, it was useful to appear aloof. If he could assume the right expressions now, Paddy might leave sooner rather than later. If you got right down to it, why couldn't Suzy be a step more detached? Why couldn't she separate herself from other individuals? Why did she always have to be so naïve? She acted like a big sister to the world, to everyone except her own husband.

She was dribbling on her pillow.

Each and every detail about her seemed to be rubbing him up the wrong way at the moment. He'd like to sit her down and tell her, lay it out logically and impassively. 'Look,' he would say. 'These are the ways you don't shape up to my template of an ideal wife. These are your pros and these your cons, so how about doing something about the second column?' He was an accountant by training so perhaps it came naturally to him to want to construct a tidy balance sheet of something as flawed and messy as a wife? (Even as he thought this, he felt his ears burn: he was caught, squirming, on a pin of exquisite self-knowledge.)

But in reality, he would never speak out: what man would dare? Also, he hated scenes. Loathed them. Would do almost anything to avoid them.

You could never be sure how Suzy would react if he did voice his frustrations. That time he'd asked her to grow her hair past her shoulders, duplicate the style she'd had when he met her, and she'd begun to cry. He'd been stumped. Finally, she'd confided in a small voice, 'Sorry, I'm being stupid. I had a bad day and then I passed a building site and realised I'd reached the invisible stage.' He'd thought about that for a while. It had caught his heart in some way. And when she'd walked past him, on her way to the kitchen to make the coffee, he'd caught her by the skirt and uttered a low wolf-whistle, and she'd stopped, and subsided in his arms, and, well . . . that had developed into one of the good moments they'd shared recently.

Pity there weren't a few more of them.

Mind you, Paddy snoring on the other side of the partition wall was going to have the same effect as swallowing neat bromide before bed. 'Stuck with a stiffy? Try Paddy! The sure-fire antidote to Viagra! *Da-ta-da!*' He composed a television advertisement for her unique properties and chuckled over it, grimly.

There was no deal to be struck, no bargaining in a marriage. You had to bite the words back. You learned, slowly and painfully, there was absolutely no point itemising your partner's faults. She didn't want to rectify them.

Fay held this theory: you rowed for the first decade or so of marriage, and then you shut up because you knew there was no changing each other. You either accepted it or you bailed out. Paul had never seriously thought about bailing out, although every now and then he tried on the idea, which seemed a bit like trying on some outlandish garment. Sometimes these scenarios ended with Suzy begging him to return, a chastened and more appreciative Suzy. Sometimes Fay had featured in them. She was the junior executive at the office, an alert but very feminine woman in her early thirties, with long shiny blond hair. Several times Fay had sat across a pub table from him talking – about the office at first, and then about more.

She was working long hours, as Paul well knew, but her husband didn't seem to appreciate the fact. Her husband didn't so much as load the dishwasher. (Neither did Paul, but he skipped over that in his sympathetic murmuring. Anyway, it was different: Suzy didn't have a proper job.)

Fay wore green eyeliner and a ruddy lipstick which left smeared half-smiles on the empty glasses. It was fun to speculate about an affair with lipsticked Fay. A flight of his married imagination. A lunchtime flirtation, nothing more. He felt rather righteous about this line he had drawn. He prided himself on his loyalty. He would never actually *do* anything about Fay.

But Fay hadn't understood this. It was hard to put your finger on, but . . . the tilt of her smile seemed to alter. And the moment they sat down at their table – *their* table! – by the side window in the pub, her conversation took a lurch into intense, serious territory. She leaned forward and her foot brushed his.

He grew indignant that she had misread him so badly, that she would imagine he would make a pass at her merely because he was a sympathetic sort of person. The conceit of the woman! Puh! That Fay went right down in his estimation. The lunches petered out.

'Do you love me?' he sometimes asked his wife, after a row,

during a patch when they seemed cranky with each other. He never started their arguments. His strategy was to turn quiet. After half a day, he had noticed, Suzy grew conciliatory and would endeavour to set things right, which was reassuring, active proof of her enduring priorities.

'Are you all right?' she would venture.

'I'm fine. Why shouldn't I be?' he inevitably replied.

And after sleeping on it, he was.

But recently the crotchety, scratchy periods seemed to have extended. She wasn't trying so hard to discover why he'd turned taciturn. Perhaps she didn't care so much? That time he'd come upon her, knife clicking at a pile of herbs on the chopping board, and he had wrapped his arms around her, under the soft bounce of her boobs, and pressed his groin to the yielding warmth of her rounded bottom.

'Do you love me?' he'd said.

But instead of replying, 'Of course,' in that indulgent tone, she'd said, 'Don't be silly,' in a distracted, dismissive way.

Oh, he knew what he should have done: wheeled her around, discarded his boyish demeanour and substituted an adult one, talked to her . . . but no, he'd obeyed a petty prompting. He'd whisked away his arms and stamped off to the shed, pretending to be engrossed in compost and seed trays. He'd replied in monosyllables when she asked him questions. He'd kept it up for three days running. He'd been obstinately proud of it at the time.

Chapter Four

Often Suzy was gripped by the notion that the merest hitch in their routine would throw everything out, like a tiny spark of static garbling the insides of a computer. So the fact that Paddy did, indeed, make herself useful should have come as a great comfort.

Here she was, emerging from her bedroom just as Suzy stepped from hers. There she was in the kitchen, which hung with salty, oily smells and was scattered with frying pans, grill pans and eggy plates, while Luke — bright in the morning for once — was mopping yolk from his plate with a spongy fold of bread.

'God! It's been decades since anyone cooked me a proper fry-up for brekkie, Gran,' he announced.

And there was Paddy immediately afterwards, locking Paul out of the shower room, even as Daisy was stretching tooth brushing into a quarter-of-an-hour exercise in the bathroom upstairs.

Oh, Lord.

Seeing Paddy before she had applied her make-up was alarming, the transformation from bold to bloodless and back again. After she was lipsticked and combed, she looked in need of a day's small adventures. Suzy knew that for once she should ditch her normal schedule. She would devote some time to her mother. She suggested they went to Cambridge together. She wanted a rug for the sitting room in any case. Daisy was demanding a bra. Paul needed underpants.

She wrote out a list.

The road had turned a deeper shade of grey from an overnight shower. There was a tailback at the railway crossing even though the barrier had already risen. Suzy noticed how a vapour of sooty grime had adhered to the pebbledash of the elderly cottage by which they were stopped. New leaves, tenderly corrugated, were unfurling from the straggly beech hedge on the other side of the carriageway. Meanwhile, Paddy was chattering about various neighbours whom Suzy could barely place.

They tramped around Cambridge, completing a circuit of department stores. Paddy had a way of sailing through the crowds, her chin held high, her gaze fixed a few inches above the scalps of everyone else. The crowds streaming across Parker's Piece eddied around her, individuals stepping out of her way. Her stride was long and purposeful and Suzy, despite being a few inches taller, had to concentrate on keeping up.

Suzy remembered being left behind in a shop once, a clothes shop it must have been, for there were heavy dark coats on hangers all around her, so that, at her level, the shop noise seemed muffled. She remembered the shuffling forest of legs and her escalating disbelief as she scanned it for her mother's. After a while she had simply turned to the adult nearest to her and demanded help. He was a tall, thin man, balding, dishevelled, his wisps of hair standing at interesting angles to his skull. She'd been fascinated by his scarecrow fuzz.

'Well, let me see. Maybe I'll take you to the police station,' the man said.

Suzy had slipped her hand into his dry palm and off they'd gone, back down the High Street, until, at the big junction, Paddy's shriek resounded from the pedestrian island in the centre, her words drowned by the thunder of a passing lorry. The round-eyed faces of Paddy, Gerard and Clare disappeared behind tarpaulin, a rick-rack of rope and deep-treaded tyres, then reappeared around her, while simultaneously the scarecrow man said, 'Ah, good, your mother,' and slipped away.

Well, this was Suzy's memory. The episode was a long time ago and had probably been tinkered with. For three decades she had heard it retold by her family, who regarded it as peculiarly indicative of her trustfulness. In the same circumstances, Gerard, a skinny boy with a cool, unhurried vigilance, would have withdrawn wordlessly to a corner until he spotted a policeman or Paddy herself returning, stately and unruffled. As for Clare, she stuck to Paddy's side with a fierce, frowning concentration, one hand clenched around the hem of her mother's coat; there was no question of losing Clare.

'So, he was probably genuine enough,' Paddy said of the man who disappeared. 'He was taking you in the right direction, that's for sure.'

Paul had been appalled when at some point he had been acquainted with this story. He appeared to worry that Suzy might prove a similarly negligent mother. When Luke started to toddle, Paul returned one day with a pair of reins, pale blue for a boy, which he wanted Suzy to use on shopping expeditions. Later, it seemed to Suzy that this was the beginning of Luke's uncertainty; ironically, the result of Paddy's imperturbable mothering was untroubled, confident children.

Paddy interrupted her thoughts:

'If there's a God,' she said, seemingly addressing the branches of a plane tree, 'we'll find a rug you like at the next stop.'

But they didn't. They returned to the first department store they had visited and bought the geometrically patterned rug Suzy had been wavering over. The salesman said he would have it rolled and wrapped and delivered to customer collection.

Paddy decided she needed a jacket. They lurched to the third floor in a tiny, rickety lift, where she tried on several in succession, examining her rear view in a sloping mirror, tugging at the hems.

'Them jackets over there are good value,' said the salesgirl, a tiny bird of a girl, keen and chirpy. 'Do you want formal or casual?'

'Both, really,' said Paddy. But after she had slipped into a garnet wool blazer, she announced ruefully:

'Ah, you see. It's not a new outfit I want. It's a new head.'

Both Suzy and the salesgirl snuffled with laughter at that, but Suzy caught a glint in her mother's eye, of something tart behind the intrepid humour.

'Let's go to lunch,' she suggested.

There was a small self-service restaurant on the top floor. Suzy coasted a thin wooden tray along the metal tracks, halting by the hot section, where Paddy ordered a lasagne which was curling at the edges, sweating globules of oil. The waitress lazily lifted a row of metal lids to allow Suzy to inspect the dishes. She chose a bowl of chilli. Not much that overheating could do to a bowl of chilli, she told herself. She'd have to postpone the diet until tomorrow.

The bill came to twelve pounds forty. Paddy asked the woman at the till if she took American Express.

'Look, I'll pay if you haven't got any cash,' Suzy said hurriedly.

'Oh, I have,' said Paddy. 'It's just I'm trying to build up my air miles.'

'Cash, cheque or debit card,' said the girl behind the till.

Suzy handed her three five-pound notes.

At their wobbly Formica table, they talked of this and that, of Clare and her last letter, of Clare's new apartment and how Americanised she was becoming, of Suzy's small, nagging worries about Luke and Daisy.

'Her friends . . . all they seem to think about is boys.'

'Ah, well, it's their age. You weren't so different.'

'Oh, we were! You have no idea how obsessed these girls are. And they're only eleven.'

'You were mad about that boy with the shoulder-length hair. What was his name?'

A string bean of a teenager in tight, faded jeans stalked across Suzy's mind. His sweet, girlish face. His hair on his shoulders. His inexpert kisses.

'Bob!' she recalled.

'Bob! That's right. How I fretted about Bob.'

'Mother, I was seventeen. There was no need to fret. I always remember Daddy refusing to go to bed until Bob left. We sat in the kitchen till two one morning, just to see if he'd crack sooner.'

Suzy was beginning to smile at the remembrance, but Paddy sniffed.

'Your father was always a fussbudget,' she said.

Suzy stopped and looked at her, hesitating. Paddy changed the subject swiftly.

'Clare never gave me a moment's worry. Not on that score. Funny, isn't it? You ran through boyfriends like a child in a candy store—'

'Oh, Mother!'

'While Clare scarcely looked at them. And look at the pair of you now. You a faithful wife. And she a . . .' Paddy tailed off.

'Serial monogamist,' Suzy supplied gently.

'Is that what you call it?'

'Well . . .'

'You never judge anyone, do you, Suzy?'

'Well, I . . .' But she subsided. Paddy had sounded accusatory, that same sour note.

'Like your father, I suppose,' Paddy mused.

Plainly, this was not a compliment.

'At least Clare has my pep. We have Grandma Scannell to thank for that.'

A voice piped up inside, *I have pep, too, you know.* Surely she must have inherited something from the Scannell side of the family? Suzy always imagined her late grandmother as a caricature of an Irish working-class woman, doughty and feisty and upright, scrubbing floors to feed her parcel of kids while her feckless husband drank away his dockyard pay. She had a little difficulty superimposing her cool, slender sister upon this vital, ginger rabble-rouser.

'But there you are,' Paddy was saying. 'She stuck by my father until the day he died. He wasn't an easy man, but she managed it. She learned to handle him after a fashion.'

'More fool her,' said Suzy, who thought there was a considerable difference between Grandpa Scannell and her own father.

Paddy laughed, one soft bark, and squeezed Suzy's hand with her own.

'I agree with you there. Maybe I'd have been happier if she'd left him. She stayed because of us, of course, and the disgrace and what her mam would have said.'

'Stupid,' said Suzy, who was wondering what her mother meant by 'happier'. The conversation seemed to have whisked away, out of her control. She shouldn't have sounded so approving.

Paddy leaned forward.

'Ah God, it's hard, isn't it? I think you're doing a grand job, Suzy. Plugging away at your marriage, tucked away in the suburbs of England . . . Don't I know for myself that it isn't easy?'

'Well . . .' Suzy was left wordless once more.

'Deathly dull,' Paddy said sitting back, shaking her curls.

Something snagged on Suzy's feelings.

'Judith said to me, "I shouldn't worry," she said. "If he makes Suzy happy." '

Paddy was discussing Suzy's marriage with *Judith?*

'She said, "At least Paul's a decent provider." '

Suzy stared at her. She should defend her husband. 'But that's not—'

'I thought it was the rebound.'

'What? Me and Paul? But who was I on the rebound from? Bob?' The idea was ridiculous.

The brackets by Paddy's mouth and the lines on her forehead suddenly deepened.

'Not boyfriends,' Paddy said. 'Gerard.'

'Oh.'

Let it go, Suzy told herself. Why provoke a disagreement that might stir something up? Something dark and painful.

'Let me get us a coffee,' Paddy said, digging in her handbag for her purse. She unzipped it. 'Oh, hell's bells, I really don't have any change . . .'

'I'll get them.'

As she pushed back the plastic bucket chair, Suzy saw her life refracted through Paddy's gaze. It had never before occurred to her that it might not be universally envied. At some point, she had ceased to notice its humdrum, unvarnished reality. Paddy was right. Contentment equalled monotony. She took a tray to the counter. She ordered two coffees and pushed away a looping, wriggling, rebellious thought.

'Suzy, you're going to make us late.'

'It's only a barbecue.'

'You look fine without make-up, you know.'

Suzy was applying lipstick at her dressing-table mirror, while keeping an eye on Daisy who, cross-legged on the bed, was dabbing Suzy's blusher onto her cheeks with an expertise that was unsettling in an eleven-year-old.

'Kieran asked Tessa on a date on Friday,' she said suddenly.

'A date?'

'Yeah. He passed her this note asking her out to Tesco's.'
'Tesco's?'

Daisy sniggered. 'Mrs Butcher found out. She asked everyone what they were giggling about, and Anna gave her the note. It was hilarious, Mum. Mrs Butcher read it out to the whole class and everyone cracked up. Tessa got really angry, said it was none of Mrs Butcher's business and she was never going to speak to me and Anna again.'

'Are you ready?' Paul materialised by the dressing table, holding her black mohair cardigan which she'd left on the chair. Her hair was being a nuisance. She checked Paul's expression. It would have to do.

'Last week,' said Daisy, 'it was Edward was supposed to be her boyfriend . . .'

'These jeans make me look fat, don't they?' Suzy asked Paul.

'You look fine,' he said, after the most cursory of glances.

They called goodbye to the sitting room where Luke was hunched in a corner of the sofa, watching sport on television.

'A barbecue in bloody May,' he announced by way of acknowledgement. Both he and Daisy had been included in the invitation but had forcefully refused to attend.

Paddy looked up from the green wing chair. She was stitching up the hem of one of Daisy's slippery pink dresses.

'Have a nice time,' she called back in a cheery falsetto.

Paul marched through the cul-de-sac at an athletic pace. Suzy skittered after him. Why did all her family have to walk so fast? They had already passed the Mundays', its square of lawn edged by a garden centre range of hybrid tea roses, stalky, angular plants, which sprouted a fierce rainbow of cabbage blooms throughout the summer. The Proctors' border was a more pleasing medley of herbaceous plants and shrubs. Grant had recently tacked some bottle-green shutters to the windows.

In the lane, to their right, a row of sway-backed thatches led to the church, the pub and the shop, the nucleus of the old village. They turned left, where the pavement was swamped by nettles and weeds spilling from the foot of the hedgerow. Secretive scramblings and rustlings hinted at the presence of shy mammals. A slow breeze teased music from the green wheat field beyond. A gentleness in this day would usually have persuaded Suzy to linger, but Paul strode on, stepping into the road to leave Suzy the tapering path to herself.

The hedgerow gave way, abruptly, to a row of council houses, and then a small development of pretend period houses. They reminded Suzy of the dressing-up box and the fantasies of children, miniature toy-town houses with a certain innocence about them.

'God, I hate do's like this,' Paul mumbled.

Suzy slipped her arm through his. He was hurrying to get it over and done with, the way he arrived a quarter of an hour early for his dental appointments. She experienced a sudden surge of tenderness for him.

A gleaming caravan had appropriated most of the Cartwrights' drive. As she squeezed past, Suzy snagged her cardigan on the thorns of another hybrid tea. She extracted it from the mohair, a fleshy triangle, a Jurassic armour-plated spine. She had to be careful or it would damage the knit.

By the time she had disengaged herself, Paul had disappeared along the concrete strip by the side of the house. Bloody hell! He was so irritating! She could kick him, sometimes.

A crescendo of conversation met her as she caught up with his blue-shirted back in the garden. Angela waved at them wordlessly; she was in mid flow, enthusing about the new caravan.

'Ten thousand, it cost, but we'll make that back within five years when you count the cost of hotels or villas. Rod worked it all out quite carefully. Brian, you two must come with us to France for a camping holiday . . .'

'Oh, right, that sounds nice . . . I'll have to check it out with the wife, of course . . .'

'How does Rod reach those figures, exactly? I don't quite understand,' another male voice said. It was interrupted by a female one:

'Well, how does Angela know? Honestly, Douglas, we don't all have your mathematical brain.' But Douglas blundered on:

'He must be assuming that hotels are much more expensive than they are, you know . . .'

'Suzy!' Rod Cartwright looked up from the barbecue. 'Paul, old man! You made it!'

'Hi.' Suzy kissed his cheek, which was florid and hot from stooping over the shimmering coals. There was something touching about the enthusiasm of his greeting. Paul's face broke into a crooked smile. He handed Rod their bottle of supermarket wine. The computer-generated invitation had concluded with the words: 'Bring a Bottle!'

'White or red?' Rod asked them, his hand hovering over the glasses on a wallpaper-pasting table, two precise rows of long-stemmed goblets, a few identically filled to a middle point. In front of these was a selection of Delia Smith's *Summer Collection* salads. Suzy knew them instantly, identifying the grilled onion with rocket and the roasted tomatoes.

'Help yourself to refills,' Rod added. He slid a fish slice under the chicken drumsticks and skunk-striped sausages, which were respiring, like small rodents, on the barbecue's wire grid.

Suzy turned to Paul quizzically. Although she was the gregarious one, this time she required him to take the lead.

Paul scanned the garden, perking his face into what he hoped was a lively, interested expression. The fact that he recognised every face here should have reassured him.

They were standing in groups of fours or fives. There were

the Fishers, both bespectacled teachers, Valerie in a blue skirt that had been washed too many times, by the look of it. Her feet in sagging sandals looked white, with straggling, black hairs growing from the metatarsal bone. And Richard looked strange in jeans; Paul was used to him in corduroy, which he invariably chose for work. There were the Mundays, Will and Pat, she looking like a pantomime dame with her big nose and double chin under her feathered blow-dry. She was smoking nervously, taking deep, frequent drags, the filter of the cigarette rimmed with her sticky magenta lipstick. There were others, too, two dozen or so villagers; backs of heads which were familiar from quiz nights; profiles that could be identified from the shop; children who swooped and dived like gulls, looking healthier, somehow more themselves than when they stood hunched and miserable on the silvered verges on nippy winter mornings, waiting for the school bus.

They looked so pleased to see each other, these people, so interested, so animated. 'We found these gorgeous heritage colours which we thought we'd use for the sun lounge,' a woman's voice was saying. Another, close by, said, 'You should treat yourself, it's so relaxing. I had this stinking cold and she mixed up . . . now . . . let me see, lavender, basil and something else . . .' Paul identified Will's voice in the middle of a proud monologue about his son. His smile began to crisp around the edges, like a day-old sandwich.

Paul was steering Suzy towards a university lecturer they knew vaguely and rather liked, but the crowds shifted and a figure on their right, Mick Gray, a pale-skinned, beaky sort of a man, something in the City – Paul could never remember these details – waved an earthenware platter under their noses.

'Pork pie, you two?'

The group surrounding him undulated, engulfed them, assimilated them.

'Not for me!' Valerie Fisher stepped back as the plate wafted under her bosom. 'I'm on a diet,' she informed them. 'I started it last month and I think it might be working. I've lost four pounds already.'

'We all seem to be on her diet. Nothing but salads she serves up these days,' said Richard through a mouthful of gelatinous crust.

Valerie clicked her tongue, shaking her head and amiably rolling her eyes to the trees.

'Oh, I don't mind,' Richard added. 'No pain, no gain.'

'What a terrible idea,' Paul ventured.

'Er?' Richard frowned, munching hugely.

'You said, "No pain, no gain." ' Paul explained. 'Awful notion, that you can't have any pleasure without sacrifice.' A short silence ensued as the group considered this. Eventually, Mick Gray broke in:

'That was the idea behind school swimming lessons, wasn't it?' He addressed the two teachers. 'The colder the water, the faster you swam, that was the theory.'

'I hated my swimming lessons.' This was Valerie. 'You're bringing it all back to me.'

'Do you remember life-saving badges?' Mick Gray, again. 'You had to dive in in your pyjamas, remember? You had to bring your pyjamas into school, get changed and dive into the pool to save the life of a brick . . .'

'You're bringing it all back to me!' Valerie exclaimed. 'Only I didn't have any pyjamas. I wore nighties. My teacher said, "You can't do life-saving in a nightie," and my mum said —'

'They don't teach swimming at schools, these days, do they?' said Mick. 'It's one of the things that's been cut.'

'No, no,' said Richard. 'It's one of the things we manage to squeeze in at all costs. Oh, no, not swimming. It's music that's been cut. Music, art . . .'

'I learnt the piano, once,' said Valerie.

'I played the guitar,' said Richard. 'Folk group. What did we call ourselves? Legolas, that was it.'

Paul decided on a note of gentle teasing. 'So you didn't make the big time.'

'Pardon?'

'Legolas. It didn't make the big time, did it?'

'I got up to grade five,' announced Valerie.

'Very enterprising.' Mick smiled at her. 'Kids today don't learn the piano any more. They play the "keyboard" and just pick it up without the bother of lessons.'

Paul searched the back garden surreptitiously: the man they had meant to attach themselves to was now beyond reach, near the back boundary by the conifer hedge, talking to a woman who had recently moved into the big tithe barn, which a developer had converted. She was young and very pretty and was wearing a flowery dress with a square, low-cut neckline. He definitely approved of her. The Fisher's son and two other primary school boys had climbed to the top of the climbing frame; they were trying to look down her cleavage.

Suzy was being unnaturally quiet, Paul realised. Normally, he could rely on her to fulfill the lion's share of their conversational obligations. (This was how he thought of it.) But she was in another world, with her gaze on the grass. Most unlike her. *Buck up, Suzy*: Paul tried to send his message telepathically, with a sideways glance, the faintest frown.

'These days, poorer kids don't get any music in their lives,' Richard was saying. 'If schools don't have any money for music and the parents don't.'

'Ach, don't get me on the cost of children,' Mick said, adopting a Scottish accent, presumably because he thought it sounded parsimonious. 'Each kid costs you a hundred grand according to those surveys they do. And these days, there are no tax breaks for families. Quite the opposite. If you want trouble with your bank manager, have a child is what I say.'

'Do you think so?' said Valerie. She thought for a beat. 'We had trouble with a bank manager, once . . .'

'Suzy! Paul!'

Angela, materialising by her elbow, made Suzy jump. The button brightness of Angela's round, child-like face was hardly affected by the deep lines skirting her eyebrows and lips. 'I was just telling the others about our new caravan. Did you see it?'

'Couldn't miss it,' Paul said roguishly.

'Oh, you. It's like a palace inside, you know. The storage is amazing. You wouldn't believe the clever receptacles and pouches they build into these things. There's a loo, there's a shower, oh, and a fridge. We're berthing it in Norfolk for a few months, lovely site, twenty miles up the road.' Angela paused in thought. 'You want to come on a nice weekend away with us. A little break would do you the power of good.'

Suzy faltered over an excuse, managed something about being manically busy.

'We've got her mother staying,' Paul announced.

'Ah. Perhaps after she's gone then?' Angela suggested.

'Puh! Whenever that will be.'

Angela changed tack.

'Paul, you're interested in cars . . . We were thinking of upgrading to a four-wheel drive for the pulling power. We got all these brochures . . .'

Suzy tucked herself behind Paul's back, her cheek brushing the old, downy cotton of his shirt and beneath it, the hard angle of his shoulder bone. She was protected from the need to make small talk. Paul nodded and murmured, which Suzy experienced as a tensing and a vibration in his back. Thankfully, he was pretending an interest in torque ratios he didn't possess.

It was irksome, it was downright discombobulating, this business of seeing your life through someone else's perspective.

Why did Paddy have to open her mouth? Suzy had always thought of herself as different from her neighbours in some essential way. A little more aware, perhaps? A little more amused? But what if she wasn't?

Right at this moment, she felt ponderous and plodding, her jeans too tight and her hair too wiry. Look at her! She merely kidded herself that her job was a polished, urban career. As for her children, the moment the clock had chimed midnight on his fourteenth birthday, Luke had been transformed into a rude, expressionless vegetable. She hardly dared to correct him. And Daisy, sweet and uncertain as she was, was far too influenced by those ghastly little madams at school. And her marriage? Well, that had unquestioningly been through a bad patch recently. No. Revise that. For the past two . . . no, three years . . .

'That's very kind,' Paul was saying, swivelling to include Suzy in his exchange. 'We'll, er, certainly bear that in mind.'

'I must just see what Rod's doing,' said Angela. 'The fuss he's made over that barbecue. Honestly, men are such big babies! Two o'clock and not a sausage ready to be served . . .' She headed off towards the wallpaper-paste table.

Paul shot Suzy a stealthy, amused glance. She didn't feel like smiling. She could see her life boiling away to nothing. It was simply a matter of time.

At the centre of the lawn, two young girls in thin cotton frocks were spinning around their linked hands. Faster and faster they turned, leaning against each other. The outer child had long, fair hair, which flowed behind her. Suzy watched them speculatively. If one of them let go, the outer child would spin away, carried by impassive forces to the inevitable bumpy landing.

Chapter Five

———◆———

Luke had a way of marking his territory – with a jock strap, which should have been dropped into the linen basket several weeks previously, with trainers respiring malevolently under the bed. His presence was so total, so robust, so sprawling, so malodorous. She didn't have time to do more than close the door on his room. She had hit a busy patch. Her diary was spiky with black ink entries. Sasha called several times during the week with new commissions, in Dorset, in Docklands, in Kensington, and Suzy said yes to them all. She had never mastered the delicate art of refusal.

Daisy tried to help Suzy load her cases, her tripods and lights, into the Golf, although, to be honest, she was more of a hindrance, dumping down the heavy metal camera cases at every third step. The legs of the light stands made a hollow, percussive clanking inside their long canvas bag.

'When will you be back, Mum?' Daisy asked. The vestiges of Daisy's infant dependency never failed to touch Suzy. She brushed away a wisp of hair from her daughter's forehead. Her skin, so pale, so easy to flush, was soft as suede.

'I really can't say. You walk back from the station with Luke. Granny is making supper tonight.'

'Oh. OK.'

In her wing mirror, as she pulled away, Suzy caught a glimpse of her daughter walking back up the drive in the netted, early morning light, her shoulder blades like the stubs of wings which had dropped off, eleven years ago, when she fell to earth.

Suzy turned out of the close and hauled her mind on to other objects. There was a long drive ahead of her. Half an hour later, she was bowling down the motorway, Bruce Springsteen on her tape deck, singing about sex. She liked to warble along to the choruses, to join the backing singers for the oohs and aahs. Normally, if she was unable to meet her children from school, she would deliver them to some cocoon deep in her mind. She was followed wherever she went by a nagging, spectral protectiveness for Daisy, in particular. Today, though, she was buoyed by Paddy's promises to hold the fort. She had shuffled off some of her care. Oh yes, she was going to make the most of the remaining days of Paddy's stay: only eight left by her reckoning.

The people whose garden she was photographing were tense. The Pickerings were a retired couple who had finally acquired the leisure hours to devote to their hobby. They viewed Suzy's visit as some kind of professional validation. The wife – Emma – uttered nervous, strained laughs as she showed Suzy around. And the husband – Rupert – told her several times that she should really see it in high summer, *then* it was really something. Suzy was accustomed to this. She had evolved an infallible method for reassuring people. Generalisations wouldn't do. Often they made people tenser, convinced that she was fobbing them off. She had to pick out a number of specific items – a striking combination of plants, a neatly clipped hedge or a thick, even lawn – to praise. Their tentative faces would change, quicken. The Pickerings melted when she admired their ornamental kitchen garden. Its geometric beds were edged with woven wattle.

'I got the idea from the garden of a French château,' Rupert told her.

'Well, it was my suggestion originally,' Emma chipped in. 'I tore this picture out of a magazine at my hairdresser's.'

'I realised ready-made panels wouldn't do; we needed a chap to construct it *in situ.*'

'That was what the magazine said, actually.'

'Oh, I didn't read that,' Rupert concluded.

On her own once more, perched on her aluminium stepladder, Suzy focused on a small clump of Stag's Horn sumachs standing sharp and dark against the high morning sun. This garden was a little manicured for her personal taste. If she had owned such sprawling acres she would have proceeded judiciously, watchful of the moment to stop, before the ramshackle romance was cut away by pruning saws.

It was one of those gardens that was divided into sections by low stone walls and high yew hedges. Suzy trailed from area to area. She framed a shot by the Rabelaisian colours of the hot border, peering into the square of her viewfinder, judging the glistening of light and the last drop of morning moisture on the buttery asphodel in the centre of her shot. Its stamens, she noticed, curled upwards lewdly, powdered with thick, fertile dust. Photographing gardens often reminded Suzy how nature directed all its energies towards procreation.

By one o'clock, the light was harsh and glaring. She found a pub further along the village's main street and ordered a ploughman's lunch. The bar, which was dark and gloomy, was almost empty. She entertained herself by eavesdropping on the only conversation. An old man, perched on a stool, was telling the barmaid, whom he appeared to know very well, about someone's death from a heart attack.

'It were that sudden,' he was saying.

'I'd like to go like that,' said the barmaid, who looked to be in her late twenties.

'Would ya?' he said. 'Would ya? I'd prefer to go on living, meself.' He erupted in a wheezy laugh, the molecules of spittle visible, for a second, in a sharp shaft of sun.

Afterwards, Suzy wandered back, past unsteady boundary walls, the stones collapsing outwards, leggy plants spilling from every crevice. She dodged a gang of children on roller-blades who let out lawless yells as she approached, then swooped past her in a rumble of diminutive wheels. A younger girl trailed them. She wore a wild, frightened expression, Suzy noticed, and she was a clumsy skater, her knees jerking up and down in a way which reminded Suzy of a heron wading, whereas the older children glided smoothly, low and fast.

The Pickerings had paused for coffee on their lichened terrace.

'Got enough?' Rupert asked her as she rounded the corner of the low stone house.

'Well, how can she?' Emma said. 'She hasn't taken any by the pond yet.'

'I need a shot of you two,' Suzy told them. 'I thought I'd take you in the kitchen garden.'

'Oh, how dreadful,' Emma fluttered, 'I hate having my photo taken.' But she was pleased, Suzy could tell. 'I better powder my nose.'

'Righty ho,' said Rupert, unfolding his long legs.

'It won't take long,' Suzy said.

But it proved a more difficult shot than she had envisaged. Rupert and Emma did not stand close enough together, and when she asked Rupert to lay his hand on Emma's shoulder, Emma seemed reluctant, inching down the stone bench on which she was sitting. Suzy was used to this, too, but it saddened her, none the less. Frequently, a hidden antagonism revealed itself to Suzy's lens. The little squabbles between a couple told her nothing, but the way they inhabited space together, their unconscious, public *pas de deux*, often said too much.

It would be better not to pose the Pickerings as a couple. She let Rupert stand behind the bench on the right, leaning against an apple tree. Emma settled herself in the centre of the seat, her plump, nylon-encased knees together. She stared fixedly at Suzy's lens from beneath her wispy white fringe. Suzy measured years of resentment in that two feet of space between them. And Rupert, oblivious to the fact that his wife couldn't bring herself to stand in the same block of air as him, stood up straighter and sucked in his tummy.

'Watch the birdie, Emmie,' he bellowed.

It was enough to break your heart.

'Suzy, you've got to talk to your mother about hogging the bathroom in the mornings. She's got to slot in with our routine. It's not fair on me otherwise.'

'I'll mention it to her.'

'She doesn't think.'

'I'll talk to her . . . Anyway, you enjoyed that roast dinner she cooked tonight. Admit it.'

'Hmm.'

Paul was sitting up in bed, idly leafing through *The Times*. The light of his lamp had sent a concave sun rising beneath Suzy's closed eyelids. She considered if she should raise the subject of showers with her mother. She had tried yesterday. She had indicated that Paddy was a family member and therefore . . . But, before she had finished, Paddy had looked up from her book with an offended expression. Her lips looked pinched.

'I can go and stay with Judith, you know. If it's too much trouble,' she said.

'No,' Suzy had cried instantly. 'No, you must stay with us.'

Although Paddy staying with Judith was a marvellous idea, one that would have been welcomed not only by Paul but by Suzy herself. Constant intercession between her family members was such a strain. Ah, well. Paddy must have seen her point. Not long afterwards, she had volunteered to make dinner.

Paul had turned a page; the bedsprings bobbed, a faint sea-surge.

'What's going on between them, do you know?' his voice asked.

'Oh, it's one of their annual upsets. *You know.* She'll be gone in a week, just you wait and see.'

'Hmph.'

Suzy opened her eyes:

'I must telephone Clare.'

'Why? What's she going to do about it? Seems to me she's baled out and left all the onus on you.'

'I'm sure she didn't do it on purpose,' Suzy said, despite the fact that a similar thought had occurred to her at exactly that moment. Clare adopted a carping, questioning manner at times like this, acting as if their parents' troubles were Suzy's responsibility. 'What are you going to do about it?' she would say. It was so annoying . . .

Suzy opted to change the subject.

'Would you like to go out to dinner at the weekend, just the two of us?' She turned towards her husband, slid her hand over his hipbone, resting it on the faint bulge of his stomach.

'Us?'

'We haven't done something like that in ages. And we wouldn't have to worry about the children squabbling while we were out. Shall we? There's that new restaurant opened —'

'Can't afford it.' There was a pause, during which Paul turned several pages before settling upon Anatole Kalestsky's column.

'Exactly,' he told the newspaper. 'At last . . . Thank God someone displays some common sense.' Suzy rolled over, warming the small of her back against his bum.

'You realise she's wearing far too much make-up.'

'What?'

'All that black stuff around her eyes, and her hair dyed that colour. She's beginning to resemble Barbara Cartland.'

Suzy propped herself on her left elbow.

'Paul, that is just so unfair. Just because she doesn't give in at the first wrinkle. She's trying to cheer herself up a bit, that's all. It isn't a virtue to resemble a knitting pattern, you know.' Paul's mother had always been as respectable as a Fair Isle pullover with matching mittens, but this dig went right over his head.

'She looks like some brassy actress,' he continued complacently.

'Well, what's wrong with looking like an actress?' Suzy subsided on her pillow.

'Nothing, providing you're on the stage.' He paused and added in a diverted tone, 'I wonder what the neighbours make of her . . .'

'Well, if that's your concern . . .'

'It's not my concern, I'm just . . . amused by the notion.' In profile, his block of a head looked particularly smug.

'Are you going to be long?' she asked him. 'Your light is disturbing me.'

'Not long,' he said. The rustle of his newspaper told her he had resumed reading.

The brief jabs of anger in Suzy's chest jerked and went out. Eventually, Paul switched off the lamp and settled down. An animal squawked in the sable depths of the wood behind the river. The curl of the river around their garden was the reason Suzy had agreed to move to this charmless box of a house.

Through a gap in the curtains, she watched the moon caught in the branches of a tree. She willed her mind to drift her towards sleep, but it seemed to be snagged on their last conversation. Staccato snatches of it echoed in Suzy's ear. It struck her as absurd. A tickle of laughter bubbled in her chest. She tried to suppress it but her shoulders were shaking, the mattress was bouncing.

'Whassa matter?' Paul's tongue curled inaccurately around the words, though there was an edge slicing through the sleepiness of his voice.

'Nothing,' Suzy said, with a telltale snuffle.

There was a movement from Paul, another buoyancy of bedsprings. 'You're not crying, are you?'

'Crying? No.'

'Good. Go to sleep.'

Suzy concentrated on motionlessness, though her mind still dipped and swerved. Paddy's bright head loomed, but she veered away. She mustn't think of her parents; she would never get to sleep. She alighted on the film she'd watched on television, a romantic comedy in which the woman fell in love with the man on the strength of hearing his voice on the radio. For some reason, this made her sigh.

She could remember the exact moment she had decided to marry Paul. He had been sharing that house by then, a ramshackle Tudorbethan terrace backed by a patch of unkempt garden on the southern outskirts of London. She used to come up to London on Friday nights and stay over, returning home on Sunday afternoons. The journey itself was tedious, involving two changes on the Underground and, if she missed her connection, an hour-long wait at King's Cross station. But it was preferable to his visiting her, with Paddy brightly assigning Paul to the spare bedroom – Gerard's old bedroom.

'Maybe she thinks I put you in a spare bedroom when you come to stay with me?' Paul speculated.

'Don't be silly,' Suzy snapped. They were already behaving as an established couple. There was no need to disguise such flares of irritation.

Paul had been sitting by the window at his battered desk, his spine, long and defined through his blue shirt, forming a graceful curve over his revision. She was sitting on his bed, had finished filing her nails and was looking around for something to do.

Even today, the prickly scent of polish, its marzipan and creosote, brought the scene back to her.

She examined the books on the shelves above the bed although she knew the titles by heart already. She had acquired the hope that an engaging novel had tucked itself between the military histories, the few dusty autobiographies, the chess manuals . . . No. One had not. He had said he would break at three, take a walk in the park before she had to leave. It was Sunday afternoon and the other occupants of the house were out.

'You're brilliant,' Paul told himself, as his problem worked out.

Suzy found the stash of folded letters between two books and opened them in the certainty they were from Jan.

'My darling Paul,' said the handwriting.

She read it from the greeting to the random, naïve spattering of kisses, like jacks thrown onto the page.

The vertebrae in Paul's neck were still arched composedly above his sums and figures. Suzy found she wanted to attack him. It was an easy matter to take one book from the bed and hurl it at his blond head.

'You kept them!' she accused.

Paul wheeled around, rubbing his ear. His mouth formed a slack crescent.

'All this time you've been going out with me! Two years and I discover you've been hankering after her!'

'Hankering! That's ridiculous!'

But he'd known instantly who she meant. There had been quite a scene.

From a distance of years, she felt rather fond of that strange, jealous Suzy and that fervent Paul. That Paul who took her so seriously. It was this that had decided her on marriage.

For some charge between them had changed. He explained that he wasn't preserving Jan's letters but had merely forgotten to throw them away, and as he talked she began to feel foolish.

'I don't believe you,' she said, but there was something in her tone, something subdued and truculent which seemed to act as a signal to him, for he put his arms around her.

'Yes, you do,' he told her, and his breath was warm on her neck.

How had she whisked herself into such turmoil over a few insignificant letters? On occasion, even after sixteen years of marriage, she could recreate the lurch she had experienced when she had unfolded those flimsy sheets and read their baby talk. For what had shocked her was discovering how different his intimacy with Jan had been from the callow, rub-along, early fling she'd imagined.

Lovers' infancy, that was what Paul and Jan had shared. Babying and spooning and teensy weensy endearments, these were what Suzy had glimpsed of their togetherness. Paul did not behave in such a fashion with her. He could be boyish with her, of course, and there were times when her tenderness for him was almost maternal. But there was a joky, self-knowing air to his outbursts of juvenility. After all, he had begun by wanting to protect her.

From time to time, though, she wondered: what would have happened had she not unfolded that letter? Had continued to lie upon the mattress, night after winding night, unaware of Jan's breathing presence above? Would the Winslow family story have advanced to the exact same ending?

Odd, the random twists and turns that propelled people into marriage. Why had Sasha, at the end of one seven-year relationship, decided upon marrying the very next man who had entered her life? Was she really more suited to Gary than to Sean? Or more in love? It did not seem so to Suzy, who had listened, over a sequence of lunches, to the chapters of Sasha's love life.

Sometimes Suzy wondered whether it was because of a bout

of jealousy that she had married Paul. Without it, they might have drifted apart, time and inattention separating them, and then: no church wedding, no peals of Mendelssohn, no Luke, no Daisy, no house in the suburbs, no life in its inevitable present, only amorphous possibility.

But it was impossible for Suzy to imagine life without her children, and so, with only the faintest sigh over lost opportunities, she gave up trying. She told herself that she was glad. She was, to all intents and purposes, a happily married woman.

Paul was asleep. His breathing had grown regular and stertorous. She listened to it for some time, the regular nightly music of her marriage.

Chapter Six

'Don't you ever consider anyone but yourself?'

Even in his imagination, Paul's voice had risen an undignified half octave. His features, glimpsed in the mirror above the wash basin, looked faintly preposterous, rearranged in a way that suggested some crass, heightened emotion. He sloshed cold water over his face, scrubbed at his teeth. It came to him in a flash that he'd save time by shaving in the car.

Thanks to Paddy, the queues at intersections were already building; he waited two minutes at the junction where the village lane joined the trunk road, drumming the steering wheel with his thumbs, hunting that elusive gap in the traffic. At last! But he was still going to be late. He turned the dial on the radio, whirling through a babble of voices and dissonant music. As he glanced up, a white van cut in front of him. He stabbed the brakes.

'It will be another fine, dry day for all of southern England,' said a rich, Fenland accent and Paul's fingers froze on the dial. 'Five days on the trot. We could be in for a long, hot summer, Mike.'

'That won't please my missus,' said Mike. 'She's a gardener, you see . . .'

Paul puffed to himself. They could never just say it was good news, could they? They always had to put a downer on everything. He had been hoping a traffic report would succeed the weather, but a melody began to play, a mournful love song, which caught him unawares. This tune had once been significant to him and it brought with it a gentle evocation of Suzy in younger days.

He glanced in the rear-view mirror, half expecting to see her younger self as he fondly remembered her, her grey eyes challenging him, surrounded by long, blackened, fibrous lashes. But, of course, he met only his own heavy-lidded glance, his own wan, stubbly cheeks. That reminded him. He felt on the seat next to him and found the battery shaver he had thrown down with his briefcase. He directed his attention to the road. It stretched ahead, true and straight. Up in front was a brief parade of shops fronted by parking spaces, their concrete surface regularly ridged. They reminded him of raked seed beds. He should weed the vegetable patch when he had a mo.

With his left hand he flicked the switch of the shaver. It purred in his hand, the note changing as it vibrated over his jaw. With a bit of luck he'd make the meeting on time.

A police car overtook him. The officer in the passenger seat was pointing at him. The left-hand indicator began to wink. Shit! He was being pulled over.

He had no choice, after that, but to abandon his car at the end of the Underground and take the tube in. What time was it? How many stops? He traced the line on the back cover map of his *A to Z*. At two minutes between them . . . yes! He might just do it. He swung the car into a back street in front of somebody's Tudorbethan semi. Briefcase under one arm, car keys in the other hand, even as he pressed the button and heard the locks clunk, he was turning to pound down the pavement. Wouldn't you think the police would be more observant? Surely they were trained in these things?

'Search me, go on, search me,' he'd invited them, when the taller, skinnier one with the purple rash had insisted he'd seen Paul talking on a mobile phone while driving.

'I don't have a mobile phone,' he'd told them. 'Bloody awful things, going off in railway carriages, theatres. Do you know? I was at a wedding the other month and one went off in the middle of the service! Not only that, but the man took the call!'

'He never!' said the shorter, rosier officer. 'I'd lynch anyone did that at my daughter's wedding.' For it turned out his daughter had just got engaged.

Well, by that stage, they'd shrugged apologetically and let him go. If they'd noticed the shaver on the floor of the passenger well, they didn't mention it.

The houses in this street looked the same: you could draw the line of symmetry in the centre of the semis and scarcely a door or window frame was different from its partner's. Sometimes they were the original fittings, sometimes modern plastic frames with fake leaded lights. It gave Paul a curious sensation of time freezing. He had run down this street for aeons, passing the same houses, making no progress.

Paul thought of himself as a reasonably fit man. He wasn't overweight. He looked years younger than most of his contemporaries in the office – Reg, for example, with his beer gut and receding hairline, or Al with his nicotine habit. Attempting to run in a business suit was the problem; in training shoes and joggers, had he owned them, he wouldn't have felt so constrained. The pavement smacked the soles of his feet. He tried to visualise himself as a fighter pilot, blond and brave, enduring with sealed lips the torture of the vicious Japanese camp guards.

His chest was bursting. But there, at last, was the entrance to the tube station. With a high gasp of relief, he pattered back to a walk. He was conveyed by the escalator past posters that asked him if he was happy to be pregnant, or that boasted in single word exclamations – 'Magnificent!' 'Unmissable!' – of stage shows he would never see. He always studied the diagonal procession of advertisements; it was preferable to watching the doughy, closed faces of the passengers passing on the up escalator, just feet away.

He inhaled, sucking air into his rib cage. His heart was still fluttering wildly. *Breathe deeply*, he told himself. *Regularly*.

By the time he reached the bottom, he felt almost normal.

The train was a modern one, with doors that slid smoothly apart with a muted hiss. A female computerised voice announced the stops. 'This train', she told him, 'is for Ealing Broadway.'

Paul settled himself in the last remaining free seat, between a hefty woman with gunmetal-grey hair and a black girl with shoulder-length ringlets. The woman was wearing pink suede T-bar shoes, which seemed inappropriately young, especially as her arches had fallen to the floor. The black girl's nails, curled around a paperback, were long, painted a sparkly purple.

Paul wondered idly if souls had colours, like skin. If so, he suspected there'd be more black souls than white in heaven. They seemed so much better at praising the Lord, for example. Occasionally, he'd caught one of those wild, joyous gospel sing-songs on the God spot and been transfixed for a few random minutes before he came to, flicking through the channels in search of Sunday evening diversion. As the image changed, he always felt that he changed back into himself, a restrained and manly figure, leaving behind the yearning individual who wished he could forget himself long enough for such abandon.

The girl must have sensed him contemplating her; her eye flickered in his direction. He snapped to. *Well,* he chided himself, *mustn't sit here day-dreaming.* He clicked open the twin gold locks on his briefcase, extracted a briefing document. He couldn't quite focus on the words. Five-year audit. Evaluation. Conclusion. The sub-headings were typed in bold. He drew his fountain pen from his inner breast pocket, fiddling with the cap as he read.

Paul's firm, which he had set up with two old friends, checked the dealings of banks, hunting out mistakes and over-charging. It was amazing to Paul how often they were able to claim substantial refunds, where, for example, a bank had wrongly calculated interest payments in its own favour. Paul saw himself as a number doctor, his painstaking care resuscitating small companies brought to the brink of bankruptcy. At heart he felt he had given a Robin Hood swagger to accountancy. He had always known, even while sitting the exams, that he wasn't cut out to be an ordinary accountant. To grow fat on smoothly extracted, inflated fees made him feel fidgety and uncomfortable. At first, he'd thought about starting his own business, putting his expertise with cash flow to his own use. But what would he do? Property development was the obvious possibility. Suzy could oversee the interiors; he could manage the money, hire the builders, control the projects. But his teeth clamped together merely thinking about this. He anticipated the rows, the bother of it. Builders never did what they said they would when they said they would. And it would be his lot in life to bawl them out, or act matey, whatever was the right combination to prod them into action. Hell! He wasn't good at motivating people.

Then, one night in the pub, Reg was miserable and pre-occupied. The bank, he said, was pursuing his father. They had called in his overdraft. His father's business was about to go belly up. Reg thrust his chin up. 'The bastards seemed to change the rules to suit themselves,' he said.

'Let's check the figures,' Paul suggested, on a whim. 'Let's see if we can find anything on them.'

A light switched on in Reg's eyes. 'All right,' he said. 'Now you're talking.'

Paul could still taste their excitement as they'd poured

through Reg's father's flimsy bank statements, plucking them from the cardboard boxes in which they'd been so carelessly stuffed.

'Look over here,' Paul had said. 'This doesn't add up.'

They'd saved Reg's father's future by what they'd done, at least in the short term. The truth was, he was a disorganised man, a florid, paunchy figure in his blue shirtsleeves, scuttling obliquely away from his mounting problems. Five years later, his business folded despite their efforts. But unknowingly, he had done them a favour. Through trying to help his company, they had founded their own. Paul, Reg and Al agreed there was a gap in the market here.

It had seemed like such a bright idea but for the first five years they had struggled. They were met with incredulity. Banks making mistakes? Surely not. But suddenly there was a sea change in the prevalent opinion; banks became villains. The telephone rang continuously, the voices on the other end crabbed or anguished or, sometimes – this was the worse – sprightly and joky. Fact was, he could sense the sleepless nights that these last callers were trying to disguise. Paul tried to avoid answering the calls himself. He felt inadequate in the face of all that naked emotion, umming and ahing as they explained their troubles. Sometimes, his callers were carried away in the release of confession, and they would reveal how the money troubles had led to marital problems, drinking . . . intimate stuff Paul had no wish to know. On the contrary, he wished to save their face, to restore their exterior dignity. Luckily, Al had the knack for dealing with these calls. The load divided up quite neatly. Soon, Paul, Reg and Al were so stretched they had to expand, renting new offices and hiring new staff.

The beauty of numbers, Paul often told himself, was their simple, clean precision. As long as people were methodical, kept proper records, he could trace the mistakes of years gone by. In perhaps a fifth of the cases he investigated, he was able to clear the bank of any wrongdoing. The client whose report he was perusing now was one of these lucky ones. Six years of accounts they'd combed through, and only the most minor errors discovered.

Paul became aware of his neighbour examining him, covertly. What was the matter with – ? A recollection sparked in his mind's eye: his own face, one side smooth, the other prickly with stubble. How odd he must appear! How unprofessional! It was Paddy's fault, of course. Suzy had better speak to her today or else . . . or else he'd take matters into his own hands. There was considerable satisfaction in imagining himself expelling Paddy from the house, like Eve from Eden, though he knew in his heart it would never happen.

It turned into one of those days. The client sprang to his feet when Paul was still in the middle of his summary. Frank Keswick was one of his more recalcitrant clients, with a twitchy, suppressed energy and an ignorance of normal social forms. At first sight, Paul had thought him rather distinguished, his hair had turned silver grey and he was tall and thin. Today, he was wearing a quiet grey pinstripe of which Paul thoroughly approved. But somehow, as always, he fell short of distinction, betrayed by aggression and the adenoidal blare of his accent. He had seated Paul on the subordinate chair by his desk rather than meeting him across the bland circle of a boardroom table, which was what most of the clients chose to do. Now, he towered above Paul, gnawing a small flap of skin from his lower lip.

'Nothing!' he squealed as Paul finished. 'Not a bloody sausage!'

Paul experienced a dainty, acidic twinge in his stomach.

'Er, there is no evidence of any mischarging,' he said.

'You must have got it wrong.'

'We do double-check . . .'

'If you think I'm paying you good money to come up with fuck all, you have another think coming.'

'Mr Keswick . . .' Paul hesitated. 'Frank, erm, I have to say, you are one of the fortunate few. Surely you can continue trading against a background of increased confidence . . .'

'On your bloody bike, son.'

Paul could feel a tide of blood washing from his neck to his face. Frank Keswick was at the window now, through which London roof-lines, grey and sooty, were visible. Intemperate words such as 'cheated' and 'ripped off' were spraying from his mouth onto the plate glass. Paul saw the city through a miasma of spit and disgust.

Paul rose. He slipped his papers back into their briefcase and clicked the lock. He let himself out of the door soundlessly. He had had enough. Al could call Frank later.

There were delays on the Central Line and a tailback on the M25. His gut had tied itself in a knot and he found difficulty in concentrating. He was scarcely aware of the creeping lines of cars, the grimy bulk of the lorry in front of him with its heart and arrow and two sets of initials drawn in the dirt; he was too busy replaying the scene with Frank Keswick over and over. He had to remind himself there was no reason whatsoever for his uneasy sense of guilt. They were not in the business of invention. They could only reveal the truth.

Why did he feel so depressed then? The truth was, reactions such as Frank's were becoming more common. People expected more. Expected money they were not entitled to, the rapacious bastards. Bust had turned to boom and clients approached the firm not in desperation but in greed. Better face it: he was Robin Hood no longer. These days, he was a hero nowhere, not in the office and not at home. He was an average guy in an average job in an average house; the illusion he had constructed had blown away, leaving him to face the naked truth in his middle age. It was an unpalatable sight.

He tried to explain some of his unease to Reg later at the office. Pointless. He realised this almost as soon as he opened his mouth. Reg was in one of his dynamic moods. There followed a few dismissive Reg-isms about Frank Keswick and he launched straight into a discussion of the Glasgow project. Paul had known Reg would pressure him to oversee it. 'C'mon, Paul,' Reg said. 'It's difficult for me at the moment.' This was a reference to the new baby expected imminently by his third wife.

'Why can't Al do it?'

'Finding premises? Hiring staff? Al may be a wunderkind with clients but Mr Methodical he isn't,' Reg said and winked.

Paul resented the implication of that. He loathed Reg's phrases. He resented the way Reg was lolling back in his chair with his feet resting on the edge of his outsize chrome wastepaper basket. 'Wunderkind' indeed. Why did Reg always have to pretend that he and Al were younger than they were? Reg's braces, his loafers, his near shaven head, adopted to disguise a hairline that had started to recede a decade previously, were getting on his nerves. They were in their forties, the three of them; why not admit it, forget it, display a little dignity?

'I think Al could manage just fine.'

'You're the obvious choice.'

'But that's what I was saying. I can't work up any enthusiasm about anything.'

Reg tipped forward, neatly side-footing the wastepaper basket into the kneehole of his desk.

'This is just what you need, then, mate' he said earnestly. 'A new challenge, a change of scene. If I could've gone, I would. I mean, this could make a real difference to us. Give us a break, mate.'

Paul felt very tired. Just considering the work involved was enough to make him yawn. It would take two months at least, maybe three, to accomplish everything.

'I'll think about it,' he said, rising from his chair.

'Fubulous, fubulous,' Reg said. This mispronounced burble was akin to his catchphrase.

'You could take who you wanted,' he suggested. 'Take Mark, he'd be a help. Or Fay. Hey, what about taking Fay?'

Paul closed the door before Reg could wink at him again.

In the car on the way home, he played a game: if Paddy didn't leave when Suzy expected her to, he'd go to Glasgow. If she went, he would refuse. There. Simple.

The sounds of home had altered into a cloaked silence punctuated by the soft whirr of an electric mixer and Chester's panting as he waddled across the hall, his backside shifting with pleasure. Paul patted his smooth, bony head. He pushed open the kitchen door, expecting Suzy. Paddy glanced at him over a foaming bowl of meringue.

'Good evening,' she said.

Suzy was working, Paul remembered, would not be back till later. A warm aroma of spices bubbled in a saucepan on the hob. Paul shuffled over and lifted the lid, the dog shadowing him expectantly.

'My own chicken Tikka Masala,' Paddy told him. 'But the pudding's a surprise.'

'Pudding!'

A chime of delight echoed in his voice. Paddy smiled.

'Men always have a sweet tooth,' she said. 'By the way, there's some post for you. I put it on the side table.'

The living room was different, too. It had been dusted, vacuumed and tidied, but more importantly, the television was turned off. He fancied he could detect a studious concentration leaking from his children's bedrooms. Paddy appeared with a glass of Scotch.

'I'd guess you could do with this,' she said. There was

something deeply feminine about the smile tugging at the corners of her mouth.

'Well,' Paul said.

Paddy pottered from the room, trailing contentment, a queen in charge of her demesne. Paul wondered if she got a kick out of waiting on men. It occurred to him she was of that generation. Of course, he supported a woman's right to work, but it was no use denying the pleasure most women took in the small, domestic skills.

'How did you win the battle of the *Simpsons?*' he called to her. She reappeared in the door.

'It's easy when you know how.' She gave him a Lauren Bacall look – that was the comparison that popped into his mind – and disappeared. He caught himself in a private smirk.

The post offered him two new credit cards and a half-price sofa at a local sale. He laid it on the arm of the chair, his mind drifting. Reg's puckish head and perky tics came back to him. Take Fay, indeed. Irritated, Paul sucked a tide of whisky through his teeth. It was his own fault, of course. He shouldn't have made his partiality so obvious. Reg and Al could never resist an innuendo.

Nor could he pretend that the expansion wasn't vital to them. It was Paul who had suggested Glasgow as a second base. Not as staid as Edinburgh, convenient for Manchester and Leeds as well as Newcastle, that was what he had argued. Reg had seen his point immediately, but Al had taken some persuasion.

The glass was lifted from his hand.

'The other half?' Paddy asked playfully.

Paul smiled at her.

'Yes, please,' he said.

Obviously, he'd been rather unfair to her. She wasn't a bad old stick at heart. Surveying the calm of the living room, he began to see advantages to her staying. He didn't mind having her here if she was going to make an effort.

No need to flee his own house, then.

Except, except . . .

Reg was right: Al would foul up the important details. He was all style and no substance.

All at once he made a decision. He was going to Glasgow. He rose from his chair, followed Paddy through to the kitchen, where she was pouring a generous, honeyed measure into his glass.

'I've got to tell you what happened today,' he began, and she looked up, her pale eyes all concentration. The scents of the curry were making his mouth water. He began to tell Paddy about the company's expansion and his own role in it, experiencing a new enthusiasm as he did so.

'I don't know if Suzy told you,' he said, 'but I've been feeling for some time that we ought to open a branch up north.'

The ice tinkled in the glass like a celebration she had handed to him. Inexplicably, Paul had been rejuvenated.

Chapter Seven

There was a row of pellet holes above the window of the sitting room, dark and regular in the blank ivory wall, where Paul had screwed the curtain rail too high, had had to relocate it two inches lower, and had never, despite many promises, got around to filling the tell-tale cavities. As a child, Suzy had invented a tiny alien species who inhabited the household cracks and crannies. They had come to earth but no one had noticed them because they were microscopic beings who lived so unobtrusively. A little puff of laughter escaped her at the recollection. Though it was funny how neither of her children had inherited her whimsical, dotty imagination. Neither had liked the books that were Suzy's favourites as a child. Sometimes she could believe her whole life had been taken over by aliens.

Ah, well, better get a move on. She had been standing here rooted by inactivity for a good half hour since Paul's taxi had departed. She and Daisy had waved him off. It had surprised her, the catch in her throat as she watched his lean figure stooping over the boot, handing his cases to the driver.

He must have felt the same, for he started playing the fool, his usual mask for sentiment. He'd stood outside the window, pulling Quasimodo faces at Daisy. Inside, his daughter responded by curling her lip and crossing her eyes.

'Oovavu!' she growled.

Paul pressed himself against the wall so that only his head was visible, craning around the window frame. His hand appeared at his throat and he leapt backwards, out of sight. Daisy shook her head, pretending to be distressed that Dad was such a gimboid.

'Bye,' Suzy mouthed silently. 'Love you.'

The taxi diminished. Daisy wandered away. The sun darted between feeble clouds, raising fierce reflections from the sheets of water lying on road and pavement, the last reminders of an overnight shower. Droplets on leaves and on window panes glittered fiercely, making Suzy blink. She reached for the tissue stored up her sleeve.

And she had been so robust when he'd told her! Glasgow, he'd said. A few months. It won't be so bad. No, she had agreed. Inside, a sensation of release flitted. It seemed, suddenly, that a break from each other's company would do them good. The crusty, scabby accumulations of sixteen monogamous years might drop away, leaving sensitive, virgin skin beneath.

It was because of Paddy that he'd left, of course. She'd tackled him about it and he'd denied it, but she knew, in her heart of hearts, that it was so.

Tackled him about it? No, she hadn't. What she had said was:

'It isn't because of my mother you've accepted this job, is it?'

'No, of course not,' he'd said immediately. 'Reg can't go. Julie's going to drop the sprog any week now. Third time around he's determined to be a better father.' He sniffed, a brief, cynical puff of air. 'We discussed Al going, but frankly he's not up to it. Actually, in case you haven't noticed it, your mother and I have been getting on swimmingly.'

'You have?'

'Don't sound so surprised. She's been making a lot more effort just recently.'

He was trying to be nice, she knew, so that she should not feel guilty. He was a good man, a decent man; whenever she was tempted to forget this, he would prove it to her anew, with a significant nicety of behaviour.

There was a scraping sound, metal on brick. Will Munday appeared in his front garden, to her left, straining to carry his hover mower around the edge of his garage. He was a small round man in his fifties who seemed to gleam: over decades, his forehead and bald spot had achieved the shiny patina of old hide. Today he was wearing a short-sleeved plaid shirt but with thick, grey socks rolled over the top of rubber boots.

He inserted the plug into the socket of an extension lead. The mower began to hum as he guided it across his thick, damp, bowling-green sward. Will's girth meant he walked with a shambling, bowing gait. Suzy watched as he progressed across the turf. A fine spray of wet clippings, like iron filings, collected on the toes of his wellingtons.

He was obsessed with his lawn was Will, forever watering and feeding it, raking and mowing it. He reached the front border, with its hybrid tea roses, and executed a clumsy half-turn, flicking the orange cable away from the blade. The silly old sod, Suzy thought, he'll electrocute himself one day.

Suzy's elusive emotions seemed to condense around Will's stocky figure. Throughout the daily chafing of marriage, she said to herself, I have never yet met a man I have preferred to Paul. She paused, acknowledging this thought with something like satisfaction. Then a second sentence passed through her brain, unwilled, unexpected. *You never meet any men*, it said.

In the week following Paul's departure, Suzy came alive to her landscape and its inhabitants, as if it, or they, held a clue to the shape of her marriage, this comfortable, bagging thing, worn, scuffed, patched as it seemed to be. She encountered dozens of tiny, significant changes in her routine, which continually reminded her of Paul's absence. The list for the supermarket had altered. No beer. No garlic sausage. She opened mail addressed to him with a clear conscience, for she paid the bills. His car was now in the garage, stored away for the duration, while hers was parked on the drive.

Loading equipment into the hatchback, she was freshly conscious of a group of children playing on the pavements. Their game involved pedalling around the cul-de-sac at full pelt on their bicycles, while the oldest of them, a scraggy, freckled boy called Kevin, occasionally shook a large stick and yelled. He was rarely seen without this staff of office, and Luke and Daisy had dubbed him 'Kevin with a stick'.

Suzy paused to watch the group. Kevin's blue-grey veins were visible through his thin, pale skin. His knees were grained with permanent goose bumps. She was struck by the notion that this would be the most authority Kevin would ever yield, that he would dwindle from the tribal warrior of his imagination into a bank clerk, or a salesman, or what? A market researcher, perhaps. It seemed likely he would fret about his pension or which model of company car he would be permitted next time around. He would measure his success by GLS or GXi. Her heart bled for him. It was sad to watch children. On the one hand, there was promise, on the other, only decline.

Later, posting a sheaf of letters, Suzy turned from the box and cannoned into Ron Bestic. A grunt of air left him, as he pattered to a stop before her.

'Sorry, Ron.'

In response, he merely heaved for breath. Ron had taken up jogging after suffering a heart attack last summer. He had pounded the pavements each dark winter morning, wearing a fluorescent band across his shoulders. Then, made redundant in his fifties, with small chance of a new post, he began to run and run, endless flights circumnavigating the village.

Suzy examined him anxiously. His skin was a delicate silver grey beneath the deeper grey shadow on his chin and it was beaded with sweat. There were drops of moisture caught on the long hairs that straggled from his nostrils. Sweat spread in a dark patch through his T-shirt. His legs, swarthy, knobbly with muscle, emerged from shorts and bowed significantly at the knee before entering towelling socks and outsized white trainers.

'Are you all right, Ron?'

He gave a slight nod. Breath whistled as it was sucked through the twin dark tunnels of his nose.

'You're not overdoing it, are you?'

A shake of his head. The faintest upturn at the corners of his mouth.

'Mustn't stop,' he aspirated, setting his face and resuming his jolting run.

Suzy could almost feel the impact on the crunching bones in his feet as his back view diminished.

She wanted to call out, 'Take care, Ron!' but he'd have thought she'd taken leave of her senses.

The thing was, she saw disaster everywhere. It was Paul being away that had affected her. She envisaged accidents of plane or hired car. She saw muggings in shady side streets. He would be working twelve, fourteen hours a day, she knew, and his judgement would be impaired. Before he'd left, she'd said, 'Paul, you will take care in Glasgow, won't you?'

He looked surprised, touched, gratified – she watched these emotions chase across his face.

'Me? I'm manly, I am,' he said and made strongman gestures with his arms. He grabbed an invisible yobo by the collar. 'I'll see you, Jimmy,' he declared and head-butted him.

But here she was, fretting anyway. It was his stepping outside the sphere of her care that had unsettled her, as if her daily cognisance of her family's movements afforded each member some form of protection. Silly, she knew, but she felt it.

*   *   *

77

Paddy was behaving differently. Paul's absence seemed to have altered her routine. She lay in bed until the children had gone to school, a development Suzy only discovered when she stirred under her own duvet, stretching beneath a block of sun that was painted onto the pillowcase and gummed to her eyelids. Sun? She sat up, focusing. She had overslept, and by half an hour! The house was quiet, which spelt disaster. Tying her robe around her, she fled into the corridor, banging on Luke's door, opening Daisy's. The dog whimpered at the foot of the stairs, its backside swaying.

'Where was Gran?' Luke grumbled in the car, as they waited in the station car park for the later train. 'She didn't make my breakfast this morning.'

'She's not here to be your slave,' Suzy said, although she, too, was feeling disgruntled. She had counted on Paddy's household ministry.

Paddy emerged at eleven in a short cotton nightie trimmed with lace and in pastel towelling slippers. She scurried into the bathroom. The thrum of water told Suzy she was bathing.

'We're due at the school at three,' she called through the door.

There was a pause in the sounds of sluicing.

'School?' Paddy said.

'Daisy's concert.'

Another pause.

'I'm going half demented. I'd forgotten.'

'Are you all right?' Suzy asked, but there was no reply. And, 'Are you all right?' she asked once more, when they were settled in their seats in the front row of the school hall. There was something lackadaisical about Paddy today. Normally, any performance by the children would see her smiling and nodding fiercely from a prominent position, clapping so hard her palms turned red. But today Paddy was all for slipping into a middle row and it was Suzy who had found them their vantage point.

For the second time, Paddy ignored the question. She was inspecting the ranks of children in grey and green on the benches to their right, in front of the climbing frames on the wall. Her chin was tilted at an imperious angle.

'Will you be looking at those girls' hemlines,' she whispered. 'I told you.'

Suzy glanced in the direction of Paddy's chin and caught Tessa, of course, slipping into a row. Suzy guessed she had rolled her skirt waistband over and over under her emerald sweatshirt.

'If she bends over, she'll be arrested.'

Paddy sounded fascinated.

The hall was filling. It echoed to the chattering of mothers in flowing skirts or jeans and the higher voices of young children, the siblings of today's performers. A girl danced across the parquet in front of Suzy, her shoes squeaking on the varnish. Plump and plain, she twirled her skirt elaborately. A smaller boy in shorts – wasn't it refreshing to see a boy in short trousers? – trailed after her.

'You look stupid,' he told her dispassionately.

'So? You are stupid. Your head looks squashed under water.'

'Doesn't.'

'Does. I was watching you at the swimming pool.'

Suzy smiled. Oh, the similar squabbles that she had heard between her own two.

Three slender figures were mounting the dais in front of them. Suzy nudged Paddy. Daisy, chin down, shot them a glance. The high colour was playing in her cheeks and forehead, an aurora borealis of blushing. Little flutterings skittered across Suzy's stomach.

The girls perched themselves on three high stools arranged around a microphone, Anna with her violin on the left, Daisy with her recorder in the middle and Yuheng with her flute on the right. Mr Barrett, the headmaster, hovered by the edge of the dais. He clapped his hands three times, slowly. The whisperings and chattering that lapped the walls of the hall subsided.

Daisy leaned towards the microphone.

'Allegro by Bach,' she announced and tipped back. The over-amplification was a surprise.

Another teacher rushed forwards, stepping over a snaking cable. She fiddled with the dials on a metal box into which the heads of the cables burrowed.

The children raised their instruments. As they did so, the end of Yuheng's flute fell off. It landed, with a neat clang, on the floor. Daisy and Anna exchanged sneaky glances and began to giggle.

Yuheng retrieved the part and pushed it into place quickly, but she, too, was tittering. Many of the audience were laughing, too, including Suzy. There was something so grave and pompous about their first flourish that had been punctured by the subsequent mishap. Yes, it was really very funny.

But then it reached the point where the audience had settled itself and directed its attention expectantly to the stage, only to find that the girls couldn't stop laughing. Nervousness had made them susceptible. Oh, they tried. But every time they raised their instruments, they collapsed again in silent sniggering, their shoulders heaving, hands clamped over their mouths. Daisy's face was flushed. There were beads of perspiration on her forehead.

The audience was growing restless. A child wailed. Mr Barrett came to have a quiet word with Yuheng. Suzy willed the trio to sobriety. By her side, Paddy was fidgeting, and when the girls broke down once more, she clucked her tongue.

In the end, Mr Barrett chivvied them from the stage and announced that the second group, a quartet, would open the concert.

'Well,' said Paddy as they left an hour later. 'That was a waste of time.'

Suzy placed her arm around Daisy, who was now tearful and sheepish.

'*You* were always a giggler.' Paddy turned to Suzy. She made it sound like a crime. Suzy could feel her teeth clamped rigidly.

'Are you and Granny going to have a row?' Daisy asked as Paddy stumped ahead of them, across the parquet, out of the large double doors.

The next day, Paddy borrowed Suzy's car, saying she was going shopping.

'My car?'

'If it's not too much trouble.'

'But you don't drive.'

'I have been recently. I started again.'

'Oh.'

So Suzy lent it, and used Paul's clumsy estate herself.

Later, while she was checking her bank statements, she was interrupted by Muriel Bestic on the telephone. The WI wanted someone to photograph the village for their millennium book and Suzy was the obvious choice.

Suzy agreed to drop by Muriel's to discuss it. She had to locate Paul's car keys. A pile of transparencies she was sorting through lay fanned across the conservatory table, dark squares in white frames. Her stride felt bouncy and yielding on the cork soles of her sandals. She closed and locked the door to the garden from the outside and walked around the side of the house. When she emerged from the chill shade, the sun burst in her face like a bomb.

Muriel could not have been more pleased to see her. She was a mild, greying woman with pale watery eyes who wore soft gathered skirts in what Paddy would call 'Queen Mother pastels'.

'This is so good of you,' she said. 'Come and have a cup of tea.'

In her kitchen, Muriel busied herself with canisters and an old-fashioned kettle. She carried the tray into the dining room. Suzy glanced around; she'd never been inside the Bestics' house before. A soft Dutch rug in faded blues and pinks was spread across the table as a protection. On top lay a long sheet of parchment imprinted with a black wax rubbing of a medieval knight. The curling ends were weighted with two hardback books, a John Grisham and a Joanna Trollope.

Muriel set the tray down next to it, pushed the books aside and rolled the brass rubbing up.

'Ron's latest hobby,' she said, nodding towards a series of three hung in narrow black frames on the pink wall. 'You could say they're taking over the house.'

Suzy pretended an interest in them.

'There are more next door in the study, and up the stairway, if you like that kind of thing,' Muriel continued behind her.

Suzy mimicked a polite gaze through the open door, then pulled out a chair with a tapestry seat and stirred her tea.

'No, me neither,' Muriel said tartly.

'How long has he been interested?' she asked.

'Hah, only four months,' Muriel said. 'He's like a man possessed. If he's not jogging, he's driving all over the country to collect new examples of gravestones or whatever you call them. He makes all his own frames, you know, out on his workbench in the garage. He'll start one later. He's gone on a run now – one of his long ones,' she added.

'Ah.'

'Been gone yonks.'

'I saw him yesterday.'

Muriel took a sip of tea. 'Funny, I thought his early retirement would mean a new phase in our marriage. I was quite looking forward to it, not that I could tell him. He was wittering on about scrap heaps and ageism, and I was thinking, well, you've got your redundancy, we've got our nest egg, the mortgage is paid off . . . I don't know, I envisaged us pootling around together, taking a driving holiday through France, staying at *pensions*, going away for the weekend on a city break. You know, finally spending some time together. Being a couple. Fact is, I don't qualify for a passing thought . . .'

Suzy blinked. Muriel's descriptions of retired togetherness so neatly matched Suzy's own expectations that she was rather at a loss. She had made a little promise to herself. So what if their marriage was at a jog-along, commonplace stage? This was the usual effect of children. The deep and satisfying companionship would come in their later years. Suddenly, Suzy was startled by her own complacency. Look at Muriel's experience. Look at her mother's. Perhaps her mother's explosions were not the dramatic ploys of an egoist? Perhaps they were born of desperation and loneliness? Was that what Suzy was headed for?

Muriel's eyes were watery with unshed tears.

'He forgot our anniversary,' she announced. 'Got up early and went off to take one of his impressions. So you see, dead people, that's what he's concerned with. Morbid, I call it. Plain morbid.'

Suzy tried to think of something soothing to say. She examined the knight above her, his melancholy eyes.

'They have a timeless quality, don't they?' she ventured. 'Immortal.'

'Huh! Maybe that's what appeals to him, then,' said Muriel. 'You'd think he was the only man in the world who's suffered a twinge of angina. The stupid sod.'

Paddy had not returned home by the time Suzy did.

She told herself not to worry.

By the evening, Suzy was tense and irritable. Where was she, for heaven's sakes? She grumbled to Paul on the telephone and he laughed at her.

'She's sixty-what?' he reminded her. 'I believe she can take care of herself.'

'But what if she's distracted? Think of all the turmoil she's been through recently. She's not familiar with my car, any car.'

Suzy twined the hard sinuous cord between her fingers. She had taken his call in the hall. Above her hung an old, carved oak panel she had picked up at an auction. She noticed the pleats in the wood, their crisp geometry. Paul was telling her, in excessive detail, about several offices he had viewed. A filament of a cobweb was strung from one corner of the panel to the base of a stair; it was undulating in the invisible weather patterns created by the radiator.

'I'm doing a great job up here,' Paul told her.

'Oh good,' she murmured.

'Are you all right, Suzy? You're not still worrying about your mother? She'll be fine, I told you.'

In the kitchen, she chopped the corner from a plastic packet of oven chips and poured them onto a baking tray. She was visited by a sudden abstraction. Paul and Paddy were off and about while she remained behind, trapped in the work triangle of sink, cooker, 'fridge. It was a dangerous place to be; your head might go under. You could drown and leave not a trace behind you.

'Ma? When's tea?' Luke bayed from the other room.

She thought she sensed the vibration of an engine on the drive. The door clicked, the lilt of conversation in the sitting room. At last.

'Where've you been?'

Paddy appeared wan and dishevelled, her lipstick worn off and her hair flyaway.

'I've been seeing a film,' she announced. There was a certain quality to her voice, as if she had done something daring. 'With Judith. And then she wanted to talk. Michael's been sending her solicitor's letters.'

She was undoing her rubberised coat. Suzy was suddenly aware of how large and knobbly her knuckles had grown, that they were roped by charcoal veins. She noticed a liver spot and a bracelet of lines around Paddy's wrist. These made her seem vulnerable. Normally, vulnerability and Paddy were two words that were never to be found in the same sentence. Then she noticed that Paddy was not wearing her wedding ring. A stab of fear chased the pity through Suzy's chest. She found that she had lost the inclination to say whatever she had been going to.

'No dinner for me,' Paddy told her, as she slipped out of her coat. 'An early night is what's called for.'

Suzy was nagged by concern as she fried eggs. The children bore their plates off to the television. She had lost her appetite. Quietly, she mounted the stairs. Paddy's door was open and she was sitting on her bed, brushing her hair with a wooden-backed brush. The curtains were open so that the cul-de-sac, at dusk, stretched behind her bright head, the silent bulk of its brick houses, the quiet hummocks of bushes in front gardens, the sulphurous glow of downstairs windows. Suzy paused in the doorway.

'Daddy's home tomorrow,' she said.

Paddy stopped brushing her hair abruptly.

'Yes,' she said.

She examined the brush, turned it over in her palm, laid it on the coverlet.

'He's in for a shock, poor man,' she added quietly.

'You're not going home.' It was suddenly clear. Why had she ever thought otherwise?

'Of course I'm not going home,' Paddy said irritably. 'I told you I'm not going home.'

'But what about Daddy?'

'What about him?'

'This is ridiculous,' Suzy said. She felt close to crying. In fact, her vision was blurred with tears. Paddy's hair and the window-scape had transformed into rosy smears of light.

Paddy said, 'Oh, no,' and rose from the bed.

'You're really leaving,' Suzy said. 'You're leaving Daddy.' Her throat seemed to be bruised.

She saw the Paddy shape come closer, with its arms outstretched, felt those strong, bony hands on her arms. Paddy held her. It was a long time since Paddy had last held her. She smelt of sandalwood and hairspray.

'This is awful,' Suzy said, sniffing back the tears. 'My family's breaking up.'

'Baby, now,' Paddy said.

Suzy endeavoured to get a hold on herself. She extricated herself from Paddy's embrace and went to perch on the bed. Paddy closed the door behind them.

Before Paddy drew the curtains, Suzy saw a car pull into the close, its headlights swinging left: Will in his Daewoo, coming home.

Chapter Eight

———————•———————

At first, Paul was buoyant. He was enjoying the challenge of the Glaswegian enterprise, just as Reg had predicted. It had been a long time since he had felt so energised about work. He had gloated over his solitude, which left him able to concentrate. No need to ring home to warn he would be late. No risk of Suzy asking him to pay a bill in his lunch hour. No children demanding he ferry them around the country on his weekends.

Even the poky flat he had rented, on the top floor of a blackened Victorian terrace, had its consolations. The ceiling was curved with age in a way that reminded him of his mother's bowing back. The anaglypta wallpaper was painted a colour which Paul recognised as 'white with a hint of apricot', the same shade as their hall and landing at home.

Above his bed, right above his head when he woke in the morning, there was a patch. The first time he lay on the bed it had pleased him. If the tile above had leaked, here was a matter that had nothing to do with him. He need not fret over the quality of the builders' repair. He need not worry if its failure was the first indication of the failure of the whole roof. He need not grapple with mental arithmetic, late at night, bowed under the responsibility of middle age.

Now, however, when he trudged back to the flat in the

evenings its shabbiness depressed him. At the new offices, his first recruits bustled around him, busy and jocular, relishing the agitation of a new job, and his own spirits sagged. He glanced out of the window and an alien city, under strange, cold, clear light, was spread beneath his view.

If he was honest, he could pin-point the moment when his unaccustomed pep had faltered and expired. It was that phone call from Suzy a few days ago.

'Left him?'

'She says it's very unlikely she's returning.'

'I don't believe it.'

'I know,' she said.

'So it was more serious than you thought.' He should have resisted that. 'What's your father doing?' he added.

'It was awful. I spoke to him on the phone and he sounded so . . . heart-broken.'

Suzy's voice had wobbled at this point. Paul bit back what he was going to say, which was, 'No, what's he going to do?' It was time, it seemed to him, that Ted took charge and brought Paddy into line. Huh! And what was that pink object with a snout flying past the window, he added to himself.

'Good God,' he substituted instead.

He should have been more sympathetic but he was a touch irritated that Suzy should be so upset. The eternal daughter, who had never really broken free, she would fret about her parents till the day they died. Also, that early suspicion, which had stuck to his back like a burr, was shown at this new angle to be only too real. Paddy would still be there, in his house, when he returned. She had moved in permanently. Abruptly, he was restored to the pleasure of disliking her as much as ever, that familiar, bilious reaction she provoked in him.

On the following evenings, too tired to face the walk, Paul hailed a taxi back to his barren, dusty accommodation. Hanging on to the strap, he slid precariously on leather bench seats as the cabbies hurled their vehicles like dodgems through the lanes of traffic. The reverberations of a thousand petrol engines went unheard by his ears. The greasy rain of the city coursed unnoticed down his skin. Each evening, a driver's soliloquy passed unremarked.

He made the mistake of speaking two days later. The radio in the taxi was switched to a talk show. A stammering voice explained. 'My wife . . . she doesn't seem to want me any more . . .'

'Join the club,' Paul told the radio, and found he had told the driver, a small, neat, slim man with bright, nervous eyes, which were regarding him inquisitively in the rear-view mirror.

'Oh, not me,' Paul explained to the mirror. 'My mother-in-law has left my father-in-law.' He was aware that he didn't sound very convincing. 'Moved into my house.' Indignation possessed him. He was getting worked up. 'After forty-odd years of marriage, you'd think they'd have worked their problems out by now.'

In the mirror, the driver's forehead pitched as he nodded. His eyes narrowed.

'It's incomprehensible,' Paul continued. 'It's bloody bizarre.'

The driver was wincing in sympathy.

'Ach,' he said, rolling phlegm deep in his throat. 'Ah ken whit ye say. Ef-er ma He-er tuk mae won lad, ah wisnae ma-sel whan ah cam ben ta hoose an' saw. Mae wan toty bi' o' scunner an' she ben awa'.'

At least, that's what it sounded like.

The strange thing was, Paul understood every word.

'Patricia,' her mother had said to her when she was growing, when too much leg showed between the top of her socks and the hem of her school skirt. 'Patricia, don't you go marrying a man for his smile, like your Mam did, don't you go thinking that you can change him.'

'No, Mam,' she'd said, cramming moist, doughy bread sprinkled with hard granules of sugar into her mouth. It was a new one this, her father smiling. There were deep brackets around his lips, to be sure, but they cast his mouth in a set piece of misery. He was the most miserable man in the world.

'So did he used to smile then?'

'Smile? Certainly. He had a smile for all the girls, but I knew he liked me best. I was honoured when he asked me out to the pictures, that first time.' The corner of Mam's mouth jerked and her eyebrows seemed to form a bitter, straight line.

Patricia drew a pattern in sugar on the old deal table. She wanted to keep her mother talking; it was rare to hear her like this, truthful and confiding. It was even rarer to get Mam on her own. Drawing a heart in the sugar, her cuff got snagged on the big screw that held the wobbly leg on. She extricated the strand of wool carefully, while her mam's back was turned.

Mam was trying to light the front burner of the stove, poking the matches tentatively towards the gas as she always did. Pop, it went, flaring blue. Mam jerked her hand away with a little cry. She dropped the wizened matchstick on the dark, crumbling lino. 'Get that for me, there's a good girl. And fetch our Renie, she'll do the potatoes.'

So the spell was broken anyway. But she remembered that interlude. It seeped beneath her skin, the warning, the sour smile, the pop of the gas.

She thought she'd paid good heed to her mam, working hard for her qualifications, moving south and landing that secretarial job, marrying a man so dependable and steady. It was Mam's strategy, though she hadn't realised at the time: she went to work in an office and she met an office man. She had bettered herself. 'Our Patricia's got some lovely things.' Mam bored the neighbours back home with her specious pride.

The things Ted had liked in her at first – her quickness and her disorder – began to chafe on him, in time. You couldn't say this was all her fault, though she would dearly like to. She'd be happy to carry the guilt, to say, yes, he is a good man and certainly deserves better than me. But it simply wasn't true. He was a narrow man, whose horizons had shrivelled. He worried about the condensation that puddled the windowsills. He liked his socks turned inside out from the heel and neatly bundled. A man who wrote the pence in words as well as the pounds when he filled in a cheque. The money had slipped through her father's fingers like water, so she'd picked a man who knew how to manage this slithery, treacherous substance, little thinking that a quality could be carried so far as to become a fault.

'Exactly how many of your family will be coming for Christmas?' he asked in that leading tone, and she knew he was resenting the outlay.

'Ah, well, just a couple.' But in the end, it had been more trouble than it was worth, trying to keep in touch with her family. One by one, they'd given up on her, frightened off by Ted's quiet, pinched disapproval.

Her father boozed, turned maudlin or impatient. His temper was a jumpety, eager thing. So she picked a man who'd never raise his voice to her, never thinking how inert and contracted that man might be.

She'd roar at him. She's scream and cry and throw things. She wasn't going to be cowed. She would not lose her own essential self. Once, she consulted the divorce lawyers, just to shake him, like, shock him into seeing her point of view. But he was a most unsatisfactory person with whom to fight. As she grew voluble, he grew taciturn, his lips a thin line, his face impassive. She followed him from room to room, needling and poking, destined never to trigger the reaction she craved.

'Accept every invitation you receive. Join every club.' That was the advice Penelope, her friend, had been following since being widowed at the age of fifty-four. She had set about filling her time with fortitude and Paddy began to accompany her. She gaily said yes to coffee mornings. She enrolled in the local medieval arts society, attending lectures where the slides of gaudy treasures glowed dimly against pale, bare parish hall walls. She was not a widow but she might as well be. She might as well be, she said bitterly to herself, scrubbing at her old withered body in the shower before leaving for another engagement. Ted seemed to believe they made a good couple, that they complemented each other, she so gregarious, he so solitary. He pottered on in his lonely interests, happy to think that she was occupied, that he need not give any portion of his time and thought to her.

Her father's eye had languished on the ladies at the race-course bar and the working men's club, so she had picked a man who never noticed women, in time not even his wife. He had ceased seeing her. If she bought a new dress, his only comment was, 'I always liked you in that green, filmy thing,' which was an outfit she'd last worn in the seventies. It was as if she had turned invisible for the last two decades of their married life. This was a man who'd lost all interest in sex at about the same time, and whose only reference to the fact had come some years past.

'Thankfully, hah, we agreed not to mind about that sort of thing,' he'd said, as two naked bodies coupled, raw and vigorous, on the television screen. They'd been watching a film that was a little more adult than they'd expected.

On the television screen, in gaudy colour, a back arched and fell. Paddy reflected on her recent past. When had she agreed to celibacy? Unless it was the tacit consent of her silence as she rolled over in bed, turning her back to him?

Ah, no wonder she couldn't explain to Suzy why she had left. She'd begun to. She'd wanted to. Clare could be told the bare facts when all was done and dusted and she'd say, 'Well, it's your life.' But Suzy was different. She feared that Suzy would judge her. Suzy loved her best and she didn't want to lose that. So she drew her tearful, adult child into the room and closed the door and sat her on the bed. While Suzy sniffed, reaching for the bulge of a tissue in her sleeve, Paddy had started to explain.

'What you have to understand is that your father's mildness is skin deep,' she said. 'He's a self-centred body, at heart.' She heard her voice in its litany of complaint. 'He has me listening to his accounts, for sure. You know how long-winded he can be; I'm forever watching people's eyes glaze over in the middle of his tales. But there's no escaping for me. I'm to listen to every minor battle of the parish council, how he's going to phrase each letter. If he goes out shopping, he tells me why he bought Anchor butter instead of Lurpak. "It may be saltier but it was considerably cheaper." "Oh, good," I say. "Quite right," I say. But many's the time I come home from the arts society and you wouldn't know he'd noticed. He doesn't ask what I've seen or what I've learned. "I made myself some supper," he says, "so you needn't worry about it." Do you see what I mean? Can you understand what I'm saying?'

'Yes,' Suzy had said. She had dried her face but her eyes and nose were red. She looked a right mess, poor baby. 'Yes, I can,' she said. 'Funny, somebody else said something similar to me recently. Or did I read it?' A look of confusion passed across her face, as if she couldn't keep up with these unhappy marriages she had encountered, all stamped from the same mould.

'He isn't any use –' Paddy began, but she let her words trail away. How could you run the child's father down to her? How could you impress his faults on her? Suzy loved him, after all. Paddy reminded herself: when she'd arrived here, she'd promised herself she wouldn't run Ted down.

'Ah, well,' she said, brushing a hand through the frizz of her daughter's fringe. 'Let's not go into the details.'

'No,' said Suzy, making to stand.

She had stayed with him too long, that was the truth, convinced that otherwise he would fall apart. But he wouldn't. He would potter on. He'd endure.

She'd stayed with him because Gerard had died.

'Oh, let him have the car,' she'd said.

'Do you think that's wise? It's a pub they're going to.'

Ted's pernickety caution always infuriated her and made her contrary.

'He's nineteen. You can't drop him and pick him up like he's a kid, Ted,' she'd snapped. 'He's a sensible lad. You be sensible now, Gerard.'

That was what she had said.

Never, over the years, had her silent husband reminded her of this. It was the one time in their marriage his voicelessness had been welcome, the one time he had not disappointed her. She had ceased to love him long before, but she had stayed with him because of this.

Chapter Nine

Suzy decided to travel to Glasgow to spend the weekend with Paul. She telephoned the travel agent and booked a flight on a new, cheap, no-frills airline. Paul thought this was a mistake.

'They don't allocate the seats at check-in,' he warned. 'There'll be an unholy scrum. It's a very basic service, too. You won't like it.'

Was he trying to put her off?

'I won't come if you don't want me to,' she said.

'Now did I say that? Did *I* say that? What's got into you?'

Suzy was silent. She thought he ought to be able to guess.

'I know,' Paul's voice sounded unbearably smug. 'It's that time of the month, isn't it? I can always tell.'

'You're wrong, actually,' she replied crisply.

At the airport, everything went smoothly. The Mundays said they'd drop her off on their way to the Lakeside shopping centre. Will liked to leave in plenty of time. He worked out her schedule and added on plenty of time for potential hazards. Wriggling his stumpy fingers into string-palmed gloves, he drove there in his gleaming Daewoo at a measured forty-five miles per hour. Pat sat placidly by his side, watching the verges flick by. Suzy remembered how much her father hated the motorways around

London. He never ventured on to the M25, planned all his journeys to avoid it, no matter how long the detour.

'She's a funny lady, isn't she?' Pat said to Will abruptly.

'Margaret Bradley,' Will said. Clearly, they were picking up some conversation they'd left off when Suzy had pressed her finger to their musical doorbell.

'She takes it so seriously.'

'It's only a game, for God's sake.'

'I said, "Don't take it so seriously." '

'About time.'

Pat swivelled in her seat. An eye, rather bulbous, painted with gleaming green shadow, looked at Suzy.

'This is bridge,' she told her.

'Ah.'

Will took fifty minutes to complete a journey that took Paul half an hour. Nevertheless, he deposited her at Stansted before a dedicated check-in desk had opened.

Suzy wandered around the terminal, pretending to window shop. The sound here was always surprisingly muffled as it drifted away into the high spaces under the glass canopy. Heathrow was so much noisier and angrier somehow.

A gaggle of plump young women was standing near the entrance, by a mound of luggage, scanning the slip road. They were wearing sports clothes and trainers, with frizzy hair erupting in fountains from their crowns or the napes of their necks; their wrists jingled with gold bangles and their ears with hoops. Suzy caught a snatch of their conversation as she wheeled her trolley neatly past them and away.

'It's a shame we didn't do Anne Frank.'

'Yeah. Still, you can do her when you go back with Del.'

She was heading for the restaurants; that unmistakable fast-food fug prickled her nostrils. She steered left, instead, and was heading down an avenue of shops, stopping by one to feel the silk in a multi-coloured scarf, and by another to read the poster in the window.

'Aromatherapy,' it said, 'relieves your stress.'

She debated whether to buy a phial. But at the counter, the sales assistant was relating a lengthy anecdote to her companion.

'So she went to the acupuncturist to stop smoking and at the end of the session, this woman says to her, "Is there anything else I can do for you?" and Marion, that's my friend, she says as a sort of a joke, "Not unless you can cure broken hearts." Well, the acupuncturist doesn't laugh; she makes Marion get back on the couch, and she talks her through all that's happened, the drinking, the marriage break-up, everything. Then she sticks a whole lot more pins in her and at the end of the session, Marion said she could feel that her heart had mended. She climbed off the couch and knew in an instant that her burden had lifted. Years of pain disappeared, just like that . . .'

Suzy pushed her trolley away.

She had to fight an urge to ask for the acupuncturist's telephone number.

Paul met her at the airport. They caught a mini-cab to his rented flat. Suzy examined his profile as he leaned and ducked to catch sight of various, personally significant landmarks.

'Down that slip road to the left is the Malmaison, where I stayed for the first four nights. Very reasonable, it was, and the food was brilliant . . . Right, just round the corner is the office. You can't really see it from here . . .'

Paul didn't look as if he was caring for himself properly. He'd grown hollow-eyed and his skin had a pale, pasty tone, as if he'd wrapped himself in Clingfilm – the result, probably, of too much take-away food. Perhaps she was seeing him anew? A fortnight's absence couldn't account for his slight unkemptness: his hair breaching his collar, his shirts rumpled in the area around the buttons where he couldn't ease the iron, his white sports socks a

puddled grey where some other dye had run during the launderette wash.

The flat dismayed her, too. From the outside it looked like a
dour old man with its grey granite and sooty face, the attic
windows, like circumflexes, marking their surprise at Paul's
occupation. And the inside was so small and so patched and,
well . . . seedy. The carpet was a drab grey, the pile flattened from
years of wear except at the edges of the room where no one walked.
There was a good mahogany chest against the far wall, the home to
a portable television. The sofa was a plump, frilly, over-elaborate
affair, the sort that used to be advertised in the back of the Sunday
supplements. Of course, she knew the company didn't want to
throw its money around, but you would have thought they could
have stretched to something halfway decent. She bet Reg wouldn't
have moved into a dive like this. And Al, well! He grumbled unless
he travelled club and stayed in five-star. Paul should try sticking up
to those two. He was far too accommodating.

'Bloody hell, it's good to see you,' he said suddenly and a
squeeze of affection overtook her.

He was pointing out the old, chintzy chair by the window, its
seat comfortably sagging, where he relaxed at the end of the day.

'The kitchen,' he announced, throwing open a door upon
white Formica units. The grouting between the tiles looked
greasy. The sink was missing its plug.

'And this,' he steered her through a flimsy board door facing
her, 'is the bedroom.' Her eyes swept over the varnished pine
wardrobe, the dressing table, the bed with a geometrically
patterned duvet standing under the window. She crossed the
floorboards, which gave with a little sprightly bounce under her
feet. The view gave onto another street, another sooty façade.

She could sense Paul at her shoulder. His arm snuck around
her waist.

'Luckily, it's a double,' he said. There was a suggestion caught
in this sentence, a hopeful note.

She turned her head. His smile had taken on that particular slant. She ran her hands up his arms until they rested upon his shoulders. His mouth tasted faintly of coffee.

'You look a bit pasty. Have you been eating any fruit?'

'Fruit?'

'Vegetables, then.'

She sounded like his mother, Paul reflected. He had forgotten that feminine conspiracy to worry about his vitamin intake. It seemed to him now that he had missed it, this echo of a secure boyhood. Women were so capable in areas like these, each of them a confident nurse whose self-appointed task was seemingly to monitor a man's bowels.

So incapable in others, though. Suzy had placed her shoulder bag on the floor, he noted, just dumped it on the no man's land of carpet at the side of their table. Typical. He knew of a dozen cases where bags had been pinched in similar circumstances. He stuck his foot out a stretch and tried to hook it towards him, or possibly it would be enough to tread on it, so he'd be instantly aware if it was moved.

When he looked up, Suzy was watching him.

'Just give it to me,' she said. 'I'll put it here, where we can see it.'

The neck of her dress flopped open enticingly as she retrieved the bag, some sort of tan leather sack. She placed it on the maroon leatherette seat of the spare chair. Paul had hoped the waitress was intending to remove the third place-setting. The silverware, the glass, the mat, the empty chair, they made him vaguely uncomfortable, as if an invisible presence were hovering next to his left elbow. Now it seemed they were stuck with the chair at least. And the bag made him think of a young baby at that dangerously floppy stage, likely to slide to the floor at any minute. Suzy patted it as if it were alive.

'There,' she said. 'Happy now?'

'I like that dress,' he said.

'Oh, no,' she said lightly. 'That's quite enough of that.'

'I can't help it if you turn up after two weeks looking—'

'You ready to order, love?' said the waitress, materialising behind the spare chair. She was a heavyset woman, with a puffy, brassy hair-do, which contrasted emphatically with her black dress. She carried a little pad and ballpoint pen, her hands crossed in front of her belly. They must be trained to do that at waitressing school, Paul thought.

'Two minutes?' said Suzy, opening the large black vinyl menu.

The waitress nodded.

'Could we—?'

Paul remembered he should order some drinks, but the waitress was staring at another corner of the room, at the people at the far table. The man had raised an open hand and was tipping it in the air to indicate they wanted more wine. The waitress raised her eyebrows, smiled and nodded.

'I won't be a sec,' she said, and was off.

Paul looked around. The place was empty apart from the couple the waitress was serving and a large family party who had pushed three tables together by the open windows. Two small girls wriggled in floral smocked dresses. A very young boy had been brushed to within an inch of his life and manipulated into a jacket. A grandfather's birthday, perhaps? A fiftieth wedding anniversary? A breath of wistfulness escaped him. He was missing his family more than he had realised.

'I think I'll try the cod with tomatoes and olives,' Suzy said.

Paul opened his menu. He was surprised to find such an adventurous choice on the menu. He'd been thinking of taking Suzy to one of the smarter Glasgow restaurants, but when she'd woken after a brief slumber in his arms, the morning had slipped away and already it seemed too late for a trip into the centre of town. They'd strolled around the corner to this pub-restaurant. The sun was up and the streets looked friendlier. A faint breeze whisked through leaves in the gardens they passed.

Inside, it was gloomy, the walls were lined with oak panels and hung with ageing photographs of the western isles: a ship in a bay, a rickety bi-plane landed on a beach. The carpet was in a blue tartan pattern. They threaded their way through the bar, through the smoky babble, Paul leading. He ducked under an arch and found himself here, in the comparative quiet of the dining room. He'd thought there were tables in the garden, which was why he'd alighted on the place. He could imagine a cool green space beneath the shade of a venerable apple tree. But the waitress said he should have reserved one and now it was too late.

'Oh, no!' she'd squeaked. 'To go frew there you 'ave to book.'

'Well, you're not Scottish,' Suzy said with a little laugh.

'No, love. I married a Scotsman. We was both working at an hotel in Torquay. Then he wanted to come back 'ome and run 'is own place.'

'Good for him,' said Suzy. She always had this knack for drawing people out.

'How's the office?' she asked him, as they looked through the menu.

'Good,' he said. 'It was the right decision to expand up here.'

'Oh?'

'And to think how much persuasion it took to convince Al. We're going to do a fortune up here. Reg has had the baby, did I tell you? Another girl. He didn't sound very pleased about it. He wanted a boy to carry on the family name.'

'Shipbottom,' Suzy remarked. They both began to titter.

'Ready, then?' said the waitress, materialising by his shoulder. She unfolded her hands, ballpoint pen at the ready, as Suzy smiled an affirmation.

Paul watched Suzy surreptitiously. He was monitoring her,

ensuring he had her imprinted on his brain so that he could replay her after she had returned home: the familiar contours of her face, the light down on her forearms, her habit of flipping those strands of hair behind her ear and of drumming her nails on hard surfaces. She was drumming them on the plastic of the menu now. She waged a constant battle with her nails, he knew. When they reached the length she liked and were filed into a pretty almond shape, one of them would break, then another, and she'd cut the others back and begin again. Right now they were at their best and her rattling tattoo was her way of admiring them. He admired them, too. They seemed symptomatic of her mettle, her refusal to give in and sport short, sensible nails like the other village women.

Why had her mannerisms grated on him so? Why had he been finding fault with her so determinedly? It was amazing how nit-picking he had been. He looked across the table and her reality was so much gentler and more subtle than his remembrance of her.

'The cod, please,' Suzy was saying, her head tilted towards the waitress.

'Battered?'

'No, the one with tomatoes.' Suzy pointed to her choice on her menu.

'Oh!' said the waitress. 'That's a new one on me! Selection of veg, love? Or chef's got some nice petit pois.'

'You haven't got any rocket salad, have you?'

'Rocket? No, love. I can do you some carrots.'

'The peas will be fine.'

'Sir?'

Paul had hardly glanced at his menu. He ran his eyes down the list.

'I'll have the curry.'

Suzy widened her eyes in warning. When the waitress had finished scribbling in her notebook and left, Suzy leaned across and whispered, 'It won't be like the Star of India's, you know.'

'I'll give it a try,' he said. Her breasts were resting on the linen tablecloth. He had to restrain himself from reaching across to cup them.

'God, I've missed you,' he said, although this wasn't true – hadn't been true until she had reappeared.

He launched into his account of the past weeks. He had so much to tell her – about the two new recruits, about his problems finding secretaries, about the business he had firmed up already. She sipped the glass of wine the waitress had finally brought, nodding at the right moments, smiling as he surmounted problems or wooed new clients. He had forgotten how necessary it was to boast to someone. Now, he was reminded anew as he faced his wifely audience, her admiration guaranteed.

The chicken curry, when it came, looked stringy, and was garnished with pale, insipid raisins. The rice was dotted with peas.

Paul prodded a sliver of chicken with his fork and it sundered neatly into its component fibres. He scooped the strands into his mouth.

'Sweet,' he said. His face creased.

'Told you,' Suzy said. 'Do you want to swap? This is not too bad, although the fish has been frozen.'

'No, no,' he said. He took another mouthful. He swilled it down with beer. 'I hate sweet curry. Why do English restaurants always do that? And there's nothing worse than overcooked chicken,' he said.

'We're not in England,' Suzy reminded him.

'Mmm . . . How are things at home?' he asked grudgingly.

'Oh, just . . .' She searched for a brief summary. 'We're calm and we've agreed not to discuss it any more.'

'Hmph.'

In Paul's opinion, Paddy wouldn't talk because she had nothing to say. She'd left for no good reason.

'It'll all blow over,' he said.

He wasn't sure he believed this, but it would simply have to. He wanted it resolved before he was due home, Paddy gone and his family reduced to its four constituent members.

'I'm not so sure,' Suzy was saying. 'This is different somehow.' Her forehead puckered.

'You shouldn't worry,' Paul told her. 'You shouldn't get upset. It's not your business.'

'Of course it is! They're my parents.'

'They're two adults who should know better. Frankly, Suzy, they're both as bad as each other. Your father should have taken your mother in hand years ago, and as for her, flouncing out when the mood—'

'Oh, please don't start . . .'

'I mean, you've got two children, your responsibility is to them. I would think this is all very upsetting for them. There's your job, the house . . . you've got enough on your plate, it seems to me.'

'Yes,' said Suzy, rather lamely.

The waitress reappeared unexpectedly.

'Everything all right, then?' she said, with a bright, prompting nod.

'Fine,' Paul said, and was suddenly fascinated by rearranging his spoon, his beer glass and his coaster. 'Lovely.'

The waitress retreated, satisfied. Suzy caught Paul's eye.

'What's the point complaining?' he said sheepishly. 'It's not her fault.'

A smile escaped his wife.

'Nincompoop,' she said.

'That's better,' he told her.

*　　*　　*

The conversation had focused Suzy's mind on the precarious deep base note within her. If only Paul could understand how disorientated she felt.

'You don't . . .' she tried. 'It's not . . .'

She laid her knife and fork on the side of her plate.

'Those marriages we compared ours to,' she said. 'Remember? We went to that party at the Mundays and Alan thingy was running his wife down in public.'

'Oh, God!' Paul groaned as the scene came back to him. 'Under the guise of very unfunny jokes.'

'Yes . . . "I wouldn't say she's put on weight but going to bed with her is like Sumo wrestling." '

'He said that?'

'Yes, we were outraged, don't you remember?'

'Good God.'

'And you remember the way Maggie was having a go at Ed?' She watched Paul's face; it was taking him a moment to summon up Maggie and Ed, to attach the right faces and the correct house to the names.

'Oh, yes,' he said. 'She was saying how much he got on her nerves and making little digs at him.'

'And afterwards we got home and we were just appalled. I mean, what's the point of being married if you're so dark and angry inside that you have to give vent to those feelings in public. We said how glad we were that we weren't like that. We bet that Maggie and Ed wouldn't last another year, yet there they are, still together, and now she's pregnant . . .'

'Is she?'

'Yes, I told you . . . I did. On the phone the other week.'

Paul nodded, feigning remembrance. He often did that; he often didn't listen to what she said. She had realised this recently. She had realised this when her mother had said the same about her father. All through lunch, Suzy couldn't help noticing how Paul barely pretended any interest in her life and her doings, while she prompted him for his news and acted so fascinated in his office episodes.

But then she told that voice to pipe down. Paddy's reasons for leaving were so mundane, so very much every woman's experience.

So why has my mother left my father when Maggie hasn't left Ed? That was what it came down to. Her parents' marriage – it was better than lots and no worse than dozens. The Mundays, the Mortlocks, Sasha and her bloke . . . Suzy considered these pair bondings. None of them seemed to hold the secret to happiness. None of them seemed to be privy to something Suzy wasn't. There! She'd done it again! She'd moved from examining her mother's marriage to her own. It was so unsettling, that was the problem.

She dropped her gaze to her plate. The cod was growing cold. She picked up her knife and fork. Paul didn't say anything, just carried on forking through his curry, separating the more edible pieces of meat from the gloop.

'I know for certain that Muriel is currently wondering whether their marriage is worth the bother . . .' she began, between mouthfuls.

'Muriel? Muriel Bestic?'

'But because Ron hasn't an inkling,' she continued. 'Because Ron himself takes their continuing together for granted, she hasn't said a word and probably never will. It will all remain under the surface and the Bestics will trundle on.'

'Good grief!' She watched Paul digest this gossip. Then: 'You make marriage sound so fragile, so chancy.'

Suzy was startled.

'I do, don't I?' She had never before grasped that this might be the case. 'I suppose it is. I suppose it's a matter of luck.'

'Luck?' He sounded rather put out. 'I think luck plays a very small part. Surely compatibility comes into it. A sense of humour. Surely it's much more important to work at it.'

Suzy hated that phrase. Still, she didn't want to pick an argument with him.

'Really', she said smoothly, 'we should be proud of how long we've lasted.'

'Yes, we should, shouldn't we?' The corners of his eyes kinked upwards.

'We should certainly be proud of the two children we produced together.'

Paul's face relaxed further.

'Do you know what Daisy said to me—'

The heavy tread of the waitress approached.

'You finished, love?' She picked up Paul's plate. 'Oh! Did you not like it?'

'Sorry,' he said, 'But I found I wasn't really hungry.'

She made a sympathetic, tutting noise. 'Never mind. It's the heat. How was the cod?'

'It was fine, thank you.'

'Oh, lovely. How about pudding?'

Suzy shook her head.

'Profiteroles? Fruit salad? I'm sure I can tempt you to some treacle tart, sir?'

'Just the bill, please,' Paul said.

He left a generous tip.

Paul found he was in a good mood as they walked along the street. The sun was warming his shoulders, a finger reaching even that deep knot caused by hunching over a keyboard, manipulating a mouse. Caught in the branch of a tree, a strip of waste paper flew in the breeze looking festive, somehow, like a streamer.

He was glad Suzy wasn't getting too steamed up over her parents. He was glad to see that she was missing him. Yes, altogether he felt remarkably buoyant. He imagined the figure he presented to the slight, white haired lady who was standing in the door of the newsagent's opposite watching them, her bony fingers entwined in the wire rack of newspapers. He must look contented. He must look successful and at ease.

'Did I tell you I'm getting help?' he said to Suzy as they stepped from the curb at the crossroads leading to the flat. 'They're sending up Chris and Fay next week.'

'Oh, good,' Suzy murmured. 'Maybe you'll be through sooner.'

'That's what I thought,' he said.

He brushed aside a slight – and wholly unfounded – spasm of guilt. Look! The undulating pavement was springing slightly at his step. The heat was melting the tar and he was walking on air. For once, he was a man in charge of his destiny.

Chapter Ten

How few of Luke's clothes fitted him properly; his jeans dragged on the ground at his heel while his wrists, with their round marbles of bone, poked from the sleeves of his shirt. He had been at an awkward age for most of his life. Suzy bought his clothes on the large size but he was growing at such a rate now that he soon expanded into the extra inches, then stretched further, like Twizzle. All of a sudden, his bike was too small.

His voice was beginning to sound like an imitation of his father's and he'd begun to pay close attention during those laddish skin-wash commercials. She knew full well he'd borrowed her Ladyshave: his chin looked suspiciously pink and raw on the very same evening she'd found her shaver in the children's bathroom and when she'd kissed him goodnight – he tolerated a quick peck near the ear – he reeked of her unisex CK scent. His front two teeth were pushed inwards slightly, into a V shape, and the orthodontist who'd been so confident that the removable, invisible brace would do the trick was now beginning to hum and haw about extractions and tram tracks.

He was such a nice looking boy, with his flop of shiny hair and his bright, eager grey eyes under those long, dark lashes. He reminded her, in fact, of Gerard. The freckles across his nose were restrained, just enough to look outdoorsy and friendly, not so many as to appear pasty and nerdy. He was skinny, it was true, but he'd fill out. He meant well. That was Luke's defining characteristic, which not everyone recognised. Paul's mother, for example, had not understood at all when Luke sent her a belated card bearing the message, 'Didn't forget your birthday, Gran, just forgot the date.'

'The date is all there is to it,' Hetty had said in her quavery falsetto on the phone and Luke's head had dropped. But Suzy knew exactly what he meant.

So here he was, at his most gawky and vulnerable, a boy old enough to be finding fault with his mother.

He was bored, that was half the trouble. School had broken up and his friends had been spirited away on enviable holidays, Baz to California, Josh to Penang. Only Luke's parents had ruled out a holiday this year because of circumstances, because of resident grandmothers and absent fathers. Only last year, of course, as they set off for the fortnight in the Dordogne, he had proclaimed that he was too old to accompany them for very much longer. Now, that sentiment had been forgotten in a tide of resentment and when she teasingly reminded him, he glowered at her.

Suzy couldn't blame him. She thought she'd try to take the children somewhere they would both enjoy – Alton Towers, perhaps – when she had a spare day, a day that she would somehow engineer between shuttling off to Glasgow, between her job, between ineffectual worry about her mother and father.

'What's she said to you?' her father asked during one of their secret daily telephone calls.

'Not very much.'

'Can't you get her to talk to you?' he wanted to know.

Suzy quashed a pang, a mixture of irritation and pity.

'I am trying,' she said. 'Why don't you come here and talk to her?'

But he didn't think that was wise, not just yet.

'She told me not to. She told me not even to call her. She wants to be left alone to think.

'She'll only get mad if I turn up.'

That was true.

The Alton Towers plan never materialised. Now Luke began lobbying to be sent to an outward-bound camp, something rugged involving assault courses and canoes. Suzy imagined these unstable craft bobbing on a choppy sea. Where had he happened upon the brochure?

It wasn't entirely clear why he wanted to go. You couldn't, in your wildest exaggerations, claim that he possessed an aptitude for sport. A whole variety of painful scenes from his childhood haunted Suzy: Luke being out for a duck in the school house cricket matches; Paul trying to teach Luke the finer points of batting on the back lawn that evening but ending up shouting at him, accusing him of not trying.

'Listen,' Paul bellowed. 'Just watch and listen. You want my help and then you don't even try . . .'

But Luke hadn't wanted help. He'd wanted to crawl away to his bedroom, never again to be troubled by the innocent pock of leather on willow.

Luke liked football, but primarily as a spectator. He slept under a Chelsea duvet and a large, dog-eared poster of the team, but he rarely took a ball into the back garden and kicked it against the wall, or practised bouncing it on his knees and head as other boys seemed to. The other Christmas, they had bought him an expensive, genuine-leather football, bearing the repro- duced signatures of all the team. Paul seemed to think this would act as a necessary spur. But what with the manager leaving and various transfers, the ball was out of date before the close of the season. Sometimes, from inside the house, you heard a couple of reverberating, hollow thumps, and then a silence, so you knew that the ball and Luke's head had strangely failed to connect this time, that he was having to retrieve the genuine-leather football from a particularly awkward corner beneath a prickly bush.

It wasn't surprising that he was one of the last to be chosen when his class split into teams during games. Sometimes he came home bright with triumph.

'I made a tackle today and Heggers (this was the sports master) praised me for it.'

Then Suzy knew that these moments were so few and far apart that Luke noted every one.

Oh, Luke! How could this boy be thinking of going to camp?

Oh, and then there was the summer he got caught up in a craze for performing acrobatic tricks on bicycle. He'd improvised a ramp in the garden with a scaffolding board and some bricks. He'd hurtled towards it, his thin legs revolving violently on the pedals. The front wheel met the base of the ramp and stopped instantly. Luke went sailing over the handlebars in a front flip and landed on his back.

Pmph! All the air was expelled from his lungs. That was the first noise he made. His gymnastic flight through the air had been traced in startled silence. Except, that is, for the stifled cry of his mother, watching invisibly through the kitchen window, his impotent guardian angel.

She set him tasks. She would keep him busy. The front garden, for example, was a disgrace, a tired patch of lawn beneath a central mock orange blossom tree, whereas she was hankering for a wild, green garden, maybe a prairie garden – no, don't get carried away – settle for a nature-friendly patch. She put Luke to work scraping up the lawn. Paddy monitored his progress from her plate-glass vantage point, then announced she was going to see Judith.

She was still nervous about driving. She fiddled with the

mirror and waggled the gear lever before starting the engine. Suzy could sense her taking a deep breath. She sat up very straight in her seat as she reversed, checking behind her with little pigeon swivels of her neck, her hands at ten to two, just as she'd been taught, decades ago. All of a sudden, she seemed so plucky. Suzy waved her off with a fond smile.

'What's he doing, then?'

John Mortlock had crossed his drive. He was a man with a sad, sallow face under a thick head of oily dark hair; his eyes were a bloodhound brown, traced with fine red lines. Today, he seemed particularly perplexed.

Suzy could sense Luke listening, although he continued with his raking as if oblivious to them. Upturned seed packets capped bamboo poles: foxglove, loosestrife and corn cockles were planted in drifts marked by a snail trail of silver sand in the fine brown earth.

'Making a wild garden.'

'Suzy, you know that's not quite the ticket,' said John. 'I know it's not exactly a formal agreement . . .'

There were no fences between the front gardens in the cul-de-sac; the developer had been aiming at a duplicate of Doris Day's America. So far, the various, changing inhabitants of the close had each concurred with this vision. A lawn, a drive – in Will's case edged by hybrid teas – the odd specimen shrub, it did for all.

A ground-elder root lay visible on the dark earth. Suzy crouched and extracted it carefully. From here, she could make out silver among the black furring John's nostrils. How sad, Suzy thought suddenly, when even the hairs in your nose betray the fact of your ageing. John was not an unsympathetic man. When the Winslow's grass grew too tall for him to bear – two inches was his usual limit – his remedy was to cut it himself.

'Just doing mine,' he would call out. 'No trouble to run the mower across yours.'

'John,' Suzy said carefully, as dust trickled from between her fingers. 'I hated my front garden. I hate suburban front gardens. We've never kept it very nicely, have we? This will be a million times more practical. Besides, finally, in this area of my life, I am making a change, I am pleasing me. Please say you understand?'

Some answering emotion seemed to flicker across his face.

'Well,' he said, 'I suppose if you put it like that . . . well, I suppose I do. But, Suzy, I don't know if Margaret will understand.' Margaret was his wife. 'Or Will on the other side. It's really terribly inconvenient. I'm going to have to put up a fence, it'll ruin this nice, uniform look which has been one of the chief selling points of the whole close, as you know . . .'

The front door opened with a scraping noise where the wood had expanded in the heat. Daisy appeared in a sliver of a mini skirt and a cut-off T-shirt, which displayed her little girl's tum. She had glued a small arrangement of sequins around her navel.

'It's Granddad on the phone,' she called.

'I'm sorry, John,' Suzy said. 'I've got to go.'

Sasha was full of wedding plans. She burbled on about ivory or cream, short or long or a Prada trouser suit and a registrar. Suzy was having trouble concentrating, although luckily Sasha didn't seem to notice. The stream of minute details continued to flow from her hastily glossed lips.

Today she was wearing black trousers and a brown cardigan, a combination that on Sasha looked modish and young and on Suzy would have been hideously drab. Her haircut was tousled and gamine, with two great wedges cut at the front, which flopped over her cheek-bones. They would have driven Suzy crazy but on Sasha they looked wonderfully sharp. The difference in their ages was only some five or six years but it seemed to Suzy that Sasha belonged to a different generation. Sometimes, when she came to London to lunch, Suzy felt as if she had parachuted in from another planet.

'Seeing as we said we'd never marry, I feel I owe it to everyone to do this properly.'

'How did you know, Saski?' Suzy asked her.

Sasha was slicing into her calves' liver. 'Know what?'

'That Gary was the man you wanted to marry?'

'How did I know?' Sasha asked herself. 'Bollocks, Suzy, I don't know. He was different. He was much more adult. He didn't want to be mothered. As a little girl, you have this image of male mastery, warped but pleasant, you know? Then you discover the reality is neediness. General, all-round patheticness. Oh, and blokes and baby names. Sean, you remember him? He even had a nickname for his penis.'

'A nickname?'

'Tiger.'

'Tiger?'

' "Tiger wants a stroke." ' She had assumed a wheedling tone. ' "Tiger needs a cuddle." ' Suzy just stared at her.

'And he wasn't the first by any means,' Sasha added darkly.

At King's Cross, Suzy joined a crowd on the platform waiting for the incoming train. When it pulled in, everyone surged forward at once, funnelling towards the open doorways while the passengers alighted. As they boarded, they were barely restrained, fraying into small shunts of elbows, a briefcase carefully inserted into a gap in order to secure some tiny advantage.

Suzy tried to absent herself in her mind as she manoeuvred past a bicycle. She settled opposite two shire matrons in neat bright wool jackets, one with her hair tied back in a black velvet ribbon.

Someone's phone started up, playing buzzing, muffled music into a pocket or a bag. The velvet bow started and glanced at her quilted handbag, its gilt chain draped across her black wool stomach.

'That's not me, is it?' she asked her companion.

'I'm on the train,' said a male voice, somewhere behind Suzy. 'Say an hour. I'll give you a bell when I'm nearer.'

'I'm going to get *Captain Corelli's Mandolin*,' the woman continued to her friend, 'and hope I get the time to read it. You didn't like it, you said.'

'No, someone at the club had it and she was saying . . . I don't think I'd get into it.'

'Well, I haven't read it yet. It's probably one of those that isn't as clever as everyone thinks.'

'*The God of Little Things*,' said the other. 'I didn't understand that.'

There was a hiss of doors and the floor began to vibrate as the train moved away, emitting a plaintive, spiralling noise. *Whirrr, whirrr, whirrr.*

Suzy rested her head against the flocked foam. The wine at lunch had made her slightly woozy. She thought of Sasha's round, contented face. The railway line cut through steep walls and sooty terraces, an urban stockade of bricks relieved by the sudden jolt of twisted graffiti or a flock of gangling buddleias anchored through unseen holes in the cement.

'Anyway, Tara's getting married in pale blue,' said the plumper woman.

There was a small snort.

'Are we?'

'And he, ahh – he's not attractive at all.'

'She hasn't come to see me in ages. She saw June. June said, "If she hasn't got a man up her sleeve, I'm a China-man." June said she was absolutely glowing.'

The windows blackened. The carriage seemed to contract. They were being sucked through a tunnel. Against the dark glass, Suzy saw her own self dimly, her red-gold hair, her wide face, the

grey trouser suit with white polo neck she had chosen as right for
a trip to the city. They rushed out; time and space expanded; it
was day once more.

She drifted off, back into her mind. She was returned to the
seaside, when she was very young. She and Gerard had been
netting in the rock pools. She remembered her father kneeling
beside her on the sand, explaining what barnacles were, how
anemones fed themselves, pointing out a tiny crab. She remembered him building her a magnificent sandcastle because Gerard
had stamped on her own paltry attempt.

That time he'd helped her with her French homework. She'd
had to invent a family and describe them. The Wookies, they
decided upon. Wanda Wookie, the matriarch. They wanted a
name of some dignity for the patriarch.

'Aristotle,' suggested Ted. 'Terence.'

'Aloysius.'

'Something suave. Jean Baptiste.'

'Jean Baptiste Wookie.'

'And their sons, William and Walter.'

'Willie and Wally Wookie.'

They'd laughed so hard their sides had ached. They'd always
shared the same daft sense of humour that left Paddy shaking her
head.

The train was decelerating towards a station, descending
through its quavering, electric arpeggio, *whirr, whirr, whirr*. The
doors opened with a pneumatic hiss.

She remembered the bedtime stories delivered in his hesitant
voice with its slight Derbyshire burr, an accent that was
associated for her with safety and kindness so that she warmed
to anyone who spoke as he did.

There were a hundred fond memories, until as a teenager,
she'd become aware of his inadequacies. She hadn't been so nice
to him, then. She'd turned obstructive and scratchy. Perhaps
she'd absorbed her mother's contempt? Perhaps she'd been

following Paddy's lead without knowing it? Or perhaps – terrible thought – Paddy had been following hers? The bond between mother and daughter was so intricate, so tricksy a piece of filigree, that there was no unravelling it to see how it was made.

Suzy returned to an altered cul-de-sac. She stopped the car at the top of the close to gaze. John and Will had been hard at work in her absence. Two close-boarded fences now divided her property from the others. Within, all was bare earth; without, all was garden centre propriety. And in the middle of this scene stood Luke in an oversized T-shirt. She drew alongside and he grinned at her, his irregular teeth very white against the light tan he had acquired. It was a change to see him looking healthy, without that computer player's pastiness.

Suzy stepped out and examined her evident alienation from her neighbours from the inside of her property. The fences were stained an ugly reddish-brown; they looked splintery and the garden felt very enclosed. Luke was watching her reaction with a kind of perverse pleasure. His firmest views on the pettiness of their neighbours had been confirmed and he was longing to launch into an account of the morning's scenes. It appeared he had exchanged words with Will.

'I hope you weren't rude,' Suzy said faintly.

'Me? Huh. I didn't say a word. It was him . . .' And he was off, in full flow. 'And what business is it of his? I'd like to know. It's our bollocking garden . . .'

For it seemed that Luke's opinion of the garden had altered since Suzy had first set him to work upon it. Labouring over it seemed to have engendered a creator's pride. That night, he went back outside. She spotted him in his big, puffy trainers, aimlessly straightening a wonky seed packet on its bamboo, inspecting the soil as if at any moment the first green shoots might magically wriggle into view. And when Will appeared, he put his hands on his hips and stared at him, in what Suzy knew was an act of silent insolence. Oh, Lord. The garage needed tidying. That would serve as his next task. She hurried down the drive to yank Luke in and as she did so, she bared all her teeth at Will in what she hoped was an amicable and neighbourly grin.

Chapter Eleven

Paul had grown familiar with the machines in the launderette, the way you had to coax the coins into the slot on the right-hand washer, the deep groans that emanated from the middle dryer. He knew the inadequacies of the flat's old electric iron and the board that suddenly lurched downwards a notch if you pressed too hard. He had discovered how much loo paper he got through in a week, two whole rolls, astonishing though it seemed. (He'd always thought it was Suzy and the kids who were so heavy on the bog rolls.) He even remembered to check the soap and washing-up liquid before he went to the supermarket.

Actually, he began to suspect he was more organised than Suzy had ever been. He bet he could buy the family's weekly food for less than she spent. If you bought Edam or Gouda instead of Cheddar, if you bought a smaller size of egg. He began to play a game as he perambulated around the aisles on his weekly supermarket visits, imagining Suzy wheeling a trolley next to him. 'Now, Sooze,' he'd say. 'If you bought apples instead of grapes, you'd notch up the same kind of goodness – fibre and vitamins and stuff – but for half the price.' But soon the games petered out. He felt emasculated: here he was, reduced to such domestic assiduity.

At this point, his life began to unravel. Some outside power seemed intent on making the details go wrong, on making his whole existence an accumulation of small mistakes. But in his new mood he regarded these lapses with perverse pride. He burned his pizza and chewed his way steadily through each brittle, bitter, charred morsel with a certain grim satisfaction. He shrank his preferred pullover into a matted miniature. He remembered to take his favourite suit to the four-hourly dry-cleaners but he forgot to take his black shoes to be repaired. This last omission he discovered the night before an important business meeting. The soles seemed to be unpeeling from the toes backwards. He had casual shoes — moccasins, deck shoes — but they were no good. He had a pair of smart two-tone brown slip-ons but they didn't look right with dark-grey pin-stripe. He crouched in front of the assembled outfit, the suit on its hanger suspended over the outside of the partially dislocated wardrobe door, the shoes lined up beneath it. He needed to think laterally. He had always felt lateral thinking was an especially male virtue.

Ah! He had it! He sprang up, strode through to the kitchen, floorboards creaking in protest at his eleven-stone frame, and rummaged through one of the drawers. He returned to his bedroom with a roll of masking tape and a pair of heavy scissors. He cut strips from the tape, folding them back on themselves into two adhesive pouches. With this improvised double-sided, he gummed the soles to the uppers.

In the morning, he awoke with a hard-on and had to arrange himself in his underpants and zip up his trousers with care. He could walk to his appointment if he left promptly. It was a fine morning and he could do with the exercise.

Eventually, the quieter streets gave way to wider avenues of growling, yowling cars. Soon, he had to temper his pace to that of the tramping crowd.

But hang on! Something was amiss. He didn't seem able to walk properly. For a second, he wondered if he'd had some sort of a stroke. Then, he realised: his shoes had come untaped. They made a silly flopping noise at each step he took. He rocked on to his tiptoes, trying to press down on the adhesive. It didn't work.

Each step was like wading in flippers. If he tried to walk normally, the open tongue at his toes jabbed into the pavement and threatened to pull him over. Take it slowly, he told himself.

He reached the stainless-steel door frames of the plate-glass office building. He started across the frigid expanse of marble-lined hall, aiming for the girl in the precision bob behind the reception desk. Flip, flop, flap. He had to pick his knees up and smack his feet down. He felt like Coco the Clown.

When he returned to the office he was in the middle of an erotic fantasy about the woman with the bob who had produced some Superglue for his shoes. An expression of infinite compassion had crossed her face when he'd explained that he was miles from wife and home and that everything had been completely derailed. She couldn't do enough for him.

Fay popped her head through the door as he was trying to wrench his thoughts back to the spreadsheet in front of him. She had cut her hair in a style that was appealing: wispy at the edges, so that she looked well-groomed but tousled. She looked awfully in command of herself these days, too. She had come to check whether he was still on for 1.15. They had resumed their lunches.

She had seemed so pleased to see him, last Monday, when she'd arrived at the office. 'How are *you?*' she'd cooed, stressing the last word, as if he was special to her. He was aware of Catherine, the young secretary, glancing over at them and had made a point of greeting Chris heartily, too.

Later, Fay told him that her husband had recently confessed to a drunken one-night stand at a seminar in Birmingham. Paul rather admired Fay's defiant flash as she recounted this. She had conquered her initial hurt and humiliation. Indeed, as she whispered to him, leaning forward and fixing him with her green eyes, it crossed Paul's mind that Fay wanted her own back. Apparently, it comforted her to believe that she was on the verge of her own fling, could have Paul if she wanted him. Those signals she'd sent to him before . . . he hadn't read them wrongly, had he? She fancied him. A flutter passed through his stomach. But perhaps she thought of him as a friend rather than a man. *Well, hopefully not . . . I mean . . .*

The truth was, he didn't really know what he meant.

By the time she closed the door, Paul's erotic fantasy had altered. Now it starred Fay. He was imagining her breasts, two deliciously rounded globes, their satin skin, the nipples small and cocked sweetly towards his lips. Of course, he had no idea if Fay's breasts truly conformed to his idea of perfection, but shit! in his dreams he would bestow her with these splendid orbs. In his dreams, he bestowed her also with firm, apple buttocks in white lace panties tied by two strands above her hips. He tugged on the left-hand strap and the bow slipped open.

The telephone rang.

He swam back to the surface, watching his hand hovering above the receiver.

Afterwards, he told himself sternly to get on with his work. He was suffering, as he always did after his imaginary infidelities, from a sour aftertaste of something like remorse. He hadn't done any harm, he reminded himself. No harm at all. In fact, now he came to think of it, this must be the way all lengthy marriages survived. After the love-making had become . . . well . . . a little mechanical, you escaped in your mind. You became a blameless philanderer, a master player at the game of virtual sex.

This was the way mature men operated.

He could lunch with Fay with a clean conscience.

It seemed as if Will was tending his lawn with renewed ardour. Fresh from the commuter train, he would change into his summer gardening outfit – shorts and a pale pink polyester short-sleeved shirt, worn with khaki socks and sandals – and set to. He mowed twice, three times a week; he watered with his sprinkler nightly; awkwardly he knelt, folded around his paunch, winkling out the pernicious long-rooted weeds with the blade of a daisy router.

It seemed he didn't know when to stop. He shaved closer and closer to the iron-hard earth, until the neat stripes began to fade and sicken faintly, as if weary of his obsession. As Will waddled behind his mower in the silky evening light, Ron Bestic pounded past on his circuit of the village, two middle-aged men in perpetual motion, or so it seemed to Suzy as she gazed down at them from her open bedroom window.

'Ron,' Will said gruffly.

'Will,' Ron grunted – aspirated – in reply. He ran on.

The unmarrieds came to ask Suzy about what she was doing to her garden.

'What a brilliant idea!' said the man, whose name was David. 'Much better than this phoney neatness.'

'Shall we do something similar?' said the woman, whose name was Charlotte. Suzy shook their hands. They had moved in eighteen months previously and she had never introduced herself until now.

'We're organic,' David told her. 'Are you?'

Will chopped a neat two-foot strip from the grass on his side of the eyesore of a fence, planting a row of Cyprus Leylandii. He meant to obscure the Winslows' house from his sight entirely. When the conifer hedge grew high, he would be able to pretend it didn't exist, except, of course, when he weeded the flower beds of Casa Fina, when he would be convinced that every unwanted seedling had blown in from number four. Oh, shoot! She felt so guilty in advance. There'd be all hell to pay if Charlotte and David at number one followed her example. She would be branded a subversive. A suburban saboteur.

Luke remained convinced that Will was a prat. Paddy agreed with him.

'You can't believe that man has a drop of testosterone in him,' she exclaimed one evening. She was watching him through the picture window as he neatened his lawn edges with a half-moon slicer on a pole. 'I'm thinking that the true *vice anglais* isn't homosexuality, at all . . . It's something to do with turning into old women,' she mused.

No, Paddy did not share Suzy's vague, sad compassion for Will and his ilk. She stood with Luke in the centre of the nut-brown earth, damp from the watering can, a dusting of green hinting at new growing tips, and admired his handiwork in a loud voice so that Will would be sure to overhear. She was in danger of undermining Suzy's authority.

'Why do you want to be putting the boy to work inside on a lovely summer's day like this?' she proclaimed, as Luke burrowed in the garage. Then she marched into the back garden to sunbathe in shorts and a bikini top. Her limbs, puckered near the armpit and at the inner thigh, were turning quite pink and freckled.

But Luke was being surprisingly useful. He backed Paul's estate onto the drive – without mishap! – and excavated long-forgotten implements from beneath piles of debris. He sorted out soggy cardboard boxes containing rusty nails and an odd assortment of shelving brackets. He packed a precarious tower of old Formica kitchen cabinets into Suzy's car and helped her to unload them at the dump. He badgered Suzy into buying a plastic drum and Daisy, coming to help through boredom, rolled the hose around it neatly.

A scuffling conspiracy of anti-Will sentiment broke out between them. Suzy heard snuffles of laughter and looking in, through the heavy inter-connecting door, she saw the children in the shadowy far corner. Luke held a thin, transparent plastic pipe from the winemaking kit, a discard of Hetty's which she had forced upon them several years before. Hetty had been an enthusiast for money-saving gadgets. When each proved finicky and time-consuming – there was a certain inevitability about this – she came to the conclusion that they would transform Suzy's life instead. In this way, the Winslows had acquired a yoghurt-making machine, a soda stream with bottles of assorted flavourings, each the colour of cheap bubble bath, and a collection of demi-johns, corks and plastic tubing, along with several recipe books bearing a shower of berry stains. All were now stored in the cobwebby reaches of the garage.

Luke seemed to be measuring the tubing against his leg, saying, 'You know . . . it's a prehistoric figure,' to Daisy who was examining a miniature tap against the light of the single bare bulb.

'What are you doing?'

Luke's mouth slipped into a sideways grin.

'Nothing,' he said.

'It had better be.'

'What's testosterone?' Daisy asked Luke as Suzy turned to go.

Later, Suzy found her examining the books on the shelves in the hall.

'Have we got any guide books?' she asked.

'Why?'

'Oh, perfect,' Daisy answered herself, and disappeared with a Reader's Digest tome, another cast-off of Hetty's.

Will was examining his lawn on his hands and knees, stroking a browning line of grass, when Suzy drove home from the supermarket the next evening. Luke stole a look as he helped her with the carrier bags.

'He's killed it himself with his fussing,' Suzy muttered from behind a hefty cardboard box. Luke snickered.

The next morning, when Suzy opened her bedroom curtains, Will was in his garden once again, standing by his front doorstep, gawping at the ground. Burnt into the grass, almost certainly by a thin stream of weed killer, was an image that stretched the length and almost the breadth of the lawn. It was an image of the Cerne Abbas giant, its erect penis reaching to the level of its nipples.

It was not a faithful copy. It carried a club in one hand, like the original on its chalk hill, and in the other, a watering can.

Oh, dear God. Luke.

Will still hadn't moved; his face was blank, his mouth a lax comma of comic woe.

Poor Will. Suzy suspected Luke had broken his foolish, pernickety heart.

She rushed from the window and pounded down the stairs to his side, uttering apologies, promises to pay for the damage, promises to punish Luke so firmly he would never so much as glance at Will again. Finally she heard her voice saying shrilly, 'But don't worry, Will. I'm sending him away to camp.'

Chapter Twelve

Suzy rose early and wandered into the back garden with her cup of mint tea. She followed the lawn's gentle slope to the silver birches by the riverbank. She paused above the little mudflat, gazing upstream where the willow leaves blew grey and silver in the breeze and a sunslick swayed on the surface of the water. The leaves were rustling peacefully in the breeze. By her feet, tall strappy leaves fountained next to broad flat hostas, meadow plants dipped by the water's edge; above her, plumes of creamy Russian vine draped through branches like trailing net. It was a jungle, her garden. It cast profligate seed from papery bracts with a sigh, or from tiny hard maracas with a shifting rattle.

Suzy could smell the water, its slick, metallic scent. The wind ruffled her hair. She felt a sudden piercing burst of happiness. When she walked back to the house, she felt cleaner, as she had, when young, after confession.

Luke was in the kitchen.

'You won't forget to water my garden?' he said.

He had unwrapped the Clingfilm and was extracting the last sliver of lettuce from the ham bap she had made him for the train journey.

They were aiming for a mainline railway station from which

Luke might catch a direct connection to the west coast of Scotland. In the hall was the one canvas bag that he was taking. It was knobbly with bulges and reminded Suzy of her toes in a ballerina pump. She hoped he had included enough changes of dry clothing. Guttering misapprehensions blew shadows across the back of her mind. Luke in the drink. Luke drunk. And mainly she hoped that he wouldn't be cast as the lone figure on the fringes of all the fun.

Now that he was leaving he had turned sunny, a replica of the little boy he had been before he had morphed into this lanky, hunched half-adult. Luke's becoming an adolescent reminded Suzy of one of those werewolf films where the protagonist's face and body stretched and contorted alarmingly before settling into some oddly doggy – and therefore homely – resemblance. She envisaged him turning into his father – an updated version, to be sure – but of the same essential stamp. There he was at his wedding, to some young, modern, independent girl who wished to weld their surnames together. Luke would crack that joke to her parents in his speech, the one about not losing a daughter but gaining a hyphen. He'd help her with the weekly shop but he'd still carol, 'Aren't there any clean socks?' in a surprised, offended tone when an empty drawer confronted him in the morning panic for work. He'd nurture his own fund of witticisms, repeating them frequently. 'Why do you want a dishwasher when you've got me?' he would tell his wife.

Her lips twitched and Luke asked her what was so funny. 'Oh, nothing.'

'This is going to be so great,' he told her as he settled in the passenger seat, ramming the belt buckle into its plastic home.

It was the brief promise of independence that appealed to him. Both Suzy's children seemed in such a tearing hurry to grow up. How come they hadn't noticed what an effort it took to be adult?

'Thanks for letting me go, Mum,' he added.

She supposed she shouldn't. She had been so mortified at his prank. And he really hadn't been contrite. He'd hung his head looking sullen rather than ashamed as she'd ticked him off. But somehow she found herself providing his side of the story: he was young, he was bored, Will had been pompous and unpleasant towards him. She devised all the mitigating factors that he should have mentioned in order to earn her forgiveness, and before she had finished, her anger had melted away. Sometimes her internal monologue did not seem to be her own at all, but the voices of those around her as she strained to understand them.

It had rained during the night and the wheels of the car in front spun a fine gritty spray onto Suzy's windscreen. Every now and then she hit the stalk and sent the sediment to each extremity of her wipers' wave.

A few minutes' thought and Luke was sounding less confident.

'I suppose they give us expert instruction?' he said suddenly. She made the right, soothing answers.

'Do you suppose they'll introduce us or leave us to mingle and muck in?' he asked.

Oh, Luke. They had only travelled half a mile down the road. How she was going to miss him.

Suzy had decided to visit her father. She didn't tell Paddy though, knowing her absence would go unnoticed, that Paddy would assume she was ferrying Luke on a much longer journey. She began to watch for the sign to her parents' town. It should be the next exit. Yes, there it was. She flicked the indicator down, signalling left, and decelerated smoothly back into childhood.

There was the house where Jennie had lived, with an upturned plastic tricycle on the lawn and a tree house in the old oak testifying to its new inhabitants. There was Suzy's secondary school! She slowed the car. The flat roof had been replaced with sloping tiles

. . . how small it looked! How small and shabby! Up on the right was the parade of shops where she and Gerard had gone to buy ice cream or penny sweets. There was the turn-off leading to the park. And here was the old 'tween-wars house, which still, in some part of her brain, was known as home, her past and forever home. She pulled onto the drive. The curtains, flowery in the sitting room, plain in the bedrooms above, neatly framed the windows. She gazed up at them for a moment, their blankness reflecting ghosts and memories and absences. There was only one of the family left at home now. Ah, well. The door was still bright blue and the knocker, in the shape of a fox with a bushy tail, thudded dully as always.

Before long, she heard the creaking of an internal door, the clicking of the ratchets in the lock. The door opened inwards.

'Well, well,' her father said with his edgy, punctuated laugh. 'It's very good . . . hah . . . to see you.'

Ted looked well, which surprised her. At first, he had sounded so disconsolate on the telephone that she had expected him to have lost weight, his skin to be sallow, his eyes to be red raw . . . but if anything he had put on weight. And come to think of it, during the last week, he had recovered somewhat. His voice had grown more complacent. He had regained his self-containment. And here he was, a shortish man with ruddy cheeks and wide grey eyes, whose wiry hair was now such a mixture of grey and brown it looked taupe, hugging her, pressing his cheek to hers; he wasn't a kissy person. Suzy hugged him back and it still surprised her that she was taller than he was. His cheek was soft and smooth as an old pillowcase and came with its usual scent of fresh, disinfectant soap. He was of the generation that wore slippers and she saw, as she stood back, that he was wearing them now, below his slacks and patterned jumper. His slippers seemed an essential part of home.

'Come on through,' her father said. 'I've been cooking us some lunch.'

A smell of the past leaked from the walls and furniture, a particular brand of polish mixed with her mother's Guerlain scent and a warm, furry note from the carpets. With Paddy gone, a fringe of soft dust had settled on the skirting boards, a region a man overlooked during the weekly dust.

Suzy followed her father into the kitchen where potatoes were rumbling violently within a pan, leaking their unique starchy vapour. Ted padded over and turned them down.

'I've finished all the painting,' he told her over his shoulder as he fiddled with chops on the grill. 'Had to do the interiors as well as the outside. It took longer than I'd reckoned. You leave a place unoccupied for any length of time . . . Got all that black mould in the bathroom.' He stopped for a moment, considering something – whether relating to the decoration or the cooking, she could not tell – and as he did so, he nodded his head faintly, a little nervous habit of his.

'We're having lamb,' he told her, 'and that cabbage your mum does with the caraway seeds. I'm very partial to that. I think I've got the hang of it.'

Suzy parked herself on the bench by the kitchen table. All that sitting during the drive had made her want to sit down even more. There were rainbows caught in the suds in the sink, the traces of rainbows dried on the dulled draining board.

'Shall I lay some places?' she asked his back.

'Hah, hah . . . forgot to do that. If you would, dear. Now, how far does your mother place the chops from the heat?' he asked himself. 'She always gets the fat crisp and the insides pink,' he explained to Suzy.

Suzy forbore to tell him that she didn't like pink chops. She realised he had need of copying Paddy's ways. It kept her closer, perhaps; it paid tribute to her wifely skills. This was very much what he had done after Gerard had died. He'd murmur, 'Gerard had a knack with mechanical things,' as he faithfully followed the abridged instructions written in Biro in his son's script on the video manual. It gave him an excuse to recite the well-loved name.

'And we're having Bakewell tart for afters,' her father announced with his gentle smile. 'From the supermarket, I'm afraid.'

'That's fine,' she said.

There was something so valiant about his attempts at normality. His little acknowledgements that all was not quite as it should be.

Catching sight of her laying the kitchen table, Ted sent her off to the dining room. They were going to eat properly, he told her, mustn't let standards slip.

Suzy, her hands full, pushed through the door with her elbow. It was several degrees cooler in here. The sun blinking through leaves danced through the french windows and on to the faded pink carpet. On the Arts and Craft sideboard, the usual ranks of photographs sailed at angles on the grainy wood: Suzy on her wedding day, Clare, taken in black and white by a professional photographer in New York, Gerard with his guitar, Paddy before she had dyed her hair red, when she coloured the grey to match her original subdued gold. How mild and muted she looked, how much softer and sadder. Perhaps she was frightened she would fade away entirely if she remained?

Suzy stood inspecting the photographs carefully for some time, before coming to and hurrying to help her father dish up.

'Mint sauce?' Ted asked her as they sat down.

'No, thanks. Oh, OK. Thank you.' Suzy watched the teaspoon hover above the bowl, wheel towards her plate and in triumph dump its vinegary contents by the powdery potatoes and the shiny lamb chops.

'Oh, come on!' he cajoled, tipping the neck of the wine bottle to within an inch of her glass. 'Just the one won't hurt.'

'I'm driving . . . Oh, well, half a glass then.'

When it came to small matters, Ted took delight in insisting.

He saw it as a function of hospitality to force every item of the available food and drink on his guests. Suzy experienced a squeeze of fond pity for her father. He was so eager for everyone else to be happy, as if he thought to increase the contentment of the world by infinitesimal nudges. Oh, she could see how annoying he might be, if you were living with him, but wasn't everyone? Why couldn't Paddy appreciate his good points?

'Well, it certainly is good to see you,' Ted was saying. 'If you have a moment after lunch, I'd be pleased if you'd have a look at the washing machine for me. The instruction booklet seems to have been mislaid. Maybe you can tell me what cycles I should be using . . . I've been washing everything by hand, you see.'

'By hand? Oh, Daddy!'

'Hah, yes, well, I didn't want to ruin everything, you see.'

'We'll sort it out afterwards,' Suzy said comfortingly. She wondered when it was that she had metamorphosed from flibbertigibbet daughter to competent domestic oracle. She remembered the row there'd been when Paddy had noticed the smiley face on Ted's bald spot. The corner of Suzy's mouth kinked upwards. That was not so very different from Luke's latest naughtiness, now she came to think of it . . .

'Have you, er, spoken to your mother then?'

Suzy looked up.

'I . . .'

'Do you have any idea when she might get over this?' He chewed and swallowed. 'Erm, far be it from me to run your mother down, but it all seems a trifle undignified,' he continued.

Suzy agreed but decided not to say so. All this business of ringing each other when Paddy was going to be out. It was getting ridiculous.

'I think it's time *you* talked to her,' she said.

'That's easier said than done.' Ted twirled his wine glass by the stem thoughtfully. 'Yesterday I decided enough was enough and I called her. She said there was nothing further to discuss and put the phone down.'

'She did?' Suzy hadn't realised that. 'As I say, what about coming to see her? She may feel . . . that you don't care much about her if you're not prepared to come in person . . .'

'It wasn't me that left,' Ted said shortly.

Suzy felt a spurt of pure impatience. 'Dad,' she began, but there didn't seem much point continuing. He was getting that stubborn look, a certain set to his jaw.

He had set his knife and fork at a precise angle on his plate. Something about this gesture reminded Suzy of Paddy's asides this summer, the baleful malice in them. 'You can't believe that man has a drop of testosterone in him,' she had said. And, 'The true *vice anglais* isn't homosexuality . . . It's something to do with turning into old women.' Suzy suddenly understood that her mother was talking not about Will but about Ted, that the contempt she aimed at Suzy's next-door neighbours was really inspired by her husband. How had Paddy arrived at this angry, bleak stage? It was all so sad, so *wasteful* . . .

'I can see that I might be annoying,' Ted continued.

'Oh, no, Daddy!' Suzy exclaimed. 'Of course you're not!'

'Everybody's annoying.' A pause. 'She's extremely annoying in her own way,' he added in a very reasonable tone.

'Yes,' Suzy agreed.

'So she feels she needs a breather, I understand that, Suzy . . . hah . . . I've put up with the woman for forty-one years. I know her inside out. I can read her like a book.'

'So you definitely think she's coming back?'

'Back? I think I may safely say yes.' He picked up his knife and fork and sliced a neat square of fat. 'Give her time to climb down from her high horse.'

Suzy opened her mouth and closed it again. She decided against disillusioning him. It would break his heart. A pendulum of emotion swung within her, from dread and commiseration to a bright sliver of hope. Maybe he was right? It was true: he did know Paddy best. Oh, how she hoped he was right.

'I expect you're right,' she said.

He chewed and swallowed thoughtfully. 'I'm only sorry you've been involved. It's not fair on you and Paul, especially Paul. She can be very selfish, your mother, sometimes.'

'Headstrong,' said Suzy.

'You're telling me.'

'But loveable,' she suggested.

His little stuttering laugh.

'Very loveable,' he agreed.

Suzy perked up.

'She suddenly went ballistic,' Ted continued in a measured, thoughtful tone. 'I said we were spending the summer in Cornwall. Well, what was the point in buying the place if we don't use it? But you know what she's like; there's no reasoning with her sometimes. *She* didn't want to spend another bloody summer in Cornwall. What was there down there for her? It was all tourists and surfers, traffic jams and clotted-cream teas and pretty villages.' He gave each word a separate weight, as if he had repeated them many times since Paddy said them, searching for hidden meanings. 'I was amazed, as you can imagine. "Pretty villages?" I said. "I thought you liked them." She said, "There, I knew *you* wouldn't understand." '

He stopped and glanced over at Suzy, who was feeling a little bamboozled by this account. It did seem unfair. It did seem as if Paddy had been more than usually subjective.

'I said, "What don't I understand, Patricia?" ' Her father dropped his voice into the mild, kind tone he had used when he'd asked her this. 'Do you know what she said? "Don't you call me Patricia," she said.'

Suzy frowned, screwing her nose up.

'I know,' Ted said. 'It does seem ridiculous. I simply don't know what I've done wrong.'

'No,' said Suzy.

'I thought about it a lot while I was down there on my own . . . there wasn't much else to do without her. It was obvious that the argument wasn't about Cornwall. Ho, well, even I, obtuse as she says I am, can see that. Do you know what I think? I came to the conclusion it was all a bit of an excuse to engineer some time with you and the children . . .'

'She hasn't been very sociable, actually.'

'Really,' said Ted, without much interest. He was twiddling his wine glass again.

'Goes off to the cinema, goes to see Judith; been twice this week, taking my car.'

'Your car?' Ted suddenly paid attention.

'I know.'

'Well, that's something new.'

'She's jumpy as a grasshopper behind the wheel. It makes me so anxious.'

'Do try to stop her, Suzy. She's hardly driven these twenty years. Oh, I wish you hadn't told me that.'

'I did try, Daddy. I was . . . what's the expression Luke uses? Flamed. I was well and truly flamed. I wonder what she's talking so much to Judith about?' Suzy tailed off. On second thoughts, she didn't want to invite that speculation.

Ted sat staring at the corky dregs in his glass with a forlorn expression. Several minutes passed. Behind his shoulder, a mute and muted Paddy smiled inscrutably in her portrait. Suzy had the odd feeling that the key to everything lay in her parents' last argument, but try as she might she couldn't figure it out.

'Perhaps it's a mid-life crisis?' she suggested.

'Ho. I don't think we can call your mother middle-aged, Suzy.' That was true. Paddy was old. Suzy was middle-aged. Somehow, her consciousness hadn't managed to embrace that one.

Ted sat up abruptly. He gave her his mild, benign smile.

'How about that Bakewell tart?' he said.

Suzy wasn't really hungry but she ate everything in the bowl he placed in front of her. It was a gesture of solidarity. Her heart felt sore, from too much feeling. She had a vision of her mother climbing into the taxi and leaving this house, of the gentle gladness she had felt in escaping here.

Chapter Thirteen

Paul was tired. His nerve endings appeared to have frayed; he noticed that he was grinding his teeth together. It had been a particularly demanding week, and the last thing he needed was to hire a car for the weekend and drive to collect Luke from the west coast. Why did Suzy invent these bird-brained schemes? Didn't she realise how busy he was?

'He needs his father,' she'd said. Good God! She gave the impression that Luke was running amok after a mere two months without paternal discipline. On the one hand, it was flattering, on the other, highly unlikely.

The drive was tedious, the roads congested with caravans that speeded up when he tried to overtake but fell back to a pootling thirty when he stopped edging out to hunt for a gap. If Paul ruled the world, caravan owners would be shot. Also, the drivers of foreign juggernauts bigger than houses. Also, L-drivers who ventured out for a spot of practice during the Friday evening rush hour when they were as yet incapable of halting at a roundabout without stalling.

After a while, the suburbs petered out. He travelled past a stretch of water, an island topped by a small conceit of a castle. The speed restrictions gave way to traffic signs warning of leaping deer. The villages grew fewer and farther between. The road climbed through a rocky pass and descended to weave past a loch, squeezing between auburn mountains and the pewter lakeside. He looked up, along the great finger of water, where far away on the horizon it struck the sun in a fissure of light. Undeniably, it was pretty. He was heading towards a low, whitewashed building on his right. An oyster farm, he saw, set back behind a neat car park. Should he stop? A vision of Fay's mouth cupped prettily around a corrugated shell came to his mind, liquid dribbling down her chin. No, he would drive on.

Since that day in the office, he had been haunted by images of Fay. Fay in a short, flared skirt but no underwear . . . Fay in a lacy basque . . . Fay astride him, Fay below him, Fay full frontal, Fay taken doggy-fashion, Fay screaming with pleasure . . . Slabs of time were filled with fucking Fay, far more than were given to her real, office self. The real Fay was smart in her green suit or pretty in her navy dress, which swayed around her legs. She flirted with him transparently – as the fictional Fay did before his imagination took the next bound to a voluptuous consummation. The real Fay had leaned forward and planted a kiss on his cheek tonight.

'Drive carefully,' she had said.

Where was this leading? What was going to happen? It seemed that only a filmy membrane separated fantasy and fact.

Whoops! He had almost squashed a dilatory blackbird.

Awareness stabbed him. In his flights of fancy, he had doctored himself somewhat. He had lost that slight suggestion of middle-aged spread. His legs were tanned. His penis had grown an inch.

Up ahead, where the unbroken white line started, he spotted another caravan.

'What took you so long?' Luke exclaimed as he drew into the camp. 'I've been waiting yonks. Everyone else's dads arrived an hour ago.'

'Have you got your stuff together?'

'Oh, hang on a min. I've got a few bits to bung in, still.'

When they arrived back at the flat, Paul simply wanted to collapse on his sagging chair by the window with a cold can. But Luke unzipped the canvas bag in which he'd scrunched his entire casual wardrobe and at the smell of mildew, Paul was drawn to investigate. The limbs of damp, salt- and sand-encrusted clothes were plaited in a contortionist's embrace with unworn garments. There was nothing for it but to transport the whole lot to the launderette.

Shit!

No. Keep calm. Unclench the jaw.

Paul decided to take his son to sit in the nearest pub garden while they waited for the wash cycle to finish.

'What do you want to do during this week your mother has decreed you will stay with me?'

'Bollocks, Dad, I don't know. A mate I met at camp lives in the city. I might see him.'

Paul sighed.

'You wouldn't like to do something together? I could take half a day out here or there.'

'And do what?'

'Well, er, go to a football match?'

'The season hasn't started.'

'Well, have a think about it. Cheeseburger?'

'Cool. And get us a half pint, will you, Dad?'

'Should you? Oh, all right, then. You have the odd beer at home, after all.'

As dusk fell, Luke straddled a bench, swatting midges that landed on his bare arms and conveying chips to his mouth in a seamless train. It seemed to Paul that Luke had passed through another phase of development. His gestures had gained a combative thrust. He was divulging a questionable tale about some girls at the camp, whom he and his mates had fancied. Paul wasn't listening to the details, just the sound of his son's voice, animated and confiding. He was growing up. Four years and he'd be off to college.

'Did Mum tell you about Will Munday and my act of revenge?'

'Ye-es, she did mention a spot of bother with him.'

'What a prat. He had it coming. Gran agrees with me, I know.'

'Well, now, your grandmother—' Paul hedged.

'You and Gran don't get on very well, do you, Dad?'

This was straying into personal territory.

'Oh, I wouldn't say that. . .' he stalled.

'Why is it?'

Paul took a sup of his beer. If he started to list all the reasons, they'd be there all night. But in the end, he said, 'I think it's something to do with Gerard, your uncle – your mother's brother – the one who died. I was with him when he died, you see.'

'But it was nothing to do with you, was it?'

'No, not really. He was driving his car – your grandmother's car – while he was the worse for wear. Let that be a lesson to you, I told him not to. But I think . . .' He paused. 'I think your grandmother blames me to some extent.'

'But you were in another car.'

'I was in another car, yes.'

A peculiar metallic sculpture dumped on the verge by a lamp post – that was what he had thought it was at first.

'I think she thinks I was lying about something,' Paul said.

'That's unfair. You should—'

'I did lie, in a sense.'

Paul was examining the grass but he sensed Luke sitting taller, tense and springy, waiting to see if his father was about to diminish in his eyes.

'I told them Gerard was unconscious, that he didn't know a

thing. It wasn't true.' Paul swallowed; even after all these years, he had to take this slowly. 'It was pretty nasty, to tell the truth.' He tried not to remember the piteous sounds Gerard had made.

'But you did that for their sake,' Luke continued in his matter-of-fact tone.

'Yep.'

'Doesn't Mum know?'

'No.'

'Wow,' said Luke.

Paul almost laughed at that.

'And you are not to tell her,' he added sternly.

'Of course I wouldn't.' Luke slumped sullenly, twirling a chip in a pool of brown sauce, but just as suddenly recovered. 'I think that's really cool of you not to have told them,' he said. 'Especially under Gran's provocation.'

'Thank you.' Paul was gratified. He felt a little as if he'd won a battle for his son's loyalty.

He sat back and Luke resumed his prattling. An extended family of sparrows was roosting in the conifer near by, where the pub garden bordered the gravel parking area; their excited chatter was spilling over, the boughs were bobbing. Paul had never before noticed that the leaves of this common, prosaic conifer resembled the fronds of coral he'd glimpsed in the aquatic shop at the local garden centre. This association lent the tree a beauty it had never owned before.

He swallowed a draught of cold, yeasty beer. It chilled his gullet as it flowed downwards. He felt contented. He was, for this moment, a hero to his elder child. The glass was heavy and solid in his hand. A wasp alighted on its edge and waved a whisker at him in salutation, bending its busy, Sputnik head to sup in the alien landscape of petrified froth. Paul could not raise the energy to waft it away. Besides, he was too brimful of goodwill to all living creatures.

He noted that his own eyes were crinkling at the corners.

How good it was to be a father. He was suspended in joy by Luke, the sorcerer, his son.

The next night, they had pizzas in front of the telly, watching *Predator*, which was one of their mutual favourites. It wasn't as good in black and white, there was no escaping that, and there was a shadow beneath the picture, the stealthy ghosts of another channel. Luke fiddled with the buttons, hammered the side of the set with the flat of his hand.

'Bollocks! Why do you put up with this? Can't you demand a new one . . .? Why don't you buy a colour one for yourself, then? The little portables are bloody cheap, Dad, and I could have it in my room when you come home.'

'I wish you wouldn't swear so much,' Paul said. 'It's immature, it shows a certain poverty of vocabulary. Where did you pick up bollocks from? Your mates at camp, I suppose. Anyway, a colour telly in your room is the last thing you need with GCSEs looming. . . Do you want that pepperoni?'

Paul liked to get his chores done on a Sunday morning: pass a quick Hoover round, iron what had to be ironed, belt round the supermarket at a precise, strategic moment. If he left at 10.30, he could load all the food items he needed into the trolley and be at the end of the booze aisle more or less on 11.00, when the tapes and the signs about the licensing laws came down. That way, he also beat the worst of the crowds.

This morning, though, Luke was still asleep, lost in the peculiarly inert slumber of adolescents. It was 9.00 already. Better get on with something! Paul erected the ironing board in a corner of the kitchen and worked his way through the pile. It took him ninety minutes, twice as long as usual, thanks to Luke's ream of

T-shirts, and it had to be done quietly, without the company of
the radio, for fear of rousing the undead.

Paul couldn't quite centre some of these T-shirts on the
ironing board properly; the seams seemed to be out of alignment
somehow.

Fay had been wearing a white T-shirt on Friday. She was
wearing a bra underneath and her figure looked delicious.
Definitely she possessed his favourite sort of breasts. She'd
caught him looking at her. She'd smiled.

He couldn't imagine Fay in this threadbare flat, so he
transported the pair of them to a five-star hotel with a king-
size bed and a mirrored bathroom. Fay in the shower, now that
was a new one.

The right side of Liam Gallagher's head melted unexpectedly
onto the base of the iron.

'Bollocks!' as Luke would say. 'Bollocks! Bollocks! Bollocks!'

When Paul had finished the ironing, he telephoned Suzy. There
was no answer. He was a trifle put out. He'd said he might ring.
It didn't seem right that she and Daisy were out enjoying
themselves somewhere.

The sleeping bag on the futon was stirring. Luke's eyes
peered out as he sat up, a polyester caterpillar. He was immediately *compos mentis*.

'Shall we go out today, Dad?' he said. 'Go to the town centre
or something?'

He wriggled out of his bedding and streaked to the bathroom
in his underpants, a skinny figure composed of angular bones
and undersized muscles, the first wisps of hair in his armpits and
scrawled on his chest. Paul busied himself folding the futon,
rolling the sleeping bag, tidying the room, putting away his
ironing, and before he knew it, Luke was nagging him to get a
move on.

As they left their door, one of the girls who flat-shared opposite called out hello. She was searching in her bag for her keys, a wedge of newspapers and a milk carton clamped beneath one elbow. She was wearing one of those short T-shirt thingys that displayed her navel, tight black shiny trousers, and sandals with ungainly clompy soles. As she burrowed further, her hair swung over her shoulder, a yellow curtain. Yes, she was very pretty, too.

'What a babe!' Luke said.

Paul was a trifle disconcerted by this remark. Surely they did not share the same taste in women?

'Shall we stop at the supermarket on the way home?' he suggested, stooping to open the car door.

'What for?'

'We have to do a shop. Maybe we could pick up a curry for tonight.'

'What? A ready-made one?'

'Yeah.'

'OK. Long as it's a real bum burner. Bog rolls in the freezer, ay?'

On Monday, Paul slipped up; a basic mistake in compiling some figures, the kind of error he'd have bawled out his subordinates for making. One of the secretaries resigned. It wasn't the job she had expected, she said. There was too much work and not enough salary. Fay seemed preoccupied, nodding distractedly when he was talking to her. The new computer system crashed.

He left early. After all, he'd promised Suzy he'd try to spend some time with Luke. He couldn't find a taxi and meandered home by foot, dreaming of Fay. Fantasy sex with her was becoming an addiction. Perhaps it was because he was frustrated? After all, he'd spent months away from his wife. But he knew that was a lame excuse. Even at home, he flitted off for weeks on end screwing his latest fancy. Then, suddenly, the infatuation was over. Normally, they didn't last long, his mind's mistresses. How come Fay was lasting longer than most?

At home, Luke had drawn both sets of curtains and was sprawled across the futon, his concentration shared between an afternoon snooker match on the television and picking the black rubbery bits from between his toes. The moment Paul gained the top of the stairs, before the door was fully open, Luke said evenly, 'How am I supposed to tell one ball from the other when they're all in shades of grey?'

Paul fell back upon a familiar soliloquy of fatherhood: 'Hello, Dad, Well, hello, Luke. How are you, Dad? I'm fine, son, how are you?'

Puddles of clothing had rained on to the floor, including it seemed, one of the clean, ironed T-shirts. Paul strode to the nearer window, drew the unlined curtains on their flimsy track. A block of light sliced through the gloom; dust motes rose from the floor, fizzing like steam.

The vindaloo had been grumbling inside all day. He grabbed one of last week's unread newspapers from the table and threaded his way through the squalid domestic obstacle course to the bog. There he rifled through the pages urgently, searching for his favourite items: 'This Day Ten Years Ago', and 'Ten Things You Never Knew You Wanted To Know'.

In the interval, Luke banged on the door.

'You gonna be long, Dad?'

Paul extracted himself from an article about a donkey rescued from a Spanish festival, which had brought tears to the back of his eyes. He dropped the newspaper on the floor and yanked a wad of tissue from the roll.

Afterwards, he went to change in his bedroom. He heard muffled protests from Luke. 'Ph-orr, Dad!' Then the spitting of the Spring-Fresh-Lemon-Pine aerosol. His family always did that; he'd forgotten it while living on his own. Whichever bathroom he used at home, the cry of 'Phorr!' and the blazing of air fresheners greeted his every visit. Sometimes he felt like the only man in the world whose shit smelt.

The pocket patches of lawn in front of the stone terraces were turning brown. The leaves on the trees were brittle, rattling if you brushed against a low branch. The heat was unholy. You wouldn't have expected it this far north.

Had there ever been a month so hot, so unrelieved, so obtrusive? The tip of his nose was pink and peeling, as if he'd been sprawling negligently beneath the rays, not flitting from gloomy flat to air-conditioned office, nor, when out, drifting towards the shady side of the street as if he had an in-built bias, like a bowling ball.

The sun was a naked flame above his head, desiccating the neurones in his brain so that his thoughts faltered, turned up blind alleyways and died out. Conversely, his nerves worked overtime, like the motor on the rackety fridge in the flat's kitchen. In the middle of the night, he lay uncovered, sweating, etherised by heat, and listened to the fridge's fracas of small, unoiled metal parts.

Luke's messes were getting him down. His capacity for indolence, also. Paul pushed on the thin plywood door at the top of the stairs and stepped into a purgatory wrought by teenaged hands. In the dead, unmoving heat trapped under the thin roof slates, a family of gleaming flies was feeding on some pale adipose tissue cut from a chop and abandoned at the side of a greasy plate. A pair of stained underpants lay discarded in the middle of the room. The television was chortling over a fiendish *Countdown* conundrum. From the bathroom came the sound of water slooshing, a body sliding recklessly from one end of the bath to the other. Paul's heart sank: a lukewarm bath was the cure he'd prescribed for himself as he'd trudged along the blistering pavements, hunting vainly for a taxi.

Luke emerged twenty minutes later in a clean but crumpled T-shirt. He looked pink and fresh. He hopped into one leg of a pair of jeans.

'I'm popping out, Dad. I got hold of Josh. We're meeting in town.'

'Right,' Paul said.

He felt a bit hurt. It was Luke's last night. On the other hand, he was looking forward to Luke going home. It was odd, the range of emotions this sliver of a boy could inspire.

Chapter Fourteen

Suzy's summer was unfolding to the suburban music of eternal watering. She was at home. There was not much work for her in August: people were away, gardens were at that awkward, in-between stage. She caught up on household chores, listening to the sounds of suburbia.

Will Munday's sprinkler was working overtime. It was one of those state-of-the-art German ones, which flicked its jets from side to side in a punctuated melody, as if the fairies at the bottom of his garden played with water machine-guns day and night. It was oddly lulling. Beneath it, through the open windows, she could hear Kevin yodelling and the whirr of bike wheels, the wail of a disconsolate baby, the clunk of doors, the 'Greensleeves' chimes of the ice-cream van. *Alas, my love, you do me wrong,* Suzy accompanied it silently in her head.

Will had begun watering within minutes of finding the Cerne Abbas giant on his lawn. After his initial stupefaction, after Pat had joined him in a silent pantomime of horror, Will had retreated to his back garden and emerged with the hose on its wheel. He churned its wobbly handle, paying it out, while Suzy gabbled apologies and offered to buy turf.

Will accepted with alacrity and the turf arrived the next day. The cul-de-sac rang to the scrape of his spade and the hollow thud of him jumping up and down on planks, tamping down this grassy perfection. He was tickled pink, he told Suzy; he had been hankering after a brand-new lawn.

The next evening, Will arose from his supper table and emerged with contraptions strapped to his feet, rubber sandals with spikes on their soles to aerate the lawn as he walked. He launched a puppet's progress across his grass.

'What's he doing now?' Paddy asked, glancing superciliously over her half-moon reading glasses through the window. 'He looks as if he's engaged in some weird and solitary Morris dance.'

Suzy endowed Will with a handkerchief and bells in her imagination.

'Now how do you suppose the people who scratched the Cerne Abbas giant into a hill dwindled into fusspots like that?' Paddy asked rhetorically, laying down her book. 'Spear wielders have turned into secateur carriers . . .'

'Oh, Mother,' Suzy said. She was trying not to smile.

'These are men developing child-bearing hips,' Paddy observed.

'Don't be cruel,' Suzy said more soberly. Although no overt reference had been made, she was sticking up for her father. His figure was a little maternal.

Paddy continued her soliloquy.

'I'm thinking that they'll lose the power of reproduction entirely . . .'

'I'm going for a walk,' Suzy announced.

Paddy raised an eyebrow.

It was late to be venturing out, gone 8.00 as the theme tune blaring from the television informed her. Already, as Suzy stepped on to the porch and made her way up the drive, night seemed to be breathing over her shoulder. It was that stage of the year when autumn was just detectable even on a parched, still evening. The crows in the tall trees on the other side of the river seemed to be cracking coarse jokes, their raw voices so much graffiti in the sky. Soon she would be able to see their precarious twiggy platforms balanced in the smooth bare branches; see the gang gathering in their shiny black uniforms.

From the Mundays' house, there came a raised voice, muffled but distinct, then a loud slamming. Will had disappeared but Pat appeared abruptly on the front step, in a magenta blouse with a frill around the collar, giving an impression of ruffled feathers. She was apparently in the grip of an impulse similar to Suzy's. There was a fumbling, a tiny scouring noise as a lighter was flicked, once, twice. It caught and Pat's head came up, exhaling smoke. Suzy judged the moment safe to move on.

Pat's voice floated across to her, over the lush sward that Will was coaxing into growth above the poisoned outline of the ludicrous giant.

'I don't know why I married him,' it said. 'I wish to God I hadn't.'

Suzy shuffled past, feeling embarrassed.

So, that was the Mundays' marriage, was it? A memory switched itself on: the last time she'd seen the pair of them together, when they'd driven her to Stansted. Their disjointed conversation, its verbal shorthand, had seemed so indicative of decades of marriage. She had watched them, too, at that dreadful barbecue. Will had been enumerating their son's many triumphs. 'It's a skilled job, being a farrier, you know,' he had said to the polite, fixed faces of his listeners. 'There are yards in Newmarket depend on him, reckon he's worth an extra head in a race. Now if you ever want a tip on the Derby . . .'

Will's voice droned on. Pat stood at his side, nodding encouragement at each of Will's prompts. 'He said that, didn't he, love?' Yes, Pat affirmed. She looked a picture of devotion, Suzy had thought. They made an ideally suited couple, impervious to monotony, two peas in a pod. Who would have guessed at Pat's hidden rancour? It was amazing what double-glazing and a quarter-acre detached plot could conceal.

Suzy struck out across the footpath that led to the riverbank. The stubble, which had not yet been ploughed in, scratched her feet when she ventured on to it, as she had to a couple of times because of tides of nettles drifting over the path. Stupid really, this impulsive stroll, but she'd had to get away from Paddy for half an hour.

She sat down at the edge of the river and watched the weed shifting in the current, the clear water fast-flowing across a sandy bed. The level had dropped during the summer. There was a thick seam of deeper, khaki-coloured mud that extended right along the bank several inches above the present water level. Tired, brown, overcropped fields dipped to the bank and crumbled away. Two piebald cows were watching her, two calves with them, one of which was making haphazard, lumbering charges at shadows. A concert of sheep in sober grey coats was posed at regular intervals in this amphitheatre.

She had talked to Paul earlier on. Twice he had brought up that Fay, making complimentary comments about her. Apparently, she was being a real help. This would not be the first time Paul had developed an ardent admiration for some other woman. That winsome vet on television, for example, and the woman in the coffee advertisements. He'd been smitten by that secretary at work, too. Why, at one time, he'd rather liked Clare. He always denied these romantic episodes when she teased him about them, lurching between indignation and sheepishness. Well, he was entitled to a secret life. She had one, after all, although she kept it better hidden. Sam Shepherd, Ralph Fiennes . . . the new vicar had occupied a niche in her daydreams for a while, but Paul had never guessed.

Suzy couldn't place Fay in her mind, although she must have

met the woman at some office function or other. She must be pretty, blonde and have a decent figure to qualify as his latest inamorata. And the pair of them were away from their respective homes. Suzy had an urge to book the next flight to Glasgow, but she told herself not to be silly. Did she believe that Paul's fidelity was based on lack of opportunity?

There was an essential decency about him. She had always acknowledged this, although she now believed his integrity to be buried beneath some highly irritating habits. He was like her father, but unlike. Where Ted dithered, Paul could be bombastic. Paul was diligent and worked far too hard; Ted knew how to relax. But she could see from a distance of sixteen years that she had married a man who came from Ted's mould. She wondered what Paddy made of that.

Perhaps Paddy's sly comments were aimed at Paul, too? This notion struck Suzy uncomfortably. It was only too likely. If Suzy saw similarities between the two men, Paddy would, certainly. She had never liked Paul. No, that wasn't true. She had liked him when he was Gerard's friend, and she had been fond of him in those raw, smarting weeks after Gerard's death when Paul had been the only one of the group to come to see them, the only one who was not too embarrassed to sit at their kitchen table reminiscing.

He had kept in touch, doggedly, even when he went back to university and his parents moved to Leicestershire. She'd sometimes told herself he did this for her. He had a soft spot for her, or so she thought. And she had been right. She had progressed through art college – just the local one, nothing special, how could she leave home when they needed her so? – and a sequence of disappointing men. Something changed one evening. He turned up. He sat and talked to her. He looked different, leaner, somehow – older. She saw her mother's face looking down at them, that cold, blank stare. Paul was tarnished from that moment. Paddy suspected him; where once she'd thought him kind, now she considered him devious.

'Now, isn't that nice?' her father had said when they announced their engagement. 'Wouldn't Gerard have been pleased?'

'Love you,' Paul used to chorus, as he left for work. This was in the early days of their marriage.

'Love you, too,' she'd got into the habit of calling back.

When had they forgotten that little ritual?

A conversation with Clare floated back to her, over the riverbank.

'I've decided on a life of promiscuity,' Clare had announced.

It must have been after her separation from Sebastian, when she left him just eighteen months after their boisterous registry office ceremony. Suzy could see her now, sitting on the sofa in a grey pullover. There was a soft sheen to her auburn hair and her skin was pale and creamy. Suzy had felt both proud and sad to see her looking so beautiful.

'I'm just not cut out for marriage, Suzy,' Clare had told her. 'I can't manage the adapting and the restrictions and the annoyingness of it. Of course, I love men, so I'll need them in my life . . .'

'Oh, dearest . . .' was all Suzy had managed to say. Her eyes had filled with tears. She couldn't bear to think of Clare's progress through such a bleak and tedious narrative.

Now, it seemed that Clare had chosen the better part. Oh, Suzy was not sure that she believed that, but everyone else seemed to. Clare was so determinedly blithe. 'You have family, I have friends,' she told Suzy. You couldn't think of her as lonely. You couldn't think of her as sad. Certainly, Paddy admired Clare's independence. Once, she had fretted over the procession of male friends through Clare's life. 'I wish she would find some happiness,' Paddy used to say, happiness being her euphemism for Prince Charming with his golden ring. But she did not mention these worries to Suzy any more. She had begun to talk of Clare's spirit and to boast to her friends of Clare's success.

'Clare always looks immaculate. Well, she can afford to spoil herself,' she'd say. So now it was Suzy who was the disappointment. The daughter who had been content to marry and bring up children. Who had opted for monogamy. The daughter who reminded Paddy of herself.

Suzy found that she had stripped the leaves from a tiny sapling struggling through the long grass. The sight of the bare stem dismayed her.

She had better go home. They hadn't eaten. She rose with a heavy sigh so that the calf opposite took fright, cantering off at speed, upsetting sheep as it went. Their snide, tremulous complaints rose into the air around her.

In the lane, Ron passed her in his running gear. A dark figure in the dusk, he pounded down the pavement, his breath coming in tattered bursts. His eyes were fixed. He swooped round her, on to the road, and was gone.

The close was quiet. Pat's outburst had been taken indoors, to be absorbed by cavity wall insulation and the cloth ears of her husband. Suzy rang the doorbell rather than going round to the back door. Daisy answered it. She was simultaneously talking on the telephone.

'You're a pooh,' she was saying amiably. 'You're a fat, long, curly, smelly pooh. Anyway, I've got to go . . .'

Luke's voice was raised above the television.

'Urr! Grim! Hey, Daise, this'll make you throw up. Did you know there are a hundred million bacteria in your mouth at any one time? And when you eat a meal, it stays in your stomach, like a festering soup, for the best part of a day . . .'

'Mum! Where've you been? I've been worried about you,' Daisy said, following Suzy through to the kitchen, where the dog was vacuuming up yesterday's leftover biscuits from his bowl.

Suzy located the tin opener in the metal tangle that was the cutlery drawer and extricated a potato peeler from between its legs. She opened a can of lamb-and-rice-flavoured dog food. She hunted through the fridge and the store cupboards, deciding to throw together some macaroni cheese. Where was Paddy? Perhaps she might deign to help?

Passing into the hall, the front cover of the topmost magazine on the shelf caught her eye. 'Your cheating spouse: the last to know,' it read. 'Try our quiz.' Suzy wondered what a quiz would tell you that your heart didn't.

Paddy was in her bedroom. She had changed into her dressing gown and was smoothing cream from a heavy glass tub into her knees and ankles. She was perched on the edge of the divan, her leg tracing an inverted V above the mattress. There was something so feminine about this pose, so angular and seductive, that it made Suzy pause. She had never seen her mother as a sexual being. What child did?

All at once, Suzy realised.

'You're having an affair,' she blurted out.

Paddy looked up, appalled. For a moment, Suzy thought she'd got it wrong, had offended her so completely that the world was about to burst asunder in the spare bedroom. She was teetering between relief and alarm. Then, Paddy sat up, swinging her leg over the edge of the bed. She wrapped her robe around her, suddenly prim. Her face seemed to have sagged, grown older in an instant.

She was right.

'Who is it?' Suzy's voice had turned husky.

'Richard,' Paddy said in a tiny voice. Then, 'Richard,' she added more loudly.

A number of Richards cascaded through Suzy's mind.

'Who's Richard?' she whispered.

'The man Judith was in love with.'

'But Judith . . .' Suzy began to say. She petered out. Judith had had an affair. Yes, she remembered it now. Not Michael but Judith. Judith had had an affair and suffered some sort of nervous collapse when she decided to return to Michael.

'Oh my God,' Suzy said. She seemed to have listed against the doorjamb, unable to support her own weight. She could see the concern on Paddy's face.

'Oh my God,' Suzy said again.

Paddy's mouth seemed to crumple. She clamped a hand with those big, creased knuckles to it.

'Oh my darling,' she said, except she was beginning to sob and the words were punctuated by little barks of distress.

This tore at Suzy's heart and she moved forward to grasp Paddy, who was trying to rise from the bed. Suzy ended up holding her rather clumsily. They rearranged themselves on the edge of the bed, Paddy's head buried in Suzy's shoulder, so all she could see was hennaed hair, bright except at the roots, which close up you could see were white.

Paddy was shaking noisily, her sobs muffled. Suzy could feel dampness seeping through the thin cotton of her T-shirt. Paddy was saying something. Suzy couldn't make her out.

'Hush,' she said soothingly.

Paddy pulled her face back. Two black rivers of mascara trailed down her cheeks. 'Please don't blame me,' she said.

'Hush,' Suzy said again. 'I still love you.'

But Paddy sobbed even louder.

Chapter Fifteen

Suzy was woken by the throb of Will Munday's motor mower thuggishly enforcing its Sunday morning stripes. The sun was up, painting blithe patterns on her curtains, hinting at a fine day to come.

Daisy lay in the bed on the spare pillow, her face pale and puffy in sleep. Upset by the household upset, she had asked to sleep with Suzy last night. Suzy's own eyes felt raw from lack of sleep. Will's mower engine, growling, diminishing, muffled, conjured a picture of his progress across his back lawn. She saw him in her mind's eye, a garden Nazi strutting back and forth – she allowed herself this one piece of bitchiness, directing her waspishness towards poor Will's round head.

A blunt silence engulfed the close. At that, Daisy stirred.

A concert of twitterings and fidgetings began. Also, the muffled sounds of someone moving around downstairs, a voice on the telephone dropped low, intended to slide beneath her notice. Paddy was up and about. Apparently, Suzy's senses were heightened: she noticed noises which were normally too banal to register, she divined motives through plaster walls and closed doors.

The latch clicked very softly. Suzy swung herself out of bed and hurried to the window. She saw Paddy fiddling with the lock of the car. She, too, looked different: her eyes piggyish from crying, her lips swollen. She laid her handbag on the passenger seat and began her routine for starting the Golf. It creaked stridently in response to the ignition key, pinning the morning with exclamatory refusals. Finally, there was a roar and a purr.

Suzy watched as her hatchback diminished and at the head of the cul-de-sac turned left. She listened until the notes of its engine had faded to nothing, subsumed into the broad morning chorus of occasional engines and avian busyness. A girl wailed, 'You think you're so clever, don't you?' From the tone and direction, Suzy decided this was one of the Woods girls, scrapping with her sisters, by the sound of it. The impassive windows of the four pink-brick houses, the two pink-brick bungalows, reflected darkly. Everything looked neat, as if it belonged in a brochure advertising the merits of modern housing, perhaps. She drank it in. She could practically taste its suburban spick and span.

'Mum?' Daisy was sitting up in bed, her face puckered with anxiety.

'Good morning, sweetheart.'

'Are you all right?'

'I'm fine, sweetie. Go back to sleep.'

'What was the matter with you and Gran last night?'

'Never you mind. Go back to sleep. It's early.'

It wasn't that early. The crystal display on the clock radio read 8:32.

In the bathroom, Suzy caught sight of her face and examined the circles beneath her eyes. She noticed her thoughts running on, latching on to incidentals, developing separately from the upside-down sensation at the back of her mind.

She padded down to the sitting room in her slippers and dressing gown and dialled Paul. She knew his complicated numbers by heart, both home and office. He took a long time to answer and after the twelfth ring – for she was counting them – her heart gave a lurch of misgiving. Where was he, if not in his own bed? But no, how silly of her, he answered on the fifteenth ring, his voice fogged with sleep.

'Darling, it's me.' She launched in. 'My mother's confessed to me. She's been having an affair.'

'She what?' he said. He sounded irritated. He was still half asleep.

Suzy found she was reluctant to repeat the words for a second time.

'My mother's been having an affair,' she said.

'You're kidding.'

'Of course I'm not kidding.'

'I mean, are you sure?'

He was wide awake now, she could tell.

'She told me.'

'Good God.'

Suzy tried to explain the events of yesterday.

'I want to tell you about Richard,' Paddy had said. She was sitting on the bed, huddled in her towelling dressing gown, while Suzy crouched on the floor, one hand resting on her mother's foot. 'He's important to me,' Paddy said. 'You must understand, this isn't something sordid.'

Suzy related this to Paul.

'Tuh! All affairs are sordid,' he said shortly.

'How did you meet?' Suzy had asked Paddy – almost through politeness – then wished not to know.

'I knew him through Judith.' She was composing herself. She was eager to talk. She mopped her eyes with a strand of loo paper, which Suzy had fetched from the bathroom. 'He was very kind to her at a time when she needed some kindness. You know what Michael was like.'

165

Suzy thought back: she felt she scarcely knew Michael.

'What was he like?'

'Jesus, so ineffectual.'

'Oh.'

'Judith was always highly strung but she was getting worse at that point. She kept having these panic attacks, you know? She met Richard, I forget how – he'd just been widowed – and he was so sympathetic. He was good to her, Suzy. Anyway, this is all wandering off the point. You see, I met him again, last December. It was Saturday the eleventh. It was the afternoon. I went to the cemetery to lay my Christmas flowers on Gerard's grave, and he was there, visiting his wife's grave, and we fell to talking.'

'I see.'

'He isn't my type. He's so upright and English. I mean, he's a fine figure of a man, but I wouldn't have looked at him except that he was so nice and so understanding . . . Decent.'

'He's had two affairs, Mother.'

Paddy gave the tiniest of starts.

Suzy had hurt her; she could see that. She'd wanted to.

'Judith,' Paddy said, 'Judith was a mistake. He was so lonely after his wife had died. He told me that. He was demented with grief after she died. Half crazy with it. He bought big bottles of her perfume and sprayed them in the house, so scared he was that he would forget her.'

Daddy was lonely after Gerard died, Suzy thought, but this time she didn't say so.

'Your father . . .' Paddy seemed to be struggling to find the words. 'Your father – it hasn't been a full and complete marriage for a long time.'

'I don't want to know,' Suzy exclaimed. She had flinched. She should just get up and leave.

'I'm sorry, I'm sorry,' Paddy said quickly. There was a sniff.

When Suzy looked up again, she was mopping at her cheeks with their tiny broken veins.

Suzy returned her hand to Paddy's foot.

'He wants me to go to France with him,' Paddy continued, her voice wavering. 'He has this cottage in Normandy. He thinks we should start again together.'

Suzy conjured up idyllic stone walls and vines flopping over terraces.

'So you're going off with him.' She realised what this would mean. 'I'll hardly ever see you.'

'Well, not as much, but it's not the ends of the earth.' Paddy sounded eager, placatory, but Suzy was in no mood to humour her.

'Oh, Mother, please, you know it won't be the same. Everything's going to change.'

'Nothing will change between us, sweetheart.' Paddy cried. 'Nothing important.' The tears spilled over once more.

'It feels as if it will,' Suzy said flatly. She felt like a child. 'We moved here because of you,' she added. 'Only half an hour's drive away. I did it because of you.'

'Oh, Suzy,' Paddy said into her tissue.

'I've lived my whole life trying to please you.'

'Oh, Suzy, no.'

'It's true.' Paul had always said so and now she was forced to agree with him. Funny, all the rows they'd had over Suzy's attachment to Paddy and how forcibly Suzy had denied it.

There was a long pause while they followed their own thoughts. Finally, Paddy said, 'I'm going to make up my mind for sure over the next week or two.' She laid a hand on Suzy's head, stroked her fringe back. 'It all just happened, Suzy. I didn't mean it to.'

'I've never believed it when people say that,' Suzy said.

'No, well, let us say, I thought I could control it. I thought I would enjoy his company and then slip away, back to being Mrs Barrett.'

Suzy could hear movement on the landing. Daisy appeared in the doorway.

'Mum?' she said. She caught sight of their faces and her own took on a flattened, anxious air. 'Mum, Gran, are you all right?'

'We're fine,' Suzy said.

'Are you sure?'

'What do you want, Daisy?' Suzy sounded a little too sharp.

'Nothing . . . Well, Luke wanted to know if there's any pudding.'

Suzy sent her away in search of chocolate mousses on the top shelf of the fridge.

The moment had gone. Paddy gave a sigh. She tucked the tissue into the pocket of her dressing gown. Then she said, with a great deal of feeling, 'Please don't blame me, Suzy. I couldn't bear it if there was a rift between us.'

Suzy squeezed her mother's foot by way of reply. It was large and homely; the skin was dry near the ankle-bone. There was a raw patch where her sandals had rubbed.

'You say I don't judge anyone,' Suzy reminded her.

'Has she told your father?' Paul asked her on the telephone.

'I don't know,' Suzy replied. 'She went off this morning and I don't know if she's gone to see Dad or gone to see . . . that man.'

'Hmph. I hope she's not expecting you to tell him.'

His tone grated.

'Of course she's not,' Suzy snapped. 'She wouldn't do that.'

How come they had immediately fallen back into their old, familiar places? Paul attributing a malice and neglectfulness to Paddy that she did not possess and Suzy defending her willy-nilly. But Paddy had lied to her, too. That was something hard to bear.

Last night, as she'd got stiffly to her feet, an inconsequential thought had struck Suzy.

'What does Judith make of all this?' she had asked.

Paddy didn't reply. She glanced away shamefacedly.

Ah, Suzy realised, Paddy hadn't been visiting Judith at all. The trips to the cinema. The excursions. They were stories to cover assignations with Richard. How gullible Suzy had been! How obtuse!

'Oh,' she said, and Paddy flushed.

'Are you still friends?'

'Not really.' Paddy concentrated on unpicking a thread in the loose-weave bedspread.

'She took it badly then.'

'She did.'

'It's something to do with this, why Judith and Michael have split up, isn't it?'

'I suppose so . . . though I don't see why,' Paddy said. 'Judith was the one who finished it with Richard.'

'You made her realise she regretted her choice.'

It all seemed so obvious now. She had been so slow; she should have realised earlier.

'I feel so sad,' Suzy told Paul. 'It's so destructive. The backwash has swept even Judith and Michael apart. I feel so sorry for everybody . . .'

'Tuh!'

(*Oh, stop tutting,* she felt like saying.)

'I don't. Not for him. Not for her either,' he said. 'How can you feel sorry for her after what she's done to your father?'

'I just do,' Suzy said. 'I can't find it in my heart to blame her.'

'I can,' Paul announced. 'It's unforgivable. There's no excuse for adultery. We all know that there are lines you don't cross. Her saying she couldn't help herself . . .'

'Well, that's not exactly how—'

'That's exactly what Reg said when he left Lorraine for Tracey. "What about the girls?" I said to him. "But what about me?" he said. "Am I expected to be unhappy for the rest of my life?" Jesus! He was a married man with young children. He should never have looked at that Tracey. Or if he had, he should have drawn back. You can always draw back from the brink. Don't you agree?'

'Well . . . yes . . .' In many ways, she did. 'Tell me,' she added without thinking, 'Is that Fay still helping you?'

'Who?' said Paul. He was pretending he thought this comment unrelated. 'Oh, her. I suppose so,' he conceded grumpily.

'But I thought she was being a great help?'

'So she thinks. Silly cow,' Paul said.

Suzy changed the subject.

He had certainly performed an about-turn in his opinion of Fay. She rang off, her heart a little lighter. At least she had nothing to worry about where Paul was concerned.

Paul headed for the kitchen to fill the kettle. He wished he could be with Suzy, take her in his arms. God, the damage an affair could do! It wasn't just the spouse who was hurt; it was the children, too, however adult. He knew that Clare would take this badly, wailing and carrying on as if this were a personal maternal snub. He could foresee the telephone calls she'd make to Suzy, late at night, with no consideration for the time difference or Suzy's weariness. And Ted, of course, would rely on Suzy.

Paul was getting hot tempered just anticipating them overburdening his wife. He felt pretty angry with Paddy, too. Yet a part of him was relieved: she might be gone before he returned. She might be out of his life, more or less, for ever.

He sat down at the rickety table with a mug of coffee and an American chocolate-chip muffin. He acknowledged that some of his concern for Suzy was truly self-concern: if she was occupied with her father and sister, she'd have less time for him. Oh, God! In-laws! No matter how decent you tried to be, a twisted, dark goblin inside would always resent them.

Paul's estate car smelt of artificial lemons from the fragrance card which dangled from his mirror. Suzy grappled with the lever beneath her seat and slid herself closer to the controls, then back again. A pack of Smints skidded across the dashboard as she swung out of the cul-de-sac. Daisy shot out a hand and caught them. In the back, the dog panted with excitement.

It was Daisy's idea to go for a walk. Suzy had agreed readily. They would go somewhere steep where she would work off her nervy energy. An image of the Gog Magog Hill formed: it was the only 'somewhere steep' around here.

She drew up at the junction with the main road. A car behind beeped her, softly. There was a confusion over her signal. She hit the wipers. The indicator stalk on Paul's car was on the opposite side of the steering column to hers. Soon, though, they were underway, gliding off, Chester barking as they passed the eldest Woods girl with their Labrador.

It was a hot day, once more. At the base of the hill, she turned into the half moon of a parking space. It was a patch of hardened mud really, deeply rutted, so that her boobs bounced against her midriff as they lurched towards the shade beneath a tree. The dog launched himself from the back seat when they opened his door. They followed him to the path, like a tunnel through the greenery.

As she entered it, Suzy walked headlong into a squadron of mosquitoes which whined and banked in the close air. They wheeled above a sea of green, where insect spittle glinted on wiry stalks. The sun came in stripes, through trees. The dog raced ahead and disappeared as Suzy swam against a stream of slapping branches, mostly of hawthorns and elders. Then she was through. A strand of beaten earth offered a passage through the surging grasses, nettles and brambles. The sharp musk of a dog fox pricked her nostrils.

She climbed in silence for some while, then found that she was panting. Her shoulder bag was smacking against her ribs with each stride.

'Are you all right, Mum?' Daisy's voice behind her asked.

'I'm fine, my sweetheart.'

They had almost reached the summit; a clearing opened, the flatlands of Cambridgeshire were spread out before them, a landscape of stubble fields and withered linseed, traversed by grey tarmac. Below, on the half-bay of the stony car park, Paul's silver car, toy-tiny, glinted in the sun. Daisy sank to the knees of her jeans in the long grass, sat back on her ankles and waited in silence. The dog bounded over to a small rock and lifted his leg.

It was surprising how much you could see from up here. Roads from the roundabout at the foot of the hills led off in three directions: one to her right, which led north, one straight ahead, leading home, and one to her left, which led south. She imagined its path, true and flat, towards London; it sweeping past the metropolis, hanging in the air on the partial cobweb of the suspension bridge above the Thames, and transforming itself into the busy, rumbling, tumultuous route which led to the Channel ports and France. Somewhere in that direction, the sea glittered and stirred under this breeze and this sun. Waves skipped in the morning. Heavy ferries rolled back and forth between the two countries, conveying lorries, containers, cars of different shapes and sizes in a primary-school palette of colours, and thousands upon thousands of intent, ant-like people. Beyond lay novelty, new tastes, textures, flavours. Differences. It was where Richard and Paddy would live.

She was going to leave, Suzy knew it. Everything so far – the cruelty and messiness and procrastination – had been caused by a failure of courage. Paddy didn't want to hurt Ted but she was still going to.

Somewhere closer, among those tree-fringed fields, perhaps, lay the village and her economy house in its imperfect cul-de-sac. An aerial view of Sylvan Close would reveal six red-tiled roofs, six tarmac drives, five patches laid to lawn and one drifting with ill-disciplined growth, lax and indiscriminate, isolated within its birch lap fencing.

Was anyone at home?

Yes, she had left Will Munday on his lawn. In Suzy's fancy, she could make him out, one man at his mowing. His rotund figure paddled back and forth, topped by a bald spot turning pink and freckled. Then Pat appeared, the bolster of her bosom, the fluff of her perm, bringing Will a cup of coffee. By the pond on the green, Kevin was brandishing a stick. Suzy could see Ron Bestic pounding past the village houses, a man running laps for evermore, trapped in his circle.

The road on the right, going north, was the direction Paul had taken, and from where he would return, steadfastly. She'd married a man like her father.

Daisy was harvesting grass seeds from a long stalk with her nails, squinting against the sun's glare. She looked uncomfortably hot. The sun was collecting in pink patches on the bridge of her nose and her forehead. Her scalp was pink, too, gleaming between the fine strands of blonde hair, in a way that reminded

Suzy of Christmas glitter. She lowered herself to the ground beside her daughter; it was rock-hard beneath the wiry, sappy strands of grass. She brushed a strand of hair from Daisy's eyes, her heart performing a quiet back flip of mother love. Chester was panting noisily.

'It's too hot for him, poor boy,' Daisy said.

'Let's go back,' Suzy decided.

The car was a mirror, the flints on the car park sparking.

They opened the windows so the breeze blew through, strapped themselves into their seats. Suzy leant forward to select a tape, one of her own that she'd added to Paul's neat, labelled pile. She inserted it in the plastic mouth of the player and a steady, vital, deep beat passed happily through feet and fingers and bone: Bruce Springsteen singing about sex.

She couldn't imagine leaving Paul. If she ventured to begin, she saw only Daisy's face, white flushing red, and Luke chewing his lower lip edgily. But perhaps her marriage was not the fine, strong thing she had imagined: perhaps it was merely a trick of the light? Better not think like that. Thinking too hard about these things did more harm than good.

She would never do what Paddy had done but neither could she blame her. Suzy was being inconsistent, perhaps, but then . . . it was hard to be constant. She understood that. What was Paddy doing now? No, she pushed away the mind pictures that this question evoked – of her mother's legs, of her mother's arms, entwined in this unknown man's. Of her mother's sagging breasts and her belly with its appendix scar . . . no, no, stop, stop, stop.

There was something else. There was a tiny chink of envy. Suzy would never know that thrill. Her heart would never race to that illicit pulse.

She was settling for deeper compensations. Or so she hoped. She started the car and turned for home and the music seemed to be mocking her with its tales of blue-collar men and its promises of dancing in the dark. How wonderful to be irresponsible once more! There was much to be said for day dreaming.

Chapter Sixteen

The expression in Fay's eyes had altered. She seemed pre-occupied and was snappy even with Paul. She seemed to think the world was conspiring against her. He heard her tearing a strip off the temporary secretary. Her behaviour was undigni-fied and cruel and he intervened. Then, she came out with something silly during an office conference, a long tirade about economic migrants and welfare cheats and being forced to work like a navvy to support them. Although he secretly agreed with a lot of it, he winced to hear it. Didn't the woman know you didn't air opinions like these in public? She sounded like an unreconstructed Thatcherite. Where had she been for the past decade?

Just like that, he went off her. It always happened this abruptly: he fancied a woman like crazy and then, all of a sudden, he didn't. A switch was flicked and he was released from his secret obsession.

He decided to put some distance between Fay and himself. A number of taciturn, peppery days followed, when she seemed as relieved as he was at this new coolness between them. But suddenly, without warning, she latched on to him once more. There was a subtle change, though: she was treating him as a sexless ear, as a friend not a philanderer.

He was astonished by what she told him. The woman had problems. Good grief! She thought she might be pregnant.

Wasn't that disturbing? She hated her husband, or seemed to, and yet she'd been having sex with him. Bloody hell. Fay's psychological contours were unintelligible to Paul. From Monday to Friday, she'd been flirting with him. Then, returning home at the weekend to see her children – she'd tended to stress the children, as if nobody else would have dragged her away from Paul – she'd been humping the despised spouse.

Thank God Suzy was a more candid character. A grumpy Suzy brushing away his sexual overtures now became a focus of complacent reverie. At least she didn't dissemble. At least he didn't have to wonder now if she loathed him in some recess of her being as much as Fay loathed her husband. You knew where you stood with Suzy.

'A day or two and I can do the test,' Fay told him in the pub.

Paul bit deeply into a cheese roll, feeling embarrassed. This conversation seemed a touch personal. His vision of Fay had never incorporated urine samples: Fay on the lavatory, Fay with her feet in the gynaecologist's stirrups. Imagining sex with her had been far less intimate.

'"I'm on tenterhooks", I told him. Do you know what he said?'

Paul shook his head as he chewed and swallowed.

'Cross, was he?'

'Cross? Huh! That would have been the sensible reaction. He said, "At least we've got a spare bedroom." He's pleased about it!'

'Oh, well, isn't that, er—'

'I mean, what do we want with another kid? The other two are almost teenagers and I'm supposed to go back to potty training? How're we going to afford it, tell me that?'

Maybe she was angling for a pay rise? Paul decided it was safer to shake his head again.

'Well, we can't. Economies will have to be made. But none of that crosses his mind. It won't impinge on his being. He'll carry on regardless, an also-ran at work, training the school soccer team on Saturdays, visiting his gym on Sundays, a snooze in the afternoon. He's like an extra kid himself.'

'Ah—'

'Do you have any idea how much extra work a baby makes?'

'Yes, I—'

'You have to vacuum the carpets daily, especially when they're crawling. This is a man who walks into the house in his muddy soccer boots, "forgets" to take them off . . . "Oh, let it dry," he says. "It won't take a moment to Hoover off." '

Paul was beginning to feel a tinge of sympathy for Fay's husband. Oh, he could see her point of view, he wasn't a chauvinist, but she seemed a touch fanatical about cleanliness, for starters.

'Maybe every other day would do?' he suggested tentatively.

'Oh, please,' Fay said. 'Have you seen the dirt which can collect on the knees of a baby-gro?'

'Can't the au pair do it?'

She shot him a look. She began to roll an ice cube around the glass with her forefinger. 'Honestly!' She was remonstrating with the ice cube. 'Nobody wants three kids nowadays; they want a lifestyle!'

Afterwards, Paul wondered why he'd put himself out. He didn't want to be cast as Fay's sympathetic shoulder. He realised that he didn't really like her. She was so two-dimensional, so sharp and self-centred. He flushed just remembering his lascivious longings for her. He felt muddled. Dissatisfied with himself in some fundamental way. In the old days, he'd have gone home to Sooze and slipped the pertinent question obliquely into some routine discussion.

'Do you love me?' he'd have asked.

Or he'd have said, in a bright, two-note tone: 'Love you,' knowing that she must reply, 'Love you, too.'

That there could be no other answer.

✻   ✻   ✻

There wasn't much left to do now. The lease had been signed, the staff had been hired, the clients from the north of England informed of their new point of contact, a raft of new clients signed. Paul called Reg to say he was packing up and heading home.

'OK, old bean,' Reg said cheerily. 'I thought you'd be stringing it out for a few weeks more. How's Fay getting along?'

'Fay?' Paul pretended to be impervious. 'Fine.'

'She been a help?' Reg wouldn't give it up.

Paul decided to strike back.

'Reg, not all of us break our marriage vows, you know. We don't all trade our wives in for newer models every few years like some people I could mention.'

'Did I say so? Anyway, don't act so bloody pompous. Tell me about the turnover.' He listened in silence for a while. 'Fubulous, fubulous,' he murmured.

Paul replaced the receiver and rested his forehead in his hand. A sense of utter futility took hold of him. Nothing had changed. He would return in two days' time and Reg would prove as irksome as ever, Al as smug, his job as predictable, his marriage as stolid. His children were growing; they had use of him only as a provider or a chauffeur. They had ceased, years ago, to seek his advice, comfort or company.

There had been a period, a couple of years ago, when he'd woken every night to find Daisy's dim outline at the end of the bed.

'There's a funny noise in my room,' she'd say. Or, 'I've had an awful dream.'

There'd be a tremor in her voice, and not just because she was shivering in her cotton pyjamas in the nippy night air.

'Come on, then,' he'd say. 'Climb in on your mother's side.'

A scuffle in the dark, a murmur from a dozing Suzy, these sounds and the trampolining of the bed would tell him when Daisy had burrowed against her mother. He would turn then, his eyes accustomed to the pale light of street lamps and the moon rooting through a gap in the curtains, and propped on his left elbow he would regard their two quiet heads before settling himself down, dropping his right arm over the pair of them, trying to enfold them both in the saving circle of his embrace. Daisy would for ever be interpreted to him by her mother, and shielded from him, too.

She had no need of him, now. She was past bad dreams, past finding excuses to infiltrate her parents' bed. She chattered to Suzy, chirruping like a jungle monkey about school friends and high-street fashions. Yes, Suzy remained a central player in Daisy's drama but he was pushed to the periphery. Sometimes Daisy humoured him, reverting to the games they used to play, the silly faces they pulled at each other, but she did this, he knew, because she felt sorry for him in some lofty, feminine way. Essentially, she had left him far behind.

He set off on the Wednesday morning. Chris had put his back out so Paul had agreed to drive his estate car on the long journey south. He spread the road atlas across the bed. Suzy had suggested he cut off the motorway when he neared Leicestershire to visit his mother in her nursing home. He sighed as he traced the squiggly arteries of his route. But she was right, of course; he ought to go.

He pulled the flimsy door shut for the last time and manoeuvred his suitcases around the dogleg in the communal stairs. He was dreading the journey and at first he made slow progress. He had to stop at the agents to return the key. The woman behind the desk kept him chatting.

'So did you enjoy your stay among us, then?' she asked.

Paul was taken off guard but she had a pleasant face, round as a dumpling beneath her grey hair, and he searched for a complimentary comment.

'Yes,' he said. 'Yes. It's been very . . . er . . . nice.'

'Ah, you'll be pleased to get home,' she said. 'Nothing like home, is there?'

'No,' he said. There was a certain lack of conviction in his voice.

A silver plane hung in the clouds somewhere above the airport. A motorbike messenger weaved through the lanes, clipping Paul's wing mirror as he passed. Once he hit the motorway, he settled in the middle lane, noting each signpost with their decreasing distances to familiar, southern cities.

He reached Leicestershire in the early afternoon and struck out across the A-roads. The green beyond his windows was a relief after the blank relentlessness of the motorway. He stole glimpses at rolling fields bounded by stone walls, at graceful woods. He'd always liked this countryside.

Soon, though, it gave way to straggling suburbs: rendered bungalows behind gravel drives, petrol stations, a video shop. He navigated the one-way system by memory and took the sharp left down to the Meadow View Home. It was a three-storey, red-brick Victorian building, two large semi-detacheds knocked into one. The front garden, which must once have been imposing, had been covered in drab tarmac. Two bedraggled rhododendrons in half barrels stood sentinel by the main entrance. Paul had never liked rhodos. Their leaves were so leathery and so funereal. It seemed nobody here had the time to weed the tubs; tufts of couch grass and sticky weed had self-seeded in the soil.

A roly-poly nurse was coming down the stairs as he entered.

'Oh, hello,' she said. Her voice was girlish and piping.

'I'm here to see Mrs Winslow,' Paul informed her.

'Her son, isn't it? It was me you spoke to on the phone. She's on the second floor, to the right as—'

'I know,' Paul interrupted. He wanted her to know he had been here before.

'Do you want a word with matron at all?' the nurse continued blithely.

She had reached the bottom of the stairs. She was wearing a white plastic apron above her blue uniform and he saw now that she was holding a sponge wipe in plastic-gloved hands. Obviously, she had been dealing with some unspeakable chore. It made Paul fidgety, her standing and nattering when she should be disposing of these unhygienic objects.

'I don't think so,' he said hurriedly. 'I'll just go up.'

'Fine and good,' she chimed.

She disappeared through a swing door. Paul mounted the stairs with their swirling, institutional carpet. There was a smell of disinfectant on the landing. Meadow View had been his mother's choice. They'd suggested she move into a home near them. Suzy had checked several out and found a pleasant one, but no, Hetty insisted she would remain in Leicestershire, within reach of the friends whose visits had mostly lapsed already. Oh, well. She was settled here now. She liked the staff. She knew their names and their faces. It struck him that his mother was going to die here, in her poky room on the second floor, with its view of the front drive, the asphalt street and the scruffy Spar on the other side of the road.

He'd worked in an old people's home once, the summer after his A-levels. It was mundane work, cleaning and making repairs. He didn't dislike it and the old folk, they had seemed to like him. But after a while going there took too much effort. It was plain depressing. There was a lady called Hilda who used to sit hunched up in a wheelchair. He could still picture her now, her red wig, her gnarled hands. Her system was degenerating but she simply wouldn't accept it. She'd eaten two slices of rich fruit cake on the morning of her seventieth birthday, refusing to believe it would pass straight through her. By the afternoon, she was calling for a commode. There was no one else around so Paul had had to run to get it. Then he'd lifted her on, all the while staring at the ceiling.

Then there was Mrs Bruce. She was dying. She lay in her bed and they lowered the blinds, but he could still see, even in the half-light, that her skin had turned yellow. And the flesh went on dropping away from her, until she was back to her skull. He used to go in there to dust and Hoover and all he could hear was the creak of her breathing. She was waiting to die and he believed that the sooner it happened, the better for her. Once, he was Hoovering round the room and he thought to himself, that's the last sound she's going to hear, me Hoovering, that will be her last knowledge of life. He even began to feel annoyed with her for hanging on. 'Go!' he felt like saying. 'Die! It's only fear that's keeping you.'

So he realised, at that point, that he was going to have to leave. He handed in his notice. He never learned what happened to Hilda, or to Mrs Bruce.

The door was ajar. His mother was in her chair, by the window overlooking the drive, resting her hands on her table, which was wheeled into place each day. Everything she might need was arranged on top: tissues, a little make-up bag and mirror, remote control for the television, carafe of water and a glass.

Her face lit up when he walked through the door. His broke into an answering smile.

'Well, look at you,' he cried heartily.

He threaded his way carefully around the furniture. There was too much of it in the room. The residents were allowed their own pieces from home and she had insisted on bringing her dressing table and wardrobe, the mahogany side table from the hall and the jardinière he'd bought his parents as a silver wedding anniversary present.

He pressed his cheek to hers and the smell of highly

perfumed talc greeted him. They must have told her he was coming. She had applied pearly pink lipstick and had drawn in a pair of brown eyebrows, he noticed, in the approximate location of the originals, which were disappearing. Virtual eyebrows, Paul silently dubbed them, as he pulled the dressing-table stool forward.

He felt he must acknowledge her efforts.

'You're looking very racy,' he said.

She smiled at him vaguely.

'You're looking well,' he boomed.

'Not so bad,' she responded, with another beatific smile.

Oh, God, it wrenched his heart to see her like this.

She was wearing a blouse in a peppy print beneath a baggy knitted waistcoat. A magnifying glass hung on its cord, resting on her bony chest. Her bosom had long ago slipped to merge with her stomach. Paul had to bat away the unnerving thought that his mother naked must resemble one of those pendulously breasted tribeswomen in *National Geographic*. Did all women come to this? To puckering pouches of skin and glimpses of pink skull through combed, colourless hair?

The stool was a little wobbly; he settled himself on it carefully.

'I've been working in Glasgow,' he told her.

She perked her head towards him; the smile had shifted into uncertainty.

'Working in Glasgow,' he repeated loudly.

'Oh,' she murmured, politely.

'Have you got your hearing aid in?'

She heard that.

'I think so,' she said. She touched her ear. 'Yes.'

The same nurse from downstairs waltzed through the door.

'How are we today?' she chirruped. 'Feeling tip-top now you've got a visitor?'

'My son,' Hetty said, with a discernible note of pride.

'Yes. That's nice, isn't it?'

The woman dumped three hardback books on Hetty's bedside cabinet. The covers were bound in some sort of sticky-backed plastic, he noticed. The incidentals of his mother's life seemed to come fastidiously coated, although her chair was stained and fraying, the fancy gilt dressing-table handles were wobbly, the mirror spotted with black at the edges.

The nurse loitered by the cabinet.

'I chose you an Agatha Christie, a Georgette Heyer and a Catherine Cookson,' she said.

Hetty seemed to understand her perfectly, something to do with the pitch of her voice, perhaps.

'Lovely,' she said.

They were old ladies' books in Paul's opinion. She never used to read Catherine Cookson. Patronising, bloody nurse.

'You used to like that Irish woman,' he prompted.

'Which one was that, dear?'

'Oh, God, I can't remember her name.'

'Maeve Binchy,' suggested the nurse.

'That's right.'

'Did I?' Hetty enquired. She looked puzzled. Sad, too. It must be sad when your past was slipping away and had to be recalled by other people.

'We've got Maeve Binchy,' the nurse was saying. 'I'll remember that. Thanks, that's a help,' she said to Paul.

'This is Terry,' his mother told him. 'She's such a lovely girl.'

'Girl!' exclaimed Terry. 'That's a new one. Huh! No wonder I like you. I slipped her a fiver earlier, you know.'

Paul gave her a wan smile. He wished she'd go. He wished she'd take her professional cheeriness to some other defenceless old dear. He shifted towards his mother and the nurse took the hint.

'You two want to talk,' she said. 'Give me a buzz if you need anything.'

But once Terry had gone, Paul hunted for topics of conversation. He realised that Glasgow might be too convoluted.

'Luke's been to camp,' he tried.

She mouthed the word 'Luke'. Paul was encouraged.

'Yes! He learned to sail.'

'Luke! Sail! Oh, goodness.'

'I know. A terrifying prospect. But he enjoyed it. It was a good break for him. He started his GCSE courses in September.'

Nothing. Paul wondered if she knew what GCSEs were.

'You know, O-levels?' he prompted.

Hetty's face fell into irresolute, anxious slants.

'How old is he?' she asked querulously. 'I didn't know he was sixteen.'

'No, he's fourteen, Mother.'

'Well, why's he taking his O-levels?'

He had no answer to that.

What else could he talk about? What had Daisy been doing recently? It wasn't only his mother's deafness or forgetfulness that handicapped their chit chat, it was the unchanging nature of her daily existence. No point pitching a question. 'What have you been doing with yourself?' was uniquely redundant in this situation.

'Daisy's growing up fast,' he intoned.

Another smile and nod.

Paul remembered the photographs Suzy had sent him to show her. He brought them out from his breast pocket and shuffled through them with her, providing captions. 'Daisy and Chester,' he said. 'Remember Chester? . . . Luke on his roller-blades . . .'

She nodded, she smiled, but she seemed to have lost the art of asking questions herself. It was a strange, lopsided business that had happened to her mind. She received his bulletins from the outside world with undisguised pleasure, but she had forgotten how to seek them out.

He left the photographs on her trolley. The nurses would stand a few of them around her room. He rose and peered out of the window. A silver people carrier, its outline unmistakable, was parking on the tarmac outside. A woman in a padded, black anorak got out. Her hair was blonde and curly and emanated from a dark whorl in the centre of her skull.

'That's Kitty Dodds's daughter,' Hetty told him, perking her chin to peek over the sill.

'Oh.'

'She comes every day, about this time. She works part time, you see.'

'Right.'

'She's very plucky, you know. Her husband is disabled.'

'What a shame.'

Funny how much she had absorbed about Kitty Dodds's daughter.

'It was an accident,' she told him. 'Involving a double decker bus.'

Her eyes wandered to the vacant wall. A frown puckered her virtual eyebrows. Her mouth worked quietly for a moment.

'Your father was getting on a bus when I met him,' she said. 'I was getting off and our eyes met, just like that. Did you know that?'

'Really?' Paul said. He leaned forward. She was smiling now and he wanted to encourage this reminiscence. 'What happened next?' he prompted.

'Mmmm?'

He waited patiently. Finally, she said, 'Our eyes met.'

It seemed there was no more left.

Out of the blue, a scene came back to him. It was the summer day eight years ago on which he had registered his father's death. He had been sitting on a slatted wooden bench in the outer office of the registrar's. There was a queue of people at the counter to his right, busy, fidgety, impatient people in bomber jackets and trainers, in pin-striped suits. But it was the reflections in the glass of the door, which was propped open, that had caught his eye. A succession of torsos moved across it dimly, cut off at the waist by the lower planking. The women were wearing hats, the men buttonholes. Some were clutching little envelopes of confetti.

A wedding. He willed them to go away. He didn't want to witness this. But the backs of the bride and groom appeared in the window, he a tall, shadowy figure in charcoal and she, small, in a beige suit, with starry white flowers pinned in her hair. Something about her stance told Paul she was wearing high, spiky heels. She looked like a pouter pigeon, puffed up with pride, her head bent back as she gazed up at her new husband. It was she who made Paul particularly angry and raw. Her oblique adoration offended him.

He addressed her in his mind.

'You're so happy today,' he told her. 'But do you not realise it can only end badly? That marriage ends either in divorce or in death?'

His mother had spent thirty-five years with his father and now she was alone. All the high hopes she'd started out with, the daily grind of cooking and cleaning for him, the squabbles, the comfort of his body on one side of the bed, all this had ended. Cancer. In the hospital room, she'd wept. She'd kissed him on the forehead. There was something right in this gesture and Paul had followed her example. He'd never kissed his father when he was alive, but he kissed him now, although his skin was cooling.

They had sorted through his wardrobe and the sight of his soft gardening shoes, moulded to the shape of his feet, had broken her composure. When they pulled open a heavy drawer, the smell of his aftershave wafted out.

Oh, shit and fuck and damn.

Suzy had lost her faith when Gerard died. She'd told him this years ago. How seeing the casket had done this to her.

'All that life and energy', she said, 'had come down to a handful of grit and ashes.'

'Why do you still go to church?' he had asked her.

She thought for a moment.

'I hope I might find it again,' she'd said. 'I would like to believe. I just don't.'

She didn't go to church much these days. Looked like she'd given up the search. Paddy didn't go to church either.

He remembered Paddy's face at Gerard's funeral: white and red, her jaw set. There was no doubt she'd grown harder over the years. It was so long ago it was hard to recall how she'd behaved before Gerard's death, but there was one scene – her throwing her head back and laughing – that he'd never forgotten, probably because his own mother never laughed so uproariously.

Poor Paddy. She was sixty-something, wasn't she? At the best, she'd got twenty, twenty-five years left? Maybe just eight or ten. Yes, he could see why she had decided to cut her way out and run. If you looked at Paddy's affair like that, you had to forgive her everything.

Chapter Seventeen

Suzy glanced out of the window and Paul was there, on the drive, unloading cases from the back of a strange blue estate car. It was a shock to see him in person again. He was an hour earlier than she had expected and he didn't quite match the version of him that had been playing in her mind. There were two heavy lines bracketing his mouth and a cushion of fat on his stomach. She had forgotten about the existence of all of these.

He didn't look pleased to be home. His face was drawn; a fastidious curl had taken hold of the corner of his mouth. She suspected his back was playing up after the journey and when he winced as he straightened up she knew she was right.

She opened the door, at the same time calling out, 'Dad's home.'

The dog hurtled out and began to caper around Paul's feet.

'Out the way,' he ordered, stumbling over it into the hall. He dropped his cases.

'What a bloody awful drive. Last favour I do Chris.'

She held out her arms to invite the embrace. It was a quick, perfunctory matter, for Daisy appeared and he turned to embrace her. Luke was bounding down the stairs in his unlaced trainers. He began to dance around Paul, shadow boxing.

'Luke.' Suzy said this with a note of warning. This was not the time. Paul was too tired and the hall was too small for horseplay.

'Phum, phum! Phum, phum!'

With each jab, Luke provided the sound of a spongy boxing glove meeting flesh. The dog tensed and whimpered.

'Come on, Luke,' Paul said.

Luke dropped his fists and a trace of hurt flickered fleetingly in his face.

'Suit yourself.'

So this reunion, which she had been anticipating so happily, had curdled slightly already. Her heart sagged a little. Luke manhandled the cases upstairs, Daisy following with Paul's raincoat and a dustbin bag of dirty washing.

'Hungry?' Suzy asked Paul.

'No, not at all,' he said, opening the door to the kitchen where Paddy was preparing a leg of lamb. 'I stopped at a Happy Eater on the way . . . Paddy!' he added, as if her presence was a surprise to him.

He gave her a lukewarm peck on the cheek, helped himself to a Scotch and trudged upstairs. Suzy trailed after him.

'Don't worry. I don't think she's staying,' Suzy said as she closed the bedroom door.

'Huh.' A little exhalation.

'She said this morning she'll make her mind up quickly.'

'I know Paul doesn't really want me here,' is what Paddy had added.

'Oh, no!' Suzy had protested. 'Don't be silly. You don't have to go!' She had said this because she feared Paddy's mind was already made up, had been decided, in fact, for these many months. She was waiting only to screw up sufficient courage to tell Ted. But if she took her time, well, maybe she would begin to wonder. She might change her mind.

'She doesn't have to make a quick decision, does she?' Suzy asked Paul now. She was sorting his clothes into piles, discarding socks with potato-sized holes in the heels, which he had carted home regardless. He lay on the bed, nursing his whisky, the dog tucked into his side.

'Make her mind up? Surely that's the best thing, isn't it?' His voice was blurred from tiredness.

'Not necessarily.' She slid open a drawer and lowered a pile of underpants into the empty space.

'It's just prolonging the agony for everybody,' he murmured.

'For you, you mean.' Suzy couldn't help herself. 'Just because you want her gone.' Paul sighed.

'We'll talk about it tomorrow.' He closed his eyes. 'Chester! Stop licking me!'

In the closet, empty hangers were being refilled, a previous version of normality was being restored.

'How was *your* mother?' she asked.

'Mmm?' There was a pause. 'Hard going,' he said. 'She keeps forgetting things.'

'But she was pleased to see you.'

'I think so. It's much easier when you're there. You better come with me next time. She'd love to see Luke and Daisy.' His voice was fading away.

She dumped dirty underwear in the linen basket, tidied clean shirts into their drawer, stacked the cases on the high closet shelf. When she had finished, she found him breathing rhythmically, the whisky lurching in his hand. She rescued it, removed his shoes and his trousers. His bare legs lay, eel-like, on the yellow cover.

She drew the curtains quietly. The dog leapt to the floor with a thud. She closed the door behind them.

* * *

The next day, Will Munday had a heart attack and died. Suzy had only stopped to speak to him a few hours previously. He called her over as she returned from posting a letter. He was seeking an admiring audience for his new sit-upon motor mower and had already hailed Ron Bestic and one of the interchangeable Woods girls – the eldest, Suzy realised, on closer inspection.

'Go on, Will, tell us the damage,' Ron was saying.

'Oh, only eight hundred and fifty,' said Will. 'It's second-hand.'

'Blimey,' said the girl. 'Your mower cost more than my mum's car.'

'I know it's a bit indulgent,' Will said happily, 'but the back is mostly laid to lawn.'

'He won't get any exercise at all now,' Pat said, amiably enough. 'Pushing the mower was his only . . .'

'Don't interrupt, dear.'

'Well, I was only —'

'Nag, nag, nag. Wives, who'd have'em?' There was a corrosive edge to Will's banter.

Pat sought inscrutability by casting her eyes to her lace-up deck shoes. The careful immobility of her face reminded Suzy of Luke.

'I'm planning to mow down your wilderness, Suzy, while you're out one day,' Will continued.

Everyone laughed, eager to smooth the moment.

It was amazing to think that later, while she was out, an ambulance had slipped into the close and stretchered Will to Addenbrooke's where he was pronounced dead on arrival. It was all so sudden. And no sooner had Suzy rushed to the village shop to buy a condolence card and been waylaid with 'Have your heard?' and 'Isn't it dreadful!' on the way home, than Paddy forestalled her at her desk.

'May I take your car, Suzy?' she said. 'I'm going to see your father.'

'Daddy!'

'Yes. I've made up my mind, but it's only fair I tell him first. So I'll be needing the car.'

'Yes, of course,' Suzy said.

It was only too obvious what Paddy had decided. After she left, Suzy wrote her card and popped it through the Mundays' door. Then she lay on the sofa on her back, staring at the magnolia ceiling until she was aware of every stroke of the brush, of each stray bristle that had been interred in the fast-drying emulsion. And when Paddy returned, looking stricken, she took the car and returned over the roads her mother had driven, as if following the traces of the tyres.

'He was that upset,' was all that Paddy had said. 'I did not think he'd be that upset.' During the drive, Suzy had plenty of time to imagine what form this upset might take, although, when he opened his door, Ted looked thankfully composed. Then she noticed that his mouth sagged momentarily before managing a weak smile. He'd hoped she was Paddy. The doorbell had raised improbable hopes.

He clasped Suzy tightly to his shrivelled cheek. His Brillo-pad hair scraped her skin.

He took her into the kitchen and insisted upon making a cup of tea, warming the pot with swirls of hot water from the kettle. He poured the milk into a china jug and tutted as he inspected the first mug he took from the pine mug-tree. She noted how his baggy cardigan, one Paddy had knitted many years ago, pouched to accommodate his pregnancy of fat. She noticed the dual creases where he hadn't ironed his slacks properly, and that he was wearing his suede slip-on slippers, which were so worn that shiny patches anointed each toe. She was conscious of all the quirks and habits that formed this man, that endeared him to his daughter and irritated the hell out of his wife.

The dustpan was on the table, the blue-and-white shards of a broken platter inside.

'Shall I get rid of this?' she asked him.

He glanced over and grimaced.

'I'm afraid I lost it,' he said, embarrassed. 'Broke Granny's serving dish.' He emptied two medicine spoons of tea into the pot and snapped the lid back on the caddy. 'Didn't make me feel any better.'

Suzy had never seen her father lose his temper. She had never seen him cry, except once, two days after Gerard had died. Sad, that had been, just awful. She swept the china into the swing bin. She didn't know what to say.

Ted set the two mugs on the table and sat down.

'Have you spoken to your mother?' he asked.

'Not really, Dadda.'

'Oh, Suzy.' His voice wobbled faintly and she tensed, willing him not to break down. He stirred his tea, round and round. 'She's been having an affair,' he said.

'I know.'

'She's leaving me. After forty-one years of marriage, she's leaving me for that awful man.'

It sounded as if Ted knew Richard. Suzy was surprised.

'Do you know him?'

Ted didn't seem to hear her.

'Did you know he's had an affair before?' he continued. 'This isn't the first time he's wrecked a perfectly good marriage.'

'Judith,' Suzy said.

'Yes, Judith. Judith first and now he's moved on to her best friend. A cosy little sequence.'

It was understandable he was bitter.

'He's a widower, isn't he?'

This seemed to distract Ted from his line of thought.

'His wife died some years back. She was a nice woman, French woman, and after that he fell in with Judith, played the sympathy card. It was the talk of the estate. It shattered Michael. Oh, yes, poor chap. I was always surprised how your mother took Judith's part. I put it down to friendship. Judith was good to her after Gerard died . . . It makes you think, doesn't it?'

It did. It made Suzy wonder whether Paddy had suspended her moral code for her friend's sake and in doing so had encompassed Richard within the circle of her tolerance. Years later, when she met him again, he must have seemed like an old friend.

But Ted was asking her something:

'Has she spoken to you?'

Suzy nodded, scarcely thinking.

'What did she say?'

'Well . . .'

'Has she said anything about that man?'

Suzy hesitated.

'A little,' she ventured.

'What did she say?'

'Oh, just that he was a widower.'

'Did she say when it started?'

'Well, she—'

'She did, didn't she?'

'You don't want—'

'Yes, I do . . .'

'Oh, Daddy . . .'

'Just tell me, Suzy! I'm your father.'

Her father never raised his voice. It was distressingly out of character.

'I'm sorry,' he said. 'I'm sorry. I didn't mean to shout at you.'

He clutched his mug, looking dismayed at his own excit-

ability. They sat in silence for a while. Suzy stared at the surface
of her tea where white flakes of hard scale from the kettle floated.
A faint drift of steam coated her cheeks.

'I feel as if everything's slipped away,' Ted said eventually.
'My son's dead. My youngest daughter is on the other side of the
world. My wife's left me.'

Suzy felt like saying – childishly – 'But you've still got me,'
but that didn't seem to offer much compensation.

'I didn't like to think of you being . . . being on *their* side,' he
added.

'Oh, Daddy. She hasn't said much about . . . what's his
name?' – she pretended to forget the name she knew perfectly
well – 'about that man to me, Daddy. I wouldn't have wanted to
hear.'

Ted nodded; something she'd said had confirmed some
private thought.

'No, she couldn't explain it to me either,' he said. 'I asked her
why. Why? Why throw away forty-one years of marriage?' He
tailed off. 'You'd think she owed me an explanation.'

Suzy could understand why Paddy hadn't provided one. It
would have meant listing every petty irritation of the past
forty-one years. Really, this was Paddy at her best and
bravest, refusing to justify herself, refusing to end her
marriage with recriminations. But her act of kindness had
left Ted dangling.

'She said to me, "Anything I say will sound inadequate." ' He
gave a puffing, joyless laugh. 'I said, "You're bloody right there!"
She told me she was seeing Judith, you know, but she wasn't. I
worked it out. It makes you question a lot of activities. She went
back to her golf, you see, oh, about six months ago . . . Or was it
more?' He was frowning slightly, chasing some detail. Suzy felt
powerless to intervene.

'It was before her birthday because I bought her gloves as her
little present. That's right, the watch as her big present and the

gloves. So it was before then, that's right. I used to put her golf clubs and her spiked shoes in the boot for her. She'd be wearing those cord trousers she used for golf, you know; it all seemed perfectly normal . . . And now I'm wondering: when I dropped her off, did she go to play golf or did she meet him? Was it all a charade for my benefit? Was he waiting in the car park to whisk her away?'

To Suzy's horror, her father's eyes turned red and shiny. She put her hand on his arm, kneading it with her thumb, kneading in courage, she hoped.

'She suddenly started wearing lipstick . . .' He stopped, extracted his handkerchief from his pocket and blew his nose noisily. 'Hah. Oh, dear. Do excuse me.'

Suzy found that she hated her mother.

'I always preferred her without lipstick.'

There was a long pause. Suzy could hear Gerard's voice saying, 'They're not your responsibility, Sooze.' He'd told her that, shortly before he died, when she was fretting about the way Paddy treated Ted, her bossiness and explosions. It had been an intoxicating thought but she hadn't believed Gerard, not then, not subsequently, not now.

Ted rose to his feet. 'I need another cup, my tea's gone cold. How about you?'

The question took a few beats to filter through. She came to and shook her head. He topped up her mug anyway.

'They're going to live in France, did you know? Some cottage his wife inherited. I bet she's turning in her grave . . . I suppose she thinks it will be one long holiday,' he added, clearly no longer referring to Richard's dead wife. 'I expect she anticipates you and the children spending your holidays there. You won't, will you? You won't let my grandchildren meet him, will you, Suzy?'

Suzy gave a little shake of her head. She hadn't thought about meeting Richard. She didn't like to think about it.

His mood had changed. He was stoking up his anger.
'She'll live to regret it, that's my opinion. She'll have cut
herself off from everything she knows. No friends, no family.
She doesn't speak the language. She'll be dependent on that
. . . that gigolo. If he's done it once, he can do it again. I hope
she doesn't think she can come crawling back here if it all goes
wrong.'

'You don't think she'll be happy then?' Anxiety sawed in
Suzy. No, it seemed she did not hate her mother.

'Happy? No, I don't,' he said bitterly. 'Do you?' he added
abruptly.

Suzy didn't want to hurt him, but she didn't want to lie.

'I don't know. I don't know, Daddy. I want her to be happy.
She's my mother. And one day, when you feel better, you'll wish
her well, too . . .'

'No, I won't. Not without me.' His face had taken on its
stubborn set.

She replaced her hand on his home-knitted sleeve.

'That's what she said to me. "If you love someone, you want
them to be happy." It's not true,' he said. His eyes were watering
once more. 'It's not true. I do love her, but I don't want her to
be—'

He couldn't finish the sentence. A flurry of handkerchief.

'I'll be all right,' he mumbled into its white folds. He took a
deep breath. 'Why don't you take a little turn outside?' he
suggested.

Suzy glanced up. It had clouded over and the first smears of
rain were streaking the window pane.

'I need the loo,' she improvised.

She got to her feet. Her face, red and white and sorrowful,
flashed past her in the hall mirror. The wooden curl of the
banister was cool and solid beneath her palm. As she mounted
the stairs, she happened to glance down through the kitchen
door.

Her father was sitting where she had left him, the dustpan and brush on the table beside him. An old man with his head in his hands, a man wearing lemon socks and suede slippers; a man with his head in his hands, weeping.

Chapter Eighteen

'Richard's coming to pick me up on Thursday,' Paddy said.

She and Suzy were weeding in the garden. Everything had gone over. The stems of the hostas ended in exclamatory seed heads. The foxgloves stalks were withered and they rattled. The first leaves were drifting from the willow towards the river; they glued themselves to the surface of the water and were borne round the turn.

'I see,' Suzy said. She hoped she had masked her slight agitation.

'I thought you might ask him to lunch,' Paddy said. She was sitting back on her haunches. Suzy could sense her solemn gaze. 'I'll be spending the rest of my life with this man, Suzanne, so I guess you'll be wanting to meet him.'

Suzy studied the shifting, glinting surface of the water. What Paddy said was reasonable. Her pangs of protest stemmed from old, deep, ingrained loyalty.

Paddy's voice continued. There was a note of unaccustomed vulnerability.

'Are you saying we'll only be seeing each other if I return to England without him?'

'Oh, Mother,' Suzy said.

*　　*　　*

That was the point at which it became a foregone conclusion that Richard would come, despite Paul's objections.

'*I* don't want to meet him,' he insisted. 'I don't want my children to meet him . . . How's your father going to feel about this?'

'Hopefully, he won't find out.'

Suzy was sorting dirty laundry from the basket while this conversation took place. The shirt she picked up was inside out.

'So we tell Luke and Daisy to lie, do we?' Paul's rhetoric slid towards ill temper. 'What sort of an example is this setting them?'

'I don't want to meet him either, but I feel I ought,' Suzy explained.

'You always do exactly what your mother tells you, don't you, Suzy?' Paul concluded. 'She rides roughshod over you and you can't see it.' He headed for the bedroom door. 'I'm going to play golf,' he informed her.

He had taken a week's holiday. He wanted to relax, not to navigate a raft of awkward family dilemmas, she knew that.

His feet on the stairs. Him rooting in the garage. The door slamming. Suzy carried the clothes, with their faint, rumpled smell of sour deodorant, down to the washing machine. Before she had finished loading them through the porthole, Paddy's voice began behind her.

'I hope Paul isn't being prudish,' she said. 'He can be a prig. You don't see it, but he can . . .'

'He doesn't want Daddy to find out.'

'Oh, sure he won't,' said Paddy.

On the course, Paul couldn't concentrate on his game. His swing was wild; at the last moment his putts veered stubbornly away from their target. The breeze streamed through the saplings planted around the sand trap; it billowed about a flap on his jacket in a particularly intrusive way. Two ponies were being ridden along the road which edged the golf course, a grey in front of a brown. As he watched, they halted. The grey pony, in particular, was observing him through keen brown eyes, its ears pricked, transfixed by the figures with their sticks and their trolleys. Its rider, a young girl, was patting its neck reassuringly. Paul watched the pony watching him. He had a discomforting sense of how curious man's activities were.

Suzy briefed the children while both Paddy and Paul were out.

'Oh, bollocks!' Luke's face had taken on a fastidious curl, which reminded Suzy of his father. 'That is gross.'

'Poor Granddad!' Daisy exclaimed, her eyes reddening.

'You're going to have to be polite, for Granny's sake,' Suzy told them.

'I'm not going to be here,' Luke said.

'Has he got grandchildren of his own?' Daisy asked suddenly. She looked immensely curious.

'I don't know,' Suzy said. 'I don't even know if he's got children.'

'Will Granny meet his children?'

'I don't know.' It was a disconcerting thought.

'She's too old to be having it off,' Luke declared belligerently.

Yes, thought Suzy, I wouldn't have phrased it in the same way but that's exactly how I was feeling.

Richard arrived almost bang on 11.30 on the Thursday morning, just as had been arranged. Paddy went out to meet him while everyone else stayed indoors. There seemed to be an unspoken agreement about this. They were largely silent, examining their feet, except when Luke mumbled something under his breath and Paul snapped, 'That's enough!' before striding out to the hall. There followed a gravelly rumour of introductions.

And then *he* actually came in. Stepped through the door into the sitting room and took on a shape.

'This is Richard,' Paddy said. She wore an air of hesitant pride that seemed inappropriate for her, like a frilly neckline. 'And this is my daughter, Suzy.'

He was tall, six-feet-something, with grey hair, brushed back, and a military moustache. He was slim, too, with a surfeit of good manners. He had brought a bunch of lilies for Suzy. His handshake was firm, vice-like; Suzy winced inwardly as her ring bit into her flesh. Richard turned to Luke and Daisy.

'And you must be Luke and Daisy. I've heard a great deal about the pair of you.' He patted the dog and addressed him directly. 'I haven't heard about you, before. You're a fine beast, aren't you?' he said.

'He's called Chester,' said Daisy.

'After the town or the comedian?' His smile was jaunty.

Daisy stared at him blankly.

'A drink?' Paul suggested. Perhaps only Suzy heard the briskness and formality in his question.

She took the lilies through and dumped them in the sink. He might be elegant, she conceded, but his teeth were yellow. At least her father's teeth were white.

She removed the lid from a pan and examined the peas. It wasn't time to turn on their burner. Perhaps she might wipe the work surface again? And while she was about it, why didn't she attack the base of the taps, which were clogged with beige gunge?

Paddy came through after her.

'I'll give you a hand, shall I?'

Suzy dropped the scouring pad in the sink.

'It's not necessary. I haven't gone to any trouble.'

'Shall I put these in a vase?'

'If you wish.'

Suzy returned to the peas while Paddy ran water into Hetty's old cut-glass vase and fluffed the flowers.

'Don't you love the smell of lilies?' she murmured and bore the arrangement out before her.

Abrupt blisters of sizzling burst behind the cooker door. An oily haze rose from the exhaust slot. Suzy didn't have to worry if the pork was overcooked; she knew her guest would feign delight whatever she put before him.

In the sitting room, Richard was sipping a sherry and Paul a Scotch. Someone had introduced the subject of cricket, a subject that would normally animate Paul rather more than it was today.

'And do you play cricket, Luke?' asked Richard.

'No.'

There was a silence, a fidgeting. Paddy finished prinking the flowers and settled on the sofa next to Richard. Both their mouths were kinked upwards at the corners into determined half smiles.

'Luke went sailing this summer,' she informed Richard.

'Oh? I sail myself,' he said.

Luke, who'd been scratching the dog's stomach, looked up. 'Really?'

'I used to keep an Enterprise.'

'Oh, cool!' Luke said, a little uncertainly.

'Down on the south coast. And what were you sailing?'

'Catamarans.'

'You should try a single hull at some point.'

'Yeah, I want to.' Luke brushed the flop of hair back from his forehead. 'It's really different, isn't it?'

Paul got up abruptly to fetch himself a second Scotch.

'Sooze?'

'Yes, please. Gin, please.'

'Well, maybe I'll take you one day,' Richard was saying. 'If you come and visit Patricia and me.'

Even though his back was turned to her, Suzy knew exactly what Paul was thinking.

'Have you owned your cottage in France for long, Richard?' she interrupted.

He held up one finger while he swallowed his mouthful of marmalade amontillado.

'Oh, let me see . . . since 1974,' he said. 'It was my late wife's mother's. We inherited it when the old lady died.'

'You know the area well, then.'

'So I flatter myself. It's a delightful corner of the country. Are you familiar with it?'

Suzy shook her head. Richard leaned forward to incorporate Daisy within the sphere of his easiness. 'Are you learning French yet?'

'*Oui*,' she said. '*Mais je ne l'aime pas*,' she articulated carefully. Both Richard and Paddy laughed.

'Some visits to France will help that accent,' Paddy said.

'The school runs an exchange,' Paul announced.

He handed Suzy her gin and tonic. The juniper and bubbles exploded in her mouth like a fountain.

Over the lunch table, Suzy decided to satisfy her curiosity.

'So what did you do before you retired, Richard?' she enquired, as she handed round the vegetables.

'Banking,' Richard said. He poured a neat pile of salt on to the plate next to his roast potatoes. 'A bit of a disappointment to my father. He was in the diplomatic service. I come from a long line of career civil servants.'

'Oh?' said Suzy in a prompting tone.

'Richard lived abroad when he was boy,' Paddy interjected. 'He spent time in Africa, Egypt . . .'

Richard swivelled towards her, smiling.

'And more at boarding school,' he reminded her. 'Sherborne,' he told the rest of the table.

'Fascinating stories,' Paddy said.

Richard turned to Daisy on his right and lowered his voice conspiratorially.

'I'll tell you one. Line of marching ants went up my trousers once. Had to whip 'em off and dance around like a dervish to get rid of the things.'

Daisy stared.

'Marching ants?'

Suzy had conjured a picture of Richard as he was now, his stalks of legs and a pair of bagging Y-fronts through which she glimpsed a curling wisp of grey pubic hair. In this light, his story seemed faintly unsuitable. It made him less military; it made him seem seedy.

'And once in Malawi, I witnessed a total eclipse.'

'Oh, mega!' said Luke.

'The cicadas began singing as the dark fell, and the tree frogs.'

'We didn't get the darkness up here,' Luke told him. 'It was only ninety-five per cent.'

'Ninety-four,' Paul corrected him, mechanically.

'Yes, I know,' Richard continued. 'But this time in Malawi, it was total. Our house boy was terrified. Hid in the kitchen whimpering.' His laugh had a machine-gun report. 'Hah, hah, hah.'

'What an eventful boyhood,' Paul said, a little needling edge to his voice. Suzy exerted herself.

'And do you have children, Richard? she asked.

'I regret not, Madeleine – my late wife – she was unable to have children, although she wanted them rather desperately.'

'How sad,' she murmured. But she discovered she was pleased to hear that Richard was childless; she couldn't begin to know why.

'I have a nephew,' Richard continued, dabbing a neat square of potato in his pile of salt. 'My sister's boy, of whom I am extremely fond . . . But I must admit, I always wanted a girl, myself. To spoil, don't you know.' A flash of his yellowing grin at Daisy as he said this.

'Ah, well,' said Paddy and patted his knee.

Suzy pretended not to notice this easy, comfortable gesture. She topped up Paddy's wine glass. Richard put his hand over the rim of his; he was wearing a signet ring on his third finger. Suzy wondered if it was his wedding ring or whether, perhaps, Paddy had given it to him.

'I'll help myself to a bit more pork, if I may,' Richard said, but he waited for Suzy to reach for the carving knife and to serve him two more slices. 'I love pork,' he told her.

'I'm afraid I overcooked it,' Suzy said, sitting down again.

'Pork's better well done.'

'There is that,' Paddy said. She had left most of hers and was dabbing at the corners of her mouth with her napkin.

'Was your wife a good cook?' Paul asked abruptly. He was piling a heaped spoonful of apple sauce onto his slices of meat.

Suzy shot him a dirty look. Paddy, too.

There was a beat before Richard said, 'Yes, she was. The French usually are.' Nothing was going to disturb his smooth assurance.

'It's easier living in France,' Paddy said. 'The little shops. The patisseries, charcouteries.' Her accent seemed rather affected.

'Do you know, Madeleine said the most demoralising thing about her futile last treatment was the hospital food. They were feeding her pap, of course.'

'Did your wife die, then?' Daisy piped up.

'Yes, she did.'

'Poor you!' Daisy's grey eyes grew round and thoughtful.

Richard gave an apologetic little laugh.

'Well,' he said. 'It takes a while to get over but,' he picked his words with care, 'I've been very fortunate.'

'You didn't even have any children!'

'Ah, now I see I was right to want a little girl,' Richard said lightly. 'I hope you'll visit when Luke comes sailing.'

'Ooh, yes,' she said. She hadn't bridled at the use of the word 'little', Suzy noticed.

Luke spoke through a mouth of roast potato.

'You're not coming in the boat,' he said.

'Don't want to,' Daisy replied.

She looked remarkably happy.

By the time Richard shifted in his seat and said, 'Time to hit the road,' Suzy was ready for them to go. She felt she could not maintain the effort of playing hostess for much longer. The delicate twists and turns that her emotions had negotiated during this visit had quite worn her out. But then, standing on the tarmac, as she watched Paddy handing her cases to Richard, there was one last jink. Paddy was leaving. Suzy's family, that old family she had grown and left, was disbanding for ever when it should not have. It should have remained constant, as if it were the background against which the bright foreground of her life was set.

Paddy was gesturing to her small, green case. 'I'll take that in the front,' she said. 'It has the wipes and the Handy Andies.'

Paddy never travelled far without these precautions against grime and greasy fingers. The car journeys Suzy could remember, she and Gerard and Clare in the back, sickening slowly in the gas mask smell of the leather, until a fresh eau-de-Cologne wipe was handed back by those big, raw-boned hands. The roll in her father's pink neck between his collar and his hair, Gerard's and Clare's sharp elbows in her side, the egg sandwiches and bananas – it all came back to her, out of the blue.

'You will take care, won't you?' she called out. There were tears gathering at the edge of her voice.

Paddy came back up the drive and hugged her. Richard approached, too. He shook Suzy's hand.

'Don't you worry,' he said. He was looking down at her kindly. 'I'll take good care of your mother.'

'Bye,' they said as Richard's Audi rolled back across the drive. Paddy had a bright smile fixed to her jaw.

'*Bon voyage*,' called Daisy.

Richard reversed into the hammerhead in front of the Mortlocks'.

'Bye.'

They pulled away. Suzy saw their hands waving and their heads angled to catch the rear-view mirror.

Paul put a hand on her shoulder as if to shepherd her through the door. It was, she knew, a good-natured gesture. She managed a smile.

'Go and sit down,' he said.

'I'll just go and sort out her room . . . the spare room,' Suzy said.

Upstairs, Paddy's absence announced itself loudly. She had stripped her bed and left the sheets neatly folded. When Suzy picked them up, she smelt Paddy's perfume. There was a half-finished bottle of coral nail varnish on the beside cabinet. Suzy slid open the drawer and found a comb with a few strands of deep red hair caught in the teeth. In the book Paddy had borrowed from her, Suzy found an old picture, a drawing done by Clare when she was a child, which Paddy had been using as a bookmark and left behind by accident. Suzy picked it up and popped it into the drawer. It would be there for Paddy to collect when she came to visit, she said to herself. But she had to fight a nagging suspicion that Paddy would not be returning.

How could anything be the same again? Suzy saw Paddy marching off into the future, a flight of imagination that placed Paddy on the deck of a ferry, although she knew they were taking the tunnel. Paddy's face was turned to the prow as the boat cut through a choppy, grey sea. There was something bold and brave about the set of her head. Why on earth would this Paddy wish to return? Suzy saw her now on a stone terrace under a vine; she was wrapped in that robe she'd been wearing all summer, her feet bare, the nails varnished in coral, and she was dipping a croissant in hot coffee. Suzy had somehow never expected her mother to move far away from her. She'd thought there was a circle drawn on a map of southern England and that neither one would ever cross it.

Suzy threw the nail varnish in the wastepaper bin in the bathroom, laid the sheets in the laundry basket. She closed the door to the spare room. The house must now readjust to a leaving; the little creaks and groans of wood and mysterious rustlings suggested the process beginning at once.

Paul was in the kitchen. He had loaded the dishwasher but was washing the good glasses by hand in an eruption of bubbles in the sink. She was surprised; she was touched.

'Thanks, darling,' she said. 'Shall I take over?'

'I'm almost finished.'

Suzy plonked herself upon the nearest beech-ply chair. She rested her forehead in her hands. She felt bloated. The wine had left a sour taste at the back of her mouth and a fuzziness at the back of her mind.

There was a puffing of laughter.

'What so funny?' she asked, looking up.

'His wife was called Madeleine,' Paul said, a smile smeared across his face as he inspected a glass against the light. Suzy failed to see why this was amusing him. 'He's gone from a Maddy to a Paddy. Helps if the old memory's playing up, ay?'

Suzy sighed.

'He calls her Patricia,' she said.

Paul pulled the lank tea towel from the peg. Suzy would have dug out a clean one from the drawer, but she refrained from saying anything.

'Doesn't suit her,' he mused. 'She's always been a Paddy . . . I must say,' he added, 'I thought Clare would make more of a drama out of this.'

'How can she say anything? Clare doesn't believe in monogamy,' Suzy said flatly.

Paul pulled the plug. Water rushed down unseen pipes.

'Smooth bastard, wasn't he?' Paul said.

'She never spoke to my father like that, did she?' Suzy said sadly. 'She was never so admiring and so . . . so prompting with him.'

'You don't know that. She might have been once, in the beginning.'

This was said gently and was intended to comfort her, she knew, but it was an unsettling thought, a disagreeable one. Where and how had the graciousness gone?

'I thought I'd choke if we had to listen to any more stories about Abroad. My fascinating life,' Paul continued. 'Public school, don't you know.' He snorted, 'Anyway, darling, look on the bright side.' He was standing glasses in the cupboard. 'At least we've got the house to ourselves again.'

'Yes,' Suzy said.

She had better turn her attention to the small matters she had been neglecting. She had a million and one things to do. The new term began in a week. There was new uniform to buy for spreading, lubberly bodies, larger shoes for enlarging feet; protractors had gone missing, as they always did; compasses had broken. Shortly, she would be informed that fountain pens,

214

which had not been cheap in the first place, had been loaned to Ella or Baz but never returned.

At her desk in the conservatory, she made herself a list. Then she made herself busy; too busy to dwell on things, too busy to think.

Chapter Nineteen

It was several weeks before Suzy realised that something had changed. Paddy seemed to have left something behind in the house, atoms of resentment, the stale smell of grudges. Her comments hung in the air, echoing in the corners of rooms. Comments about the dull, repetitive nature of Suzy's life. Hints about Paul's bombastic nature. When Paddy had been here, Suzy had cast herself as matrimony's dogged defender. Now, she was free to meander from her script. Mutinous notions infiltrated odd, spare moments of her day.

She found herself watching couples. She watched the tiny interactions of the people whose houses and gardens she went to photograph. Sometimes they divided their labours precisely, like a military operation.

'Henry does the lawn and the hedges and I do the beds,' said the woman, a string-bean blonde with chapped lips, whose garden Suzy was capturing that autumn. 'I'm not allowed anywhere near the vegetable garden or the compost heap. If I see him with a hoe, he's dead.' She gave a girlish, mollifying laugh.

Suzy wondered if they distributed the remainder of their shared life so evenly. These exact arrangements sounded like a prescription for peace. Perhaps warfare broke out otherwise?

The gay couple whose Docklands flat she photographed had had a disagreement before she arrived. It was plain that one of them had objected to her coming to photograph it, but the other, the one who had been chiefly responsible for its design, had insisted.

'Of course,' he whispered to Suzy over a cup of tea in a stainless-steel kitchen, 'Maxwell doesn't really understand the importance of what I've done. To him, form is more important than function. He'd have ornaments dotted about if he had his way.' He gave a delicate shudder.

One day, she paused by a photograph of a youth, black-haired, black-eyed, handsome. It was standing on the sill of a sweeping, steel-framed, Art Deco window. She placed the portrait on the sofa before framing the shot.

'I'll put everything back as I find it,' she told the owner, who had slipped into the room behind her. She was a thin, sallow woman with an untidy knot of iron-grey hair pinned to her skull. There was a furrow in the centre of her eyebrows.

'You must do what looks right,' the woman said. 'You're the expert. I'm sure you'll make it look lovely.'

'Oh, I will.'

'I expect you're always having to juggle around with the interiors you photograph.'

There was a question hidden in this sentence.

'Always,' Suzy said hurriedly.

'Things are never as perfect as they seem in these glossy magazines, are they?'

'No, they're not.' The light had changed. Suzy took a reading from the windowsill.

'I thought not,' the woman said more comfortably. 'I was nervous that ours was not up to standard.' Suzy raised her head from the viewfinder. The woman was examining the image in the steel frame now.

'My son . . .' she ventured.

'He's very handsome,' Suzy said. 'You and your husband must be very proud of him.'

'He is not my husband's.'

'Oh,' said Suzy.

'This causes problems.'

'Oh, dear,' said Suzy. 'I can imagine.'

'You cannot possibly imagine.'

'Bad,' said Suzy.

'Ach. Worse than bad.'

Across the breakfast table, Daisy's sweet face, blank still from leftover dreams, would flip Suzy's heart over itself. Daisy's breasts were budding, her legs elongating; through the outsize T-shirt Daisy slept in, Suzy could detect her hip bones, smooth and round like ball bearings. Luke – well, Luke was another matter. He had descended into a particularly dark and unimaginable part of adolescence, which not a finger of light relieved. Abruptly, the gloom would be punctuated by a burst of confidence, although one that seemed to be based on scant self-knowledge. Yesterday, he had strolled in and, lolling against the kitchen counter, had announced that his score in last week's geography test had been twelve per cent.

'It's a wonder that you find your way to school in the morning, Winslow,' his teacher had remarked. Luke considered this hilarious.

The gays whose flat she had photographed informed Sasha they had changed their minds and did not wish for publicity.

'What do you expect?' Paul said when she mentioned it to him. 'Bloody woofters. It's par for the course.' And off he went to the garden.

He wasn't really interested. It was plain he was scarcely listening to what she said. Oh, she knew she didn't earn very much, not in comparison to him. But there was no need to be so dismissive.

She'd been far too easy-going throughout their marriage. Downright feeble, she'd been. That was what Paddy thought. Now she came to think about it, Paul certainly expected to have his own way. She'd given in far too often when faced with yet another male sulk.

That night, he glanced across while she was grazing through the brochures she had picked up from the travel agent's display.

'I don't want to go on a beach holiday,' he said. 'I get bored lying on a beach.'

Suzy turned the page determinedly.

'What's for supper?' he asked.

'Salmon.'

'Oh.' A pause. 'I don't fancy fish. Can't we have something else?'

'Why don't *you* cook?' she said to a picture of Caribbean sands and turquoise seas. He didn't, of course, but he forked through each mouthful of salmon as if it were poisonous.

Oh, he was perpetually irritable, monosyllabic with her, snappy with the children. He hadn't used to be like this. Had he?

The dog lay by his chair emitting deadly gases and he bellowed so loudly that it woke with a start and slunk away, pressing its backside against Suzy's feet.

'Mean Daddy,' Daisy said when Paul left the room. 'It's not your fault, is it, Chessy?

'*His bottom doesn't smell that great,*' she added in a growly, grumbly tone.

'You're quite right,' Daisy told the dog.

'*And his feet! Talk about cheese!*' said the 'dog.'

Suzy couldn't help smirking.

God, he was so narrow, so pompous, such a . . . prig was the word Paddy had used. Just this morning, he had drawled, 'Suzy, do you think you'll ever get round to mending my blue shirt?' She had taken a deep, deep breath and gazed out at the garden, where a party of starlings was warring over blood-red berries.

'I've been busy,' she said evenly.

Afterwards, what she should have said occurred to her. She should have said, 'I'll mend your shirt when you fix the hinge on the cupboard.' Damn. A year that cupboard had been waiting for his screwdriver. She saw it in her mind's eye, its handle a globe of amber, its pointy blade. A sharp instrument – yes, she could imagine herself wielding one upon Paul.

Once a week, a letter arrived bearing evocative republican stamps and Paddy's even, looped handwriting. Suzy viewed these envelopes with excitement; she did not receive many newsy, personal letters among the tide of circulars, bills and official communications. But reading them was something of a let down. Paddy seemed to have adopted a new persona: that of the wide-eyed traveller.

The cottage is two bedroomed and made of stone, Paddy wrote. *It was built in the last century but Richard has renovated it completely. It comes with a hectare of land. I can't be doing with hectares, but it looks more than enough to be going on with.*

Or:

Today, Richard dropped me at the market and went on to the bank where he had business. I managed to buy apples, bread, cheese and fish. I rather overdid it on the quantities because I could only manage 'un kilo.' I was half out of my mind with panic and forgot to say 'un demi'. What a blithering eejit.

In the meantime, Suzy wondered if Paddy was happy, if living with Richard was as she had expected. If it was odd adapting to this new man having spent forty-one years with the old.

You would think it would be. You would think it was discombobulating, shape-shifting at the age of sixty-four. Look at Pat. Over the birch-lap fence, she was having trouble accepting the crack of doomsday. No one had expected her to take it so hard. She had always seemed so doughty and phlegmatic. But she didn't seem able to rouse herself. She sat at her knotty pine kitchen table for hour after hour, staring at the herbaceous beds among which Will had breathed his last. She puffed on her fags. The fug in the kitchen deepened and swirled. The grass grew. She stirred cup after cup of tea while the brew in the pot grew cold and oily, the colour of liquid mahogany.

'What are you doing, Pat?' Muriel asked her, tapping on the glass of the kitchen door and entering without waiting for a reply.

'What do you think I'm doing?' Pat said dully. Not like Pat to be so terse. 'I'm watching the grass grow,' she said.

Muriel didn't know what to say.

'I didn't know what to say,' she told Suzy. Muriel had hurried over directly. 'We should do something for her,' she said, looking at Suzy for suggestions.

'Oh, goodness,' said Suzy.

'You call on her.'

'I have.'

'But you'll go again.'

'Yes, Muriel, of course.'

'Go now. She likes you.'

She did? It didn't seem to Suzy that Pat had ever displayed such partiality. She thought Pat much preferred Muriel. They were fellow members of the WI. A pair on the rota for the church flowers. Same generation. Similar hair-dos . . .

Well, of course she would go. She would finish her filing later.

'Tell me what you think,' Muriel urged. 'I have to go home now. I'm monitoring Ron. I'm allowing him a twenty-minute run every other day. The doctor backs me. Says that's the limit for a man of his age. I can't think why I didn't intervene before, but Will's death opened my eyes, you can imagine. No more brass rubbing, I've put a stop to that. All that motoring couldn't have been good.'

'Gosh. Does he miss it?'

'Oh, pooh, what does that matter? I book a break once a month at a country hotel. I said to him: "Ron," I said, "you've got to look after yourself and that includes taking regular breaks." '

Suzy wondered why she found herself feeling sorry for Ron.

Pat had moved to the dining room by the time Suzy arrived. A spray of fine powder had spilled from the glass ashtray on to the teak table. One stump lay smouldering on its concave resting place; Pat was already drawing on a fresh cigarette. She was wearing a blue nylon quilted dressing gown, though her hair was combed and a coat of magenta lipstick applied.

'Pat?' Suzy said.

'Hello, Suzy.' Her eyes never left the window.

'I'll just empty the ashtray,' Suzy suggested. She stubbed out the stump carefully, and transported the whole mess, with its dry, choking smell, through to the kitchen. She emptied the contents in Pat's swing bin and swilled the ashtray in the sink. She couldn't find a tea towel but there was a roll of paper towel on the counter, next to the butter, the tea bags, the half-full bottle of none-too-fresh milk with curds of cream furring the glass. A long tube of ash had accumulated at the end of Pat's cigarette by the time Suzy returned. When Pat tapped her cigarette with her forefinger, it fell on to the carpet in a perfect roll.

'I'll make a fresh pot of tea,' Suzy said.

'There's no point.'

'You're sure?'

'There's no point.'

It took Suzy a beat to realise that Pat was not referring to the second pot of tea.

'Pat?' she said. She stooped down by the side of Pat's chair. Perhaps it was the housecoat that suggested it, but Suzy found herself treating Pat like an invalid. 'Would you like to go back to bed?' she suggested.

Suzy watched Pat struggling to understand the question.

'Yes,' she said after a long moment. 'Yes, I would like that very much, thank you.'

Suzy took hold of her arm under the elbow and helped her to her feet as if she were much older than her fifty-something years.

'I'm having a bad day,' Pat told her, when they were halfway up the stairs. She was heavy, bulky.

'It's only to be expected,' Suzy said.

'Thank you,' said Pat at the bedroom door. She drew herself up. She seemed to be mustering her dignity, restoring the distance that separated them.

'I'll pop in tomorrow,' Suzy said. But in fact she was not needed. The next day, Pat was dressed and the kitchen was clean, although her eyes were still glazed and dazed.

'Have they put her on tranquillisers, do you suppose?' Suzy asked Muriel.

'I don't know,' Muriel said. 'I don't like to ask.'

'No,' said Suzy.

'You could ask her, though,' Muriel added brightly. 'She'd take it coming from you.'

'You mustn't take on too much,' Paul said. 'They'll impose on you, those women. They seem to forget you're a busy working mother.'

They were lying in bed; her face was buried in the pillows, which smelt of the outdoors and of grass from their sojourn on the washing line. Under her eyelids, she saw only blackness. She was tired, drifting along that lingering cusp between wakefulness and sleep.

'Is your neck hurting?' Paul's voice asked her.

'Mmm,' she told the pillows. She was touched.

His hand began to knead her back; his fingers searched each joint in her spinal column. 'It's not as if your own father hasn't been through something similar,' he said.

Something in Suzy's mind stuttered, fell back from the brink of sleep. How concerned he was acting! How thoughtful! *You see,* she scolded herself, *he isn't all bad!*

'I'd like to invite my dad over again,' she said, her voice close and muffled.

'When?'

'I don't know, this weekend?'

'Fine.'

His hand worked up her spine and down. It travelled to her right shoulder and lingered there for a moment, then it crept around to her breast. It teased its way through the wide armhole and under her nightdress. His fingers began to pull at her nipple.

Suzy blinked and was looking at the grain of the blue cotton pillowcase. She lay for a minute longer, fighting fatigue, while his fingers continued their urgent tug and stroke. She took a deep breath and rolled over.

'Hi,' he said, and she smiled.

Later, much later, Paul almost woke himself with a snore. His arms and legs flailed, slapping Suzy rudely from sleep. She found herself deposited on her pillow. Her heart was hammering. Oh, no. She searched for unconsciousness, for the sweet path back, that she might slip down it gently. But no. The rhythmic whistle of his breath had intervened.

She turned on her side. She turned on her back. Her mind began to work. The night wore on relentlessly.

Blades of light were pointing through gaps in the curtains and birds were scuffling on the roof, whistling noisily, before forgetfulness came. It was the small things that got to you. Learning there wasn't an easy path.

Chapter Twenty

The mower spluttered, then roared into life and Suzy thought absent-mindedly, 'Ah, Will again.' A moment later, she remembered that Will was dead. The oddest people grew so ingrained in your life, so much a part of the topography, it was hard to let them go. There would always be both a Will and a Pat to Suzy. Pat would be trailed in Suzy's subconscious by a ghostly impression of her husband.

She went to the window to investigate the mowing and there was Paul, regal on the seat as he executed a turn across the Mundays' garden, with Ted and Luke standing on her drive, talking amiably together. The three of them were getting on so well. Paul was steering the mower in circles now, tighter and tighter, his jaw eased into a grin.

Suzy watched them reflectively. Ted's visits had an unforeseen complexion. She had assumed he would want to be with her but instead he hung around with Paul and Luke, leaving her to cook or to garden. She had assumed, too, that he would need nursing along. But no. He was phlegmatic, a little vague it was true, perhaps just a shade subdued. Indeed, it was startling to see how well he was managing without Paddy.

Daisy was finishing her homework on the dining table; she was drawing a cartoon of one of the classical myths. A tin of coloured pencils was open in front of her. Every now and then she swapped pencils, inserting a green into the rolling gap, selecting a blue.

Ted came in the back door, his cheeks red from the outside. 'What's that, then?' he said, bending over Daisy's shoulder.

'History,' Daisy said. 'The Roman gods.'

'I thought it was that weather man, what's his name?'

'That's Zeus with a thunderbolt, Granddad.'

'Oh. Are you sure? Sure it's not Ian Macaskill?'

'He's teasing, Daisy. He used to do that to me.' Suzy tried to catch Ted's eye above Daisy's head.

Daisy frowned.

'Oh, no. It looks stupid. I'm going to have to start again.'

'No, no, just give him a bushier beard. Ian Macaskill doesn't have a beard.'

Daisy crumpled the paper fiercely and tossed it aside. Ted pottered off sheepishly, taking the blue canvas bag he'd brought with him into the sitting room.

Her father had made only one referenceto Paddy's leaving. 'I've been arranging things,' he had said, when he arrived. Suzy had a vision of photographs being tidied away, of knick-knacks bundled into bin bags, of feminine novels taken in cardboard boxes to the charity shop. 'I'll show you something later,' he had said, with a pleased and secret smile. He seemed to be enjoying this long, leisurely sifting through a lifetime's accumulations.

'He's coping well, isn't he?' Paul had said only last week. 'I take my hat off to the old sod.' And Suzy had been forced to agree. She ought to be pleased, and she was. But when she looked at it from her mother's point of view, she experienced a bleat of outrage. No wonder Paddy had felt undervalued.

Ted was calling her from the other room, telling Daisy to fetch Luke in. Suzy closed the recipe book she'd been searching through. She picked up Daisy's discarded picture from the table and deposited it in the sitting-room bin as she went through. Ted was crouching by the television, fiddling with their video recorder. A stream of cool air accompanied Daisy and Luke as they returned from the garden.

'Remember those old cine films?' Ted was saying. 'The ones I shot when you three were small?'

'The holiday in Ireland.'

'Yes, and the others. I found them all while I was sorting out the house and I've had them transferred to VHS.'

Luke took the remote control from Ted and pressed a sequence of buttons. The television came on, an eruption of white noise and fuzzy lines before a scene of horses racing around a lush green track. The horses gave way to a grey flicker and a row of golden dots.

'Here we go,' said Ted, scrambling backwards into Paul's chair.

Suzy's hand went to her mouth. She sat herself slowly down on the arm of the sofa, her eyes fixed on the television.

The screen seemed to lurch. The three of them appeared on the lawn at home on a summer's day. They were in swimming costumes, Gerard all skin and bones in his Speedo trunks, Suzy folding her arms over her budding breasts, and little Clare, with sweetheart frills around her flat torso and bony hips. They trotted jerkily across the back garden. The colours were strangely flat and subdued, as if they had leached from the film over the years, but you could still see how milky white Clare's skin was, how grey Gerard's eyes were.

There was an abrupt change of scene: Gerard, in shirt and jeans, with his guitar.

'He's singing that funny American song he liked so much,' Ted informed her.

Yes, she could see it now. His lips saying, 'Bye, Bye, Miss American Pie.' Ted was noiselessly mouthing along, nodding faintly, as if offering encouragement to Gerard's shifting image.

The back garden again: Suzy and Clare in full skirts jiving, self-consciousness making them silly. They began jitterbugging, faster and faster, their arms sawing the air. And here was Paddy, spreading a white linen cloth on the grass. How young she looked! How slim in her trousers and sweater! How carefree! She was saying something to the camera, swatting her hand at the lens, smiling broadly. Suzy could hear her voice: 'Don't you point that thing at me, Ted Barrett.' In those days she used to call him Ted Barrett when she wasn't really cross but was pretending to be. Funny how much you forgot.

And here, the next scene – just look at the details that Suzy had let slip: the hunch of Gerard's shoulders, the width of his smile, the crookedness of his teeth; Clare's earnestness and her fondness for Suzy. Suzy could feel again that soft, clammy hand in hers, squirming like a sea creature.

Paddy was laying out the picnic. She slapped the plates of sandwiches on to the cloth. The speed of these old films was always wrong. They all moved too quickly, hurrying through this halcyon day. Paddy threw her head back and laughed silently.

'See how happy she is,' Ted said. 'See how happy we were back then.'

The back of his head seemed suddenly very dear to Suzy. A row of dots appeared on the screen. Suzy rose and went to pat his shoulder. Luke and Daisy exchanged glances; Suzy read a mixture of boredom and embarrassment in their faces as they slipped from the room.

'How do I stop this thing?' Ted asked. Suzy took the control and pressed the rewind button. A red arrow appeared on the crystal display.

'I've got another one in here,' Ted said, rooting in the canvas bag by his feet.

Suzy was not sure she was able to watch more. Replaying the past made Ted so happy but her so sad. She could scarcely bear to be reminded of it, these jerky, joking figures performing for the camera with no idea of what the future held.

* * *

'Suzy, have you seen my screwdriver?'

'No.'

She swung the metal stand of the ironing board through its protesting arabesque. They were in the kitchen. Ted had left half an hour ago.

'He seems to be coping, doesn't he?' she asked Paul.

'Mmm? Your dad. Bearing up, isn't he? He'll be sorting out the divorce soon.'

'A divorce! Do you think so?'

'You haven't been tidying away my things, have you?' He had moved to the cupboard where the kitchen rolls and cleaning liquids were stored. 'Said to me he'd been to see his lawyer,' he added.

'He has?'

'You should ask him about it.' He stood in front of the cupboard distractedly.

'I couldn't do that.'

'What?' There was a pause. 'Why not?'

'I just couldn't.'

'Did you move my screwdriver to the garage?'

'Try the shelf under the stairs,' she said.

She followed him there. She could feel a row brewing.

'You have a right to know the arrangements if your parents are getting a divorce, Suzy.' He was on his hands and knees, halfway through the cupboard door, searching through cardboard boxes. His voice sounded muffled. 'It might have financial implications for you and the children.'

Suzy gave a small snort. *Trust you to reduce everything to hard cash*, she said to herself. *You've got accountant stamped through every pore.*

He backed out of the cupboard and regarded her. There was a cobweb caught in his hair. 'What did that mean?'

'What did what mean?' she said. 'Anyway, it's none of my business.'

'Actually, it is. Is Paddy going to leave her half to you and Clare or to that Richard bloke?'

'Well, to us, I'm sure. Richard doesn't need any money.'

'How do you know? Anyway, need and desire are entirely different matters.'

'Just drop it, will you, Paul?'

'Fine, fine. That's typical of you Barretts, isn't it?'

'What do you mean, us Barretts?'

'Hide your heads in the sand,' Paul continued. 'Pussyfoot around. You pride yourself on being so demonstrative, but none of you ever discusses anything.'

'What has that got to do with it? Who are you to talk? You're not exactly a model of . . . of . . .' She had forgotten what she was going to say. She could feel the waves of indignation swelling within her.

'Let's not talk about Ted and Paddy splitting up. Let's not talk about Clare's problems. And absolutely, above all, let's not talk about Gerard's death. Not one of you ever mentions Gerard or his death.'

'We do, too. We talk about Gerard. Who would want to talk about his death?'

'Oh, well, your son, of course, might be interested in his own family history. Has that crossed your mind? But even he knows to come to me when we're in Scotland and ask me on the quiet.' There was a pause before he added, with forced patience, 'You should try talking to him. It might help, Suzy.'

'Don't patronise me. There's no one in need of help.'

'Huh.'

She wandered into the sitting room, gathered up the untidy pile of the day's newspapers from a chair and rammed them in the bin. He appeared in the door. There were two grimy oval patches on the knees of his Chinos. 'I don't know why you have to dig that up,' she told him.

'I haven't read those.'

She was about to reply, but stopped.

'Dig that up! How could I have said that? I said, "Dig that up".' She cupped her hands around her mouth and nose. This was the sort of unthinking comment that made Paddy flinch. You knew that her mind was never far from Gerard's grave.

Paul was looking at her.

'Suzy, it's just a slip of the tongue,' he said in a kinder tone.

'I can't believe I said that.' Out of the blue, tears sprang into her eyes.

'Come and sit down. Come on.' He put his hand on her shoulder and guided her to the sofa. 'You've been through a lot recently. Let me get you a drink.' She was aware of a movement of air from the direction of the hall. 'Oh, Luke,' Paul called out. 'Will you get your mother a glass of water?'

'What's the matter with her?'

'There's nothing the matter with her, just get her the water.'

'Keep your hair on. I was only asking.'

The glass appeared before her. She took a few sips. After a while, she calmed down. Paul was right. She had been through a lot. She was bound to be overwrought.

'She'd never have left if Gerard had been alive,' she said after a while.

'Oh, Suzy, you can't—'

'No. It's true. He'd have been outraged. She wouldn't have risked him thinking the less of her.'

'You mustn't think like that.'

Paul sat down next to her, his hands clasped between his knees. He glanced at her. He felt guilty for provoking her outburst, she could tell, not that he would apologise.

'I want to go and visit my mother,' she said.

'Good idea.'

'At half term. I'll take the children.'

'OK.'

'It's just a visit, Paul. I'm not going to give her an inquisition. You'll have to manage on your own.'

'Fine. I'm forty-one Suzy. I think I'm capable of boiling an egg.'

That's news to me, Suzy replied to herself. She couldn't wait to get away. She couldn't wait to leave his smug theories and his pally complacency. It would be a relief to be among Barretts: except, she reminded herself, she wouldn't be.

The air in Normandy was clearer, golden as apples, with a bite in the early morning and a chill in the evening. Richard's house was on a sheltered hillside a mile or two from the nearest village. The road ran true and straight through the fields, then twined through the village, skirting the hip of a stone bakery that jutted into its path, widening into a quiet, dusty square. A right fork in front of the church led out and up, through orchards and hedgerows, a ramshackle sign marking the rutted track that led to the cottage.

It was a low roofed, stone building, flanked by a gravelly courtyard where they parked the cars and a stone terrace where a marble table and metal chairs sat invitingly. The table was unstable and wobbled at the pressure of each forearm or elbow, spilling coffee into saucers. Paddy showed them around the cottage.

'It's only been a holiday home until now, so I'm trying to add those homely touches,' she said. There were rugs. There were dried flowers in baskets. And when she bought fruit from the market, she arranged it carefully in a garden trug, which she placed in the centre of the rough oak table. Suzy couldn't help thinking that Paddy had never bothered with these housewifely details before. Two good items of furniture, a carved chair and a small armoire, which Paddy would normally have admired, had been relegated to the narrow, dark corridor. Instinct told Suzy they were Madeleine's family pieces.

Richard walked them to the borders of the land. It was wildly overgrown, nettles and brambles surging along the stone walls. Suzy waded through long grasses speckled with seed heads, stripping them from their stalks as she went.

'This is the project for the spring,' he told her. 'Prune the apple trees. Lay that area to lawn. Vegetables over by the far wall.' He waved his arm at the green wilderness.

'We love it here, don't we?' he said, as they ploughed back to the terrace, where Paddy was setting down a bottle of the local wine and three glasses. Luke followed with a tray of bread and pâté.

'We do,' she agreed.

Suzy pushed a chair back; there was a loud scraping of metal on stone.

'It's the life, you know,' Richard declared. 'They've done things differently from Britain. So much more civilised. The right values.'

Suzy buttered a hunk of bread and spread it with a thick layer of pâté. It was delicious, the butter unsalted and creamy, the pâté rough and savoury.

Daisy spread butter on her bread but shook her head when Paddy offered her the pâté.

'I don't like it,' she said.

'You'll like this one,' Richard told her. He was standing behind them, in the military position known as 'at ease', a plate balanced on his palm.

Daisy smiled wanly and took her bread to the edge of the terrace, where she perched, dipping her toes into the eddying grass.

'I feel sorry for old Blighty now,' Richard continued. 'Who'd live in Britain now if they had the choice?' He was getting on Suzy's nerves. Anyone would think the man wasn't English. She glanced across at Paddy, who was painstakingly spreading butter to the corners of her slice of bread.

'Tiny island overrun with inhabitants,' Richard's voice continued.

Suzy decided to make an effort.

'It's certainly very peaceful here,' she said.

'Oh, peaceful! We were saying just the other night. You lie in bed and you can't hear another sound except the wind in the trees and the odd animal noise. No traffic, you see.'

'No,' said Suzy. The idea of Richard and Paddy in bed together still brought her up short.

'No crowds . . . No crime, either. No blacks, you see.'

A pregnant hush and pause grasped the table. Daisy shot Suzy a nervous glance. Suzy tried to think of something to say, but failed. She went to help herself to another piece of bread and as she did so she caught Paddy's face, self-consciously immobile. Paddy seemed to register Suzy's hand reaching for the plate.

'Yes, do have some more,' she said, smiling quickly. 'Richard, dear?'

'What? Yes, I will, thank you.'

'The Normandy beaches,' Paddy said quickly. 'We could drive there tomorrow. Luke might be interested in the museum.'

'You know about Normandy?' Richard turned to Luke. 'These are the Second World War landings.'

'Oh, right,' Luke said. He didn't sound very interested. 'Is Flanders anywhere near here?' he added.

'No, dear,' Paddy said.

'We're doing Flanders in history,' said Luke. 'Blackadder,' he added to Daisy.

'Oh.'

'Blackadder,' muttered Richard. 'Blackadder.' He shook his head. Luke flushed. 'Oh, it's not the boy's fault.' Richard addressed Suzy now. 'They don't teach English history in your multi-cultural—'

'Will you get more wine, dear?' Paddy interrupted.

'Well, there's half a bottle left . . .'

'I fancy a glass of white.'

'Me, too,' said Suzy.

'Oh, righty-ho, then.'

He put his plate on the table, which see-sawed at his touch, and strolled off to the kitchen. By the time he came back, bottle and corkscrew in hand, Paddy was deep into a description of the neighbouring farmers. Suzy watched her. The light glinted on the ruby wine in their glasses. Suzy took a sip. The red was rather good. She would stick with it.

Suzy and Daisy shared a bedroom on the eastern side of the cottage and Luke was sleeping on the sofa in the sitting room, by the fireplace where the logs smouldered. There was an awkward moment saying goodnight in the evening, with Paddy and Richard turning right up the corridor and Suzy and Daisy turning left. Suzy sat on her bed for half an hour afterwards and it took her an age to fall asleep. Daisy knew what the matter was. She came and snuggled silently into Suzy's side.

Richard's dubious comments were far enough spread that she and Paddy might contrive not to notice them. But Luke's adolescent demeanour irritated the hell out of Richard, Suzy could see.

'Do you think you might get up before lunchtime?' he said on the third day of their stay. 'Come all this way and miss the best part of the day.'

But when she and Paddy were wandering around the market, Paddy said suddenly, 'Richard is so fond of the children. He was saying to me last night how nice they both are.'

Suzy was stunned. She had a feeling that one of them must be labouring under a misapprehension.

'He will take Luke sailing next time you come.'

'Oh, don't worry—'

'And Daisy! He adores Daisy!'

Richard and Paddy repeated the same stories, again and again. Paddy's farcical mistakes at French were recounted with gusto, the kindliness of the wife of the adjacent farmer was remarked upon several times. Suzy could see Luke and Daisy fluttering, twitching like caged mice when these same subjects cropped up towards the end of the week.

One day, when they were alone in the kitchen, Paddy said, 'Did you know your father is divorcing me on the grounds of my adultery?'

'No, I didn't,' Suzy said.

'I didn't think he'd do that,' Paddy mused.

'Mother! You can't blame him, surely?'

'Oh, no. It's just . . . I thought he'd take a while before he . . . formalised the situation.'

'And will you marry Richard?'

'I shouldn't think so. I'm very happy with him,' she added hastily, 'but I've taken those vows once. It seems a bit pointless to say them again.'

Was she happy with Richard? Suzy asked herself this question as she packed the cases into Paul's estate and nudged it through the stone pillars on to the track. It was Sunday morning and the church bells were tolling down in the valley.

'Come back soon,' Paddy had said. 'Come back for Christmas. Come for a weekend.'

'Yes,' Richard agreed. 'Don't you be strangers, now.'

'Seems a bit of a lonely life,' Daisy said from the back seat.

'Yes.'

The set of Paddy's jaw, the wave of her workaday hand, had been particularly determined, it seemed to Suzy. She turned on to the road. The tolling of bells grew louder as they slipped into the village. Luke stretched out, his knees bowing into Suzy's back.

'I can't wait to get home' he said.

'Didn't you enjoy yourself?' Suzy asked automatically.

'It was all right. I thought it was really funny when he started slagging off the Irish and you pointed out that Gran is half Irish herself.'

'Mmm,' Suzy said. It hadn't been funny, not really, intercepting Paddy's furtive, pleading glance.

'If he made one more racist comment, I thought I'd knee him in the bollocks,' Luke said.

The image this conjured made Suzy puff with laughter.

'He isn't as nice as Granddad, is he?' Daisy said.

'No, I don't suppose he is,' Suzy replied.

She kept her eyes on the road, pretending to be concentrating on her driving. She was thinking of Paddy. It came to Suzy that you could choose what you saw of your partner and what you ignored. You could wilfully pull on blinkers. It didn't matter who was nicer; it was what Paddy chose to believe that counted. It was a trick. A sleight of the heart. You could live out years pretending you were happier than you were and in the end, perhaps, the reality would be moulded to your myth. Was that what Ted had done? Was that what Paddy was going to try?

Chapter Twenty-One

Paul was no fool. He knew there was something up with his wife. Initially, he'd assumed it was that time of the month, but evidently he was wrong. It dawned on him one day, driving to work, that she'd been scratchy for weeks. Not even Suzy could exaggerate PMT into a permanent condition.

Could it be the menopause? No, no, surely that didn't happen until much later . . . So, there was no excuse, then. She was a ratty old bat.

She'd eaten cauliflower cheese and suffered a bad dose of wind the other night. It wasn't exactly ladylike. It wasn't what a chap imagined in his fondest fantasies about women. There were some women you were sure never farted. Sharon Stone, for example. He imagined that Sharon Stone stuck to some sort of rigid Los Angelean diet devoid of beans, brassicas and gaseous liquids so that not a popette passed between her luscious buttocks.

Sharon Stone's buttocks, now there was a thought . . .

On the way home, he bought a bunch of red roses from a florist's he passed on the way. He was pleased he had. Suzy's face lit up as he handed them to her. Her eyes were a clear grey that reminded him of water. He knew that, he'd always known that, but he saw her anew, tonight. Under the kitchen's halogen bulbs, he noticed that there were fine, silvery lines fanning the corners of her eyes and that they suited her. He noticed, too, that the rose petals were bruised at their extremities. They probably wouldn't last long. But Suzy bent her nose to the blooms and arranged them carefully in his mother's crystal vase.

Later, passing through the living room, he stooped to inhale their fragrance. They were scentless. They stood to attention on their straight, thornless stems. He regarded them for a moment, feeling cheated. It was Suzy's pleasure in them that had convinced him of their perfume.

The next night, however, was not so cosy. He came home from work to find the table laid in the dining room. Daisy was hovering above the plates, removing the prawns from her Thai-style starter with her fingers, dispersing them around the other settings.

'You can't eat lettuce alone,' Paul told her.

'Why not? Lettuce is good for you.'

Suzy came in.

'I've told her she can't eat lettuce alone.'

Suzy stared at the table setting.

'Oh, well,' she said. 'Just this once.'

Daisy simpered.

'You couldn't just back me up, could you?'

Now Suzy was staring at him.

'You never agree with me about anything, do you?'

'Me?'

'I assume you set out to be deliberately contradictory.'

Suzy looked astonished. Daisy's face had fallen.

He turned on his heel. He knew he'd made heavy weather of that. Hell, she'd laid the table for once. The food looked presentable for once. Shame you couldn't fast-rewind these incidents and rerecord them.

She overreacted, though. When he came downstairs, she was distant and clipped, wouldn't accept that he was trying to make amends by complimenting her on the starter. These things used to blow over. She used to make it easy for him. Not any more, it seemed.

At the weekend, she had to photograph various inhabitants of the village. The idea was to record everyone living in the village in the first year of the new millennium. The WI was going to paste her pictures into a book and provide brief captions. Suzy had caught most of the villagers at home on two previous sorties; this, she hoped, would be her last.

Reluctantly, Paul was accompanying her, hauling her equipment. He'd rather have been playing golf. Unfortunately, Luke had cried off from helping out. He had contracted a streaming head cold which he claimed was flu. Paul ventured a sniff of the chill autumn wind. Mmm. He really didn't feel that great, himself. They'd probably all come down with flu, haring around till they were hot and sweaty on a bitter day like this. Why did Suzy always have to volunteer to help out?

But halfway through the first stop, he began to enjoy himself. It was Pat Munday who was being photographed, posing by Will's rock garden. Paul was struck by Suzy's tact. No one else could have persuaded Pat to be in these pictures, not on her own, Will's absence undeclared to history. But Suzy had suggested they take the shot in Will's garden and promised the caption would include his name, and all of a sudden a weak and watery smile had emerged from behind the threatened tears.

'It will always be your's and Will's garden to me,' Suzy told her. It was exactly the right thing to say.

'She is missing him terribly,' Paul said as they left.

'Yes.' Suzy said. 'They had their ups and downs, you know.'

'Well, of course.'

'I once heard her say she wished she'd never married him.'

'Really? When was this? Do you think she meant it?'

'Oh, heaven knows. I'm sure she doesn't know herself.'

'It was probably just the heat of the moment.'

'Exactly.'

'It was obviously a happy marriage . . .'

'Yes,' Suzy said thoughtfully. 'But how can we judge? Sometimes I just think it comes down to your character. Either you're happy with your lot in life or you aren't. And if you aren't, you'll always be looking for something new.'

'Right,' Paul said. He wasn't quite sure he followed her.

Everyone seemed so pleased to see Suzy. The Woods girls hallooed to her from across the street, the Cartwrights insisted they come in for a restorative whisky, the whiskery old pensioner in the skew-whiff cottage lit up at the sight of her.

'My dear,' he declared.

And then he told Paul on the way out, 'You are a lucky man.'

The old roué. But it was rather gratifying to find that everyone thought so well of his wife. It made Paul believe he hadn't chosen so badly after all, back when he was young and green and possessed no real inkling of what marriage was about.

Suzy stood the Bestics outside their neat front door with its shiny number in the dead centre: their two faces either side of the forty-four.

'Do tell me about the Chunnel,' Muriel asked Suzy. 'We're motoring over in the spring.'

'Oh?' said Suzy, from behind her lens.

'Staying in *pensions*,' Muriel announced.

Ron shifted his weight from one foot to the other.

'Not my idea of fun,' he told Paul. 'I won't be able to eat the Froggy food. Too rich for my digestion.'

'No, dear, but I can,' Muriel replied.

'Look this way,' Suzy told them. 'Smile.'

'They seem happy enough,' Paul said to her, as they walked round to the next house. 'I remember you saying they were in trouble.'

'You were listening,' Suzy said teasingly.

He grinned. He liked it when she pulled his leg.

'But don't they?' he continued.

'I think the nuances may have passed you by,' she said in the same light tone. Paul wondered what on earth she meant.

At the converted barn at the edge of the fields, Paul was pleased to be introduced to that pretty young woman he remembered from the Cartwrights' barbecue. She had the sort of open, smiley face he was most attracted to. Come to think of it, she reminded him of a younger, slighter Suzy. Her husband was a dark, energetic man in his thirties. He was on the telephone when they arrived. Paul could hear him saying, 'Hang on a tic. There's someone here. I'll give you a bell tomorrow.' He was called Ralph, except, he told Suzy as she wrote the information carefully in her notebook, Ralph was pronounced Rafe.

'Do you think you could make that clear in the caption?' he asked her.

'Rafe to rhyme with ca-rafe,' Suzy said, rolling her 'r's'. They were crunching down the drive. Paul hoisted the camera bag on to his other shoulder. He wondered how Suzy could manage its weight on her own.

'Rafe to rhyme with se-raph,' she said. 'Do you think Rafe is safe in taxis?'

He laughed. That was one of the other things he liked about her, her disdain for pretension. Her own naturalness. She was his oldest friend, after all. His truest friend.

'Hurry up, Mrs Winslow,' he said.

But she didn't. Of course, she didn't. At the bungalow on the corner of Mereview Road, she spent half an hour getting the right shot. Anyone else would have posed the couple either side of their baby, clicked the shutter and been off, but not Suzy. She had them flying the baby like an aeroplane, its face split into a grin, their smiles wide with the excitement of new parenthood.

LOUETTE HARDING

She had always been like this, he reflected. She poured herself into each new commission. She concentrated on each shot, no matter how piffling, no matter how badly paid, no matter that this particular assignment was costing her money, as he was sure it was; he was quite sure she wouldn't ask the Women's Institute to reimburse the costs of film and processing. Ah, well. Many times this had irked him to high heaven. He'd wanted her to be more ambitious, to have a game plan, to take some of the pressure off *him*. But right now, watching her knuckles, reddened with the cold, clasped around the black camera body, he was filled with sentiment. She was a cut above the rest. She cared about the things that truly mattered.

'Do you think this area is a hotbed of wife-swapping?' he asked her facetiously as they headed home.

She didn't feed him the next line but he continued with his joke, regardless.

'I certainly hope it is. I think I might swap you for a new set of golf clubs.'

'Hah, hah. Heard that one before. Many times.'

Inside, she took off her Barbour and fingerless knitted gloves and headed for the living room. Paul went to check on Luke, who was slumbering under his duvet, his curtains open to the darkening afternoon. Paul drew them. Downstairs, he found Suzy flicking through the weekend newspapers.

'You rather liked Rafe's wife, didn't you?' she said.

'What?' he said, flushing.

Good grief! What had given her that impression? He sat down in a chair. After a while, he said, 'You know I've never looked at another woman.'

Silence, just a faint kink at the edge of her mouth. She riffled through the pages.

'Ooh!' she exclaimed. 'There's a film I want to watch, later. Sam Shepherd.'

He considered this. It reminded him of something.

246

'You used to say I looked a bit like Sam Shepherd.'

'Mmm,' said Suzy. 'So I did.'

When he looked over, she was smiling to herself. He hadn't a clue what she was thinking.